By ROWAN MCALLISTER

A Promise of Tomorrow*
Cherries on Top
Cuddling (DSP Anthology)*
Feels Like Home
Grand Adventures (DSP Anthology)*
Hot Mess*
My Only Sunshine*
Riding Double (DSP Anthology)*
Uniform Appeal (DSP Anthology)*

A Devil's Own Luck* • Never a Road Without a Turning*

*Available in paperback

Published by DREAMSPINNER PRESS
http://www.dreamspinnerpress.com

Never a ROAD Without a Turning

ROWAN McALLISTER

Dreamspinner Press

Published by
Dreamspinner Press
5032 Capital Circle SW
Suite 2, PMB# 279
Tallahassee, FL 32305-7886
USA
http://www.dreamspinnerpress.com/

Never a Road Without a Turning
© 2014 Rowan McAllister.

Cover Art
© 2014 Paul Richmond.
http://www.paulrichmondstudio.com.
Cover content is for illustrative purposes only
and any person depicted on the cover is a model.

ISBN: 978-1-62798-883-4
Digital ISBN: 978-1-62798-884-1

Printed in the United States of America
First Edition
May 2014

Thank you to all the new friends I've met since beginning this journey and to Dreamspinner for still believing in me.

Prologue

July, 1826

Penrith, Cumberland

PIP CROUCHED in the shadows, keeping perfectly still and his breaths shallow so no sound would betray him. Soft footfalls from the hall alerted him that his prey approached, and Pip's muscles tensed in anticipation.

Soon. Soon he would have them.

Only a few more seconds and his patience would be rewarded. His fingers tingled, and an evil grin spread across his face as the sound of soft leather slapping against stone drew nearer. Pip coiled his body like a spring, his fingers drawing into claws. As soon as the second body came into view, he pounced.

Ear-splitting shrieks rent the air, and Pip grappled with flailing limbs. But he'd misjudged his leap, and all three of them tumbled to the ground in an untidy heap. In an effort to maintain the upper hand, Pip wrapped an arm around a slender waist and struggled to his feet.

"Put me down! Put me down, you brute!" the girl cried piteously, kicking her legs frantically but unable to land a blow.

Pip grinned in triumph. He wanted to cackle with glee but keeping his hold on the wriggling body in his arms took all his strength, and he needed to get her away from her companion before the youth could recover and give chase. Pip turned to make his escape, but the youth was faster than he'd anticipated, somehow got in front of him, and drew Pip's flight to a swift end at the point of a sword.

"Unhand her, you villain!" the youth cried, brandishing his weapon threateningly.

Pip searched desperately about him, seeking something, *anything,* he might use as a weapon. But in his distraction, he grossly underestimated the creature in his grasp. In an uncommon show of strength and bravery, the girl thrashed mightily, landing a blow to his groin that sent Pip gasping to his knees. He released his hold on the chit immediately and cradled his ballocks protectively, letting out a breathless groan as white-hot pain shot through him.

"Ha, ha! Take that, you varlet!" the youth cried, and the girl at his side giggled merrily at Pip's expense.

The youth still held his sword, but after a few moments in which Pip could only gasp and grimace, the blade wavered uncertainly in the air.

"Pip? Are you truly injured?" Peter asked.

Joanna stopped giggling and hurried to Pip's prone form. She crouched next to him and put her tiny hand on his face. "I didn't really hurt you, did I, Pip?" she asked, twisting her other hand in her skirts anxiously.

Peter, his eyes wide with concern, set his wooden sword on the table behind him and knelt on Pip's other side.

The pain had mostly faded, and Pip had enough pride he wouldn't dare admit a girl of barely seven had laid him low. Instead of proclaiming his injury and calling a halt to their game, Pip chose to ignore the ache in his nether parts as he reached for a bit of bravado.

"Of course not. Ha, ha! Ye've fallen for me treachery, and now ye are both in me clutches! Rawr!" Pip wrapped an arm around each child and pulled them to his chest, growling and pretending to nip at their necks. Delighted squeals and giggles echoed around the kitchen as they halfheartedly struggled to break free.

"Ye'll bring the house down with all that carryin' on," Maud admonished them as she stepped into the kitchen from the garden, bringing an abrupt end to their game. "Aren't the two o' ye s'posed to be at lessons with the rest o' the children?"

Peter and Joanna immediately clambered to their feet, and both children looked guiltily at the floor. Joanna paid particular attention to straightening her skirts while Peter chewed his lower lip and kicked his boot against the stone a few times. Maud stood with her hands on her ample hips and a severe frown on her lined face, but her warm brown eyes twinkled with laughter.

As he too climbed to his feet, Pip couldn't help the cheeky grin that split his face. "'Tis my fault, madam. Villain that I am, I whisked them away, all unwillin'."

Maud pursed her lips, fighting the smile that threatened to ruin her air of disapproval. But eventually the smile won out, and she snorted. "Get along with ye now. Ye two terrors go to yer lessons," she said, pointing to the children. "And *you* stay here. I want to talk to ye."

Joanna and Peter looked at him mournfully for a few moments. Then Peter took Joanna's hand and led her from the room.

Pip watched them go with a fond smile before replacing it with his usual cocksure grin as he turned back to Maud. He plopped his arse on one of the wooden kitchen chairs and kicked his feet up to rest on the edge of the worn table. "An' what can a miserable sinner like meself do for 'is beloved Maud this fine day?"

Maud snorted again and bustled over to the kitchen fires to stir whatever bubbled in the large black pot before setting the ladle aside and joining him by the table. She fussed with her starched white cap, smoothing the few silver hairs brave enough to escape the tight chignon at the back of her head. When she looked at him again, her indulgent smile was gone. She took a deep breath and let it out before she reached into her apron and produced a slip of parchment.

"A letter came today," she said with a hint of sadness, and Pip's grin slipped. "I've 'eard from Mrs. Applethwaite, 'ousekeeper of Greer Cottage in Keswick. She's accepted the reference we gave 'er and offered ye the position of groom and sometime man-of-all-work for 'er master, Major Astley McNalty."

Pip rolled his eyes as relief flooded his chest. "Ye'd think it were bad news by the gray clouds over yer 'ead," he said with all the cheekiness he could muster. "Keswick's naught but twenty mile away. I'll come back to see ye as often as I can."

The look she gave him was sad but resigned at first… until he said that last bit. At which point she rolled her own eyes at him and harrumphed. "If yer last five positions are anythin' to go by, ye'll be back afore Christmas," she muttered, as she reached out and cuffed him lightly on the ear.

Pip flinched away and had the grace to look sheepish. He wasn't solely to blame for being dismissed from so many places. If more of the country's men knew how to keep their sisters, daughters, and wives happy and satisfied, they wouldn't be so keen to avail themselves of Pip's charms. And angry brothers, fathers, and husbands wouldn't feel so damned determined to chase him out of their villages. "I'll be good this time, love. Ye 'ave me word of honor."

Instead of rolling her eyes again and fighting a smile as he expected, Maud simply continued to watch him with sad and concerned eyes until Pip shifted uncomfortably in his seat.

"I still don't understand why ye 'ave to go at all," she said. "Yer family's 'ere. Ye'll not find better masters anywhere than Mr. Carey and Mr. Carruthers. The children love ye." She paced away and then back again as she ranted. "And if ye 'ave to leave, ye should at least be tryin' for a position as a clerk or secretary or summat more'n a laborer. Ye can read and write and do figures as well, if not better than, that nervous mouse of a tutor the masters 'ired to teach the rest of us. Ye'r wastin' yerself as a common workman, and ye know it."

"Now, Maud, ye know I'd dry up and blow away sittin' 'unched over a desk, with ink stains on me fingers and me eyes gone all squinched up. And who'd 'ire me to work in their office at any rate, rough as I am?"

"Ye can ape the gents better'n anybody, if ye set yer mind to it. Ye're just too stubborn to try. An' the masters'd send ye back fer more schoolin' if ye ever asked for it… or stayed around long enough t' see it through." She reached out, but instead of giving him another cuff as he half expected, she drew one of Pip's hands between her warm, calloused palms. "Why must ye be so restless, little lamb?"

Pip gazed up into the soft brown eyes of the woman who'd looked after him like her own son for almost as long as he could remember, and his throat closed on his impudent reply. He didn't have an answer for her, and he couldn't bring himself to cloak his confusion with a pretty lie. She was right. He had everything at the Carruthers farm that he could ever hope to ask for. But he still couldn't bear the thought of staying there any more than a few months at a time.

For the last three years, he'd convinced himself that he simply had a restless spirit. He'd grown up in the tumult and fracas of London's rookeries. And though he looked back on that time with bitterness and loathing, he would not have been shocked to find the quiet of the country chafed. But of late, Pip had begun to think that had nothing at all to do with it. He loved the country, the clean air and the open spaces. He had no desire to ever return to London, not for anything. And yet, he still couldn't bring himself to settle in Penrith, or to settle anywhere for that matter. He didn't have any real dreams or ambitions for his future. He was happy working out of doors, tending animals, and fetching and carrying for the houses he worked for. He just couldn't see himself doing it at any one house for long.

"Sweet boy. Do ye even know why?" Maud cupped his chin as she spoke, and the tightness in his throat increased.

Pip put his free hand over hers and gave it a gentle squeeze before pulling it away from his face. "Once more, Maud. That's all I need. One more village, one more change of scenery, and I'll be right as rain when I next come 'ome. Ye'll see," he assured her. He knew it was a lie even as he said it, but he didn't want her to worry.

Maud's lips twisted into a long-suffering smile. She drew her hands from his and tapped his nose with her finger. "Once more is all ye'll be getting' from us, lamb. Ye mind that now. Master Carey and Master Carruthers won't be writing any more letters for ye. Nor will I or any of the rest of the staff. Ye only got this job because Mr. Myers knows that housekeeper's husband and wrote ye a recommendation against 'is better judgment. We won't be 'aving ye ruin our good names anymore with yer wicked ways."

Pip kept his snort of laughter to himself but only just. Maud had started her life as a whore. Mr. Carey, though he appeared as fine and upstanding a gentleman as could be, had spent years as a smuggler with Maud's husband, Stubbs, on the coasts of Cornwall. And all the servants in the house were unwed mothers Maud had rescued from London's streets—the many children running about the farm, their bastards. Not even including Pip's sordid history, if ever there were a house where "wicked ways" and "good names" shouldn't be mentioned, it was here.

And yet appearances and reputation counted more than truth in the country. He was smart enough to know that. Mr. Carey had spent a great deal of time and effort establishing them as a respectable household while Pip had spent far too much time doing the opposite. So perhaps the time had come to settle down and behave himself. If only he knew what he should settle *for*.

The sound of the front door closing and footsteps in the main hall brought an end to whatever else Maud might have said on the subject. Master Carey and Master Carruthers were back from their ride. Maud needed to see to their afternoon tea, and Pip should go to the stables to help with the horses and pitch in wherever else he could until he set off on his next adventure.

Maud sighed heavily as she stood and smoothed her hands down her pristine apron. "If ye think ye'll find whatever it is ye'r lookin' for in Keswick, then go with me blessin'. Just promise ye'll come back, love. I miss ye dearly when ye'r gone… and the children as well."

Pip stood and kissed her cheek. "I promise."

That vow he could easily keep. He might be restless at the farm, but it would always be home as long as his family of choice was there. He would always come back.

Chapter *One*

September, 1826
Keswick, Cumberland

PIP STARTED his day at Greer Cottage the same as he had every other in the two months since he'd come to Keswick. At dawn, the singularly unpleasant voice of Mrs. Applethwaite, the housekeeper, screeched at him through his door, rousing him from his soft, warm bed and demanding he quit lazing about and get to work. Pip, in his turn, grumbled and called the woman unflattering names under his breath. But still he crawled from beneath the linens and washed in the icy water from the basin and ewer atop his plain wooden dresser—the only piece of furniture in his tiny room other than the bed. After as quick a wash as he could manage, he pulled on his thick wool waistcoat, jacket, and trousers over the coarse linen shirt and drawers he'd slept in, then left his room in his stocking feet, and padded down the cramped and dark hall to the kitchen.

From there, however, he'd been forced to change his routine over the last fortnight. Instead of joining the housekeeper and her husband in breaking their fast, as he had done for the first month and a half, Pip now crept as silently as possible through the kitchen to the back door. Quiet as a mouse, using every ounce of skill he'd acquired during his misspent childhood plying the buzman's trade in Rat's Castle, Pip tiptoed through the kitchen. Snatching a slice of bread from the board and a steaming bowl of porridge out from under Mr. Applethwaite's snoring nose might not be as much of a challenge as picking pockets, but Mrs. Applethwaite was as fierce as any constable Pip had ever dodged.

Breakfast in hand, he continued to the door, grabbed his boots from where Mrs. Applethwaite's edicts had consigned them, and slipped outside without so much as a stirring of the air to mark his passing. Once in the open air and away from the housekeeper, Pip breathed a sigh of relief, tugged on his boots without bothering to lace them, and headed across the muddy yard to a quiet corner in the barn where he could break his fast in peace.

Mrs. Applethwaite would notice his absence and the missing food soon enough. But Pip would already be hard at work by that time, and she'd have to dirty her boots and the hems of her skirts if she wanted to give him an earful without interrupting his chores. He'd had to endure the woman's hysterics ever since she'd received the letter announcing their master's impending arrival. She carried on like a fishwife all day long, chasing after Pip, and finding more and more work to add to his already impressive duties. In the end, Pip had had no choice but to avoid her at all costs or find himself worked into an early grave. Sheer self-preservation led to his return to guile and thievery—or at least that's what he told his conscience whenever it tried to raise its thin and querulous little voice.

When Maud had originally spoken to him about the position, it had been with the understanding that his duties would revolve around the care of a single horse, a cow, and chickens, as well as a few odd chores that Mrs. Applethwaite and her husband couldn't manage on their own. Only after his arrival did he learn those few odd chores entailed nearly everything under *Mr.* Applethwaite's charge, for the man was always ailing and rarely left his comfortable chair by the fire—or his bottle of Old Tom. But Maud's warnings were clear. Pip believed her when she said he'd receive no more recommendations. So he had no choice but to accept his lot or go crawling back to Penrith, for forever this time.

At first, Pip hadn't actually minded. With only the three of them, he was not taxed by the work. He didn't enjoy being idle, and they left him to himself most of the day. In fact, if things had stayed as they were—and Mr. Applethwaite had parted with even a little tipple of gin every now and again—Pip would have been fairly content with his lot. But now with the housekeeper on him all hours of the day and her husband, the stingy old sod, guarding his bottle like his wife guarded her clean floors, they left Pip with all the hard labor and sober as a vicar to boot.

Suffering, thy name is Pip.

He tugged his jacket a little tighter around his neck and scooped warm porridge into his mouth with the slice of bread as he wiggled his frozen toes in his boots. His stockings were worn thin since Mrs. Applethwaite forbade him to wear his boots in her kitchen. Soon he'd need to buy some house slippers and new stockings as well with the meager amount he'd managed to set by from his wages.

"Tisn't fair," he groused into the empty air.

Pip shivered and sighed dramatically, pouting, though no one other than the horse and Molly, the cow, was there to appreciate the picture he made. He was saving all his blunt for the fancy russet waistcoat he admired through the tailor's shop window in the village. The waistcoat matched his auburn curls to perfection, and he'd spent many an hour daydreaming about the figure he'd cut wearing it—and the attention he'd get from the village girls. Now, if he bought the things he truly needed, the waistcoat would probably be long gone before he could save enough again to buy it.

Pip sighed once more over his loss, and the horse nickered back, making him smile. "Laugh all ye want, 'orse. But it were a pretty waistcoat, and I'm sure there ain't a man in the village who'd 'ave worn it better."

What did it matter anyway?

Tucked away at the cottage, he wouldn't have much opportunity to wear something so fine. No one would see him in it but the horse, Molly, the housekeeper and her husband, and perhaps a few of the village chits when he was sent for supplies. Every one of them—except perhaps the girls—would think he'd lost his bleedin' mind wasting his blunt on a bit of vanity. Agnes might have appreciated it but Agnes preferred him without any clothes at all, so crying over the loss of it would do no good.

Pip downed the rest of his breakfast quickly and set the bowl aside. Ignoring the screeching from the kitchen door that signaled Mrs. Applethwaite had finally discovered his theft and his absence, he tied his boots and then set to work on the duties for which he'd actually been retained, knowing it would be some time before Mrs. Applethwaite worked up enough of a temper to willingly venture through the mud to find him. Pip hoped to be mostly through with his duties in the barn by then and free to run away if need be.

He rushed through his morning chores as much to keep warm as any other reason. Some days, he doubted he'd ever become fully accustomed to the cold of the lake country, and he very much feared his wool jacket would not be enough protection, come winter. But he could ill afford the expense of a new coat, and he sighed heavily again as the pretty waistcoat moved further and further from his grasp. A job as a clerk didn't seem so unpalatable as it had only a couple of months ago. But Pip always felt that way when winter came, and then spring would show her lovely face again, and he'd be anxious to return to the open air.

When he had seen to Molly and the chickens, Pip filled a couple of buckets from the well. He slunk in and out of Mrs. Applethwaite's kitchen, unnoticed as before, and left the buckets in the corner by the door for her to find while she bustled in front of the kitchen fire, all unaware. After that, Pip stacked more wood within easy reach of the door, fetched the pail of milk he'd taken from Molly that morning, and left it beside the water.

Mrs. Applethwaite was now thumping about somewhere in the house, so Pip took the opportunity to snatch a little more for his breakfast while Mr. Applethwaite continued to snore quietly by the fire. The man had more hairs bristling out of his ears and his bulbous red nose than he had on his head, and Pip was momentarily distracted watching them shiver and dance with his rumbling exhalations. Pip had almost finished with his second heel of bread and the apple he'd snatched when the housekeeper's heavy footsteps sounded on the stairs. He took one last longing look at the bottle by Mr. Applethwaite's feet before he hurried outside again.

The autumn sun had broken through the mist in the yard, and Pip smiled in triumph as he closed his eyes and turned his face up to it. Not only had he managed to avoid Mrs. Applethwaite for the entire morning, but now nothing stood between him and seeing to his favorite duty of all. He hurried to the gray stone and thatched-roofed barn and saddled the horse quickly. Mrs. Applethwaite called for him as he led the horse through the gate, but Pip pretended not to hear. He mounted as soon as he was able and rode off without a backward glance. Exercising the horse was the only true joy he had at that lonely stone cottage, and he wouldn't be kept from it for anyone, especially not now when the master was due to arrive at any moment and would more than likely take the pleasure for himself.

The horse didn't have a name. Pip would have named the magnificent creature the very instant he met him, something like Titan or Samson to match his grandeur. But Mrs. Applethwaite insisted the prize gelding was a present to their master from his brother, Sir Edward James McNalty, *baronet*, and their master alone had the right to name him.

By now, Pip had lost count of the number of times Mrs. Applethwaite mentioned that their master's brother was a baronet. Pip supposed he should have been as proud as she to be employed by such a lofty family, but having spent many years under the patronage and in the employ of Master Carey, whose brother was a *viscount*, Pip had lost some of the awe he might once have felt for the highborn. They only ever treated him like dirt under their feet—except Mr. Carey that is. And Mr. Carey was living proof that blue blood didn't mean a man's conscience and hands were any cleaner than Pip's. A man's deeds and character spoke more clearly of his worth than anything else. If only the rest of the world saw it the same way.

As Pip rode over the fells to his favorite spot, high above the village of Keswick, he forgot all about the duties and the tongue-lashing he would receive on his return. The sky above was clear and beautiful. Derwentwater to the south sparkled in the sun like shards of glass. The air carried only hints of loam, coal, and wood smoke. And Pip sat astride the most magnificent beast he'd ever been allowed to ride. For those few short moments each day, it didn't matter that he was born a street wretch and a bastard. On the back of that horse, he was the equal of any man. He owned the world and no one could make him feel any less a man.

He stayed there, surveying his kingdom, until the sun was high enough in the sky that he couldn't put off returning to the cottage any longer. Mrs. Applethwaite might have difficulty finding someone to replace him so close to their master's return, but if Pip pushed his luck too far, the woman could and would send him packing. He had no doubts about that. With a long-suffering sigh, Pip turned the horse around and headed back the way he'd come.

New tracks rutted the muddy road leading to the cottage. And when he reached the yard, he found a carriage waiting in front of the stone archway by the front door. Pip's stomach dropped in dread. He could already feel the loss of his only pleasure, even as his breath quickened in anticipation of meeting his new master. Two men were unloading trunks from the back and top of the carriage while Mrs. Applethwaite directed them with fluttering hands. Pip dismounted reluctantly and led the horse through the open gate as quietly as he could, but it was no use. Mrs. Applethwaite spotted him before he could disappear into the barn.

"Where have you been?" she all but screeched.

"I were only seeing to me duties, Missus," Pip replied meekly, with the best northern accent he could manage. He'd learned early that neither the cant of his youth, nor the polish of Vicar Halford's schooling would earn him any friends in the lake country, so he did his best to ape the locals wherever he went.

"Well put that animal away and 'urry back as fast as ye can," she ordered urgently, a hint of her Yorkshire birth creeping into her own usually proper British in her distress. "The master has sent his trunks on ahead while 'e rests from 'is journey, but he's only a few miles away, and we expect him tonight!"

Some of the tightness in Pip's chest eased, even as he felt a pang of disappointment. His curiosity about his new master wouldn't be satisfied that day. But that also meant he might have another opportunity to ride the horse tomorrow before the man had fully recovered from his travels.

Despite the desperation in her tone, Pip noted that Mrs. Applethwaite's husband was nowhere to be found while there were heavy trunks and crates to be unloaded. But Pip kept that observation to himself. With her nerves so obviously frayed, the housekeeper wouldn't thank him for calling her attention to it. He simply put the horse into the stall built specially for it and returned to help the men unload.

When they'd placed all the trunks and boxes safely inside, stacked along either side of the front hall, Mrs. Applethwaite paid the coachmen from a small purse she always kept in her apron pocket. The men tipped their caps in thanks and climbed back into the coach. After they passed through the gate, Mrs. Applethwaite turned to Pip. "These all need to be carried up to the master's rooms," she said casually, pointing to the six trunks on the left side of the door as if she were talking about a few baskets of flowers or something equally small and easy to carry.

Pip looked between her and the disappearing coachmen for a few moments in disbelief. "Y' want *me* to do it?"

The old woman's already severe countenance pinched even more in disapproval. "Who else?"

Pip ground his teeth together before trying again. "Pardon, ma'am, but ye said I weren't to set foot in the 'ouse. Now I'm t' carry all 'is things up to 'is rooms? Ye said ye and Mr. Applethwaite were the only ones allowed—"

Mrs. Applethwaite sliced her hand through the air to cut him off and straightened to her full height, scowling at him. "Mr. Applethwaite is unwell today. This once, you will be allowed in the rest of the house to carry the master's trunks to his rooms upstairs." The hints of her accent disappeared as her haughtiness returned, and she looked down her pointed nose at him. Pip sighed in resignation and went to pick up the first trunk. "Take off those dirty boots first before you ruin the carpets!" she snapped at him.

Pip bit his tongue to keep from blistering her ears with a few choice words from his childhood. He removed his boots by the door, and then, in his stocking feet, he began lugging the heavy trunks up the stairs to where she directed. Although he grumbled a bit under his breath, Pip's temper didn't actually last long.

He'd never been allowed beyond the kitchen and the yard before, so his curiosity soon won out over his pique. Mrs. Applethwaite had opened all the doors and windows to air the rooms upstairs for their master's arrival, and Pip was able to see into each as he followed her to the master's bedchamber at the end of the hall.

None of the rooms were large, but they were all well-appointed. Each had a bed, a dresser, a chair, a washstand, and night tables. All three had been put together in similar fashion and with little imagination—Mrs. Appplethwaite's doing, Pip supposed—but they were a lot finer than Pip's little closet behind the kitchen, and they all had one very important luxury Pip's room lacked: a hearth.

When he set the last trunk down in the small dressing room at the far end of the master's bedchamber, the housekeeper shooed him out with instructions to carry the remaining crates into the library downstairs.

Pip hovered near the sturdy dark wood bedframe, reluctant to leave at first. He was dying of curiosity over what was inside their master's trunks. According to what little the housekeeper had told him and the village gossip he'd heard, Major McNalty had not only been all over the world, but he'd spent the last couple of months in London and had probably purchased the newest fashions from some of the finest tailors in the country. Pip dearly wished to see the silks and fine linens as well as any exotic apparel the man might have brought back from his travels. But once he was shooed out of the room and out of sight of those tempting trunks, the housekeeper's instructions sunk in, and Pip's reluctance fled in lieu of a greater prize. He was finally going to be allowed into the library, and without anyone looking over his shoulder. He grinned at his luck and hurried down the stairs.

What did a glimpse of clothes he would never be allowed to wear matter when the possibility of trunks and shelves full of books awaited him? Those at least he had a chance at borrowing, if only in the dark of night, without the master knowing he'd done it.

Pip fell upon the crates with alacrity, carrying them into the library as fast as he could, cracking each one open, and digging through the packing materials to see what treasures they held. He needed to be fast. He wouldn't have long before the housekeeper finished unpacking the master's things, and she'd be sure to order him out of the house the moment she discovered him still in the library.

Pip would be the first to admit he couldn't actually remember the last time he'd cracked open a book to read for his own pleasure. He'd read to some of the children on Master Carey and Master Carruthers's farm from time to time, but thus far, the pleasures of the country had proved to be distraction enough. But ever since moving to the cottage, so far removed from the village, Pip had been lonely and anxious for some distraction when the sun went down. And now just looking at the shelves lined with books and the crates heavy with more had him suddenly starving for a good novel or a bit of poetry. The smell of the leather bindings and the feel of the smooth vellum pages beneath his touch almost had his cock stirring to life, he was so enthralled.

The sound of the housekeeper's footsteps on the stairs broke the spell all too soon. Pip quickly palmed a small slender volume from the crate at his feet and slipped it into the lining of his jacket before the old woman discovered him. He'd find a way to return it somehow, but it probably wouldn't be missed, not with so many others to choose from.

"What are you doing in here?" Mrs. Applethwaite demanded, her hands on her hips.

Pip widened his eyes, all innocence and country simplicity. "I brought in the crates like ye said, Missus. I thought ye might need 'elp opening 'em is all."

She scowled suspiciously at him for a moment before she sniffed. "Well, that will be all, Pip. You mustn't ever touch the master's fine books. You'll ruin them with those dirty hands. They'll all need to be catalogued and placed in particular order on the shelves. You won't be any help with that, so go on with you. Go and fill the coal scuttles and leave them by the door. Mr. Applethwaite and I will see to the rest."

Pip took one last longing look at the shelves and crates before tugging his cap and scurrying from the room like the good, ignorant country drudge he was supposed to be. As he pulled on his boots at the door and headed across the yard to fetch the coal, Pip had one consolation at least. If he wasn't to be allowed back in the house proper, *Mr.* Applethwaite would at long last have to earn his keep tending the fires and doing the heavy work for the master. Pip whistled merrily to himself as he shoveled hard black lumps into the scuttles from the pile that was delivered once every fortnight. And he had a spring in his step as he carried them back to the house.

When the task she set him was completed, Pip took advantage of the housekeeper's distraction and stole a few hours to read the book he'd borrowed. Stretched out comfortably in a soft pile of straw in the barn, Pip lost himself in the most unusual world of Percy Shelley's poetry, only returning when Mrs. Applethwaite's strident call shook him out his fantasies.

"There you are," she shrilled from the kitchen door when Pip poked his head out of the barn. "I need you to take the cart to Mr. Cooper's shop before dark. The master has sent a list of his requirements with his trunks. Here." She handed over the small slip of paper. "Don't lose it."

"Yes, Missus," he replied, ducking his head so she wouldn't see him roll his eyes.

He strode across the yard, snatched the paper from her hand, and then happily ran to fetch the cart. He didn't have to be told twice. The cart was heavy and the walk long—and he'd never understand why Mrs. Applethwaite wouldn't allow him to hitch the horse to it, especially when the master wasn't there to complain—but any opportunity for him to be allowed into the village and away from her frowning face was to be treasured, and he wouldn't waste a moment of it arguing with the woman.

Maud may have only chosen to recommend him for this position because of its distance from the village, thus limiting the amount of mischief he could get into. But Pip could find mischief at the bottom of a well if need be, and a little distance hadn't stopped him thus far, only slowed him down a bit.

When he reached the village, Pip went straight to the shop to rid himself of the cart. Mr. Cooper, the owner, lumbered outside, his great girth barely contained within a pinstriped apron, his ginger mustache bristling like an angry hedgehog. From the very first, the shopkeeper had taken a dislike to Pip, though Pip had given him no reason for it. Mr. Cooper took the slip of paper from Pip without a word or a look of acknowledgement, but as always he was certain to place his considerable bulk between Pip and one of his two daughters, now peering shyly at Pip through the window from behind the shop counter.

A few years ago, Pip might have given the little ginger chit a saucy wink behind her father's back. He was tempted to even now, if only to answer Cooper's rudeness. But that was the only temptation Pip felt so he didn't bother. The girl was fifteen if she was a day, and Pip had no patience for hunting the chaste and timid anymore. He'd lost interest in that not long after leaving London, preferring more experienced partners to dally with. Just the thought of having to put that much effort into wooing a girl made him feel tired. The girl's grumpy walrus of a father had nothing to fear from Pip, even if Pip would probably never convince him of that.

Instead of wasting his time, Pip simply gave the man a polite tip of his cap and pretended he hadn't seen the girl. He wandered off, leaving Cooper to put the master's order together without fear for his daughter's virtue. Pip didn't need to oversee the process anyway. The housekeeper would check everything for the tiniest mistake when he brought the cart home, and she still didn't know Pip could read, so Pip would only blame the shopkeeper if something were missing. The world believed him ignorant and dull-witted, and Pip was more than content to keep it that way.

As he walked away from Mr. Cooper, the tailor's shop window called to him first, like always. The russet waistcoat was still in the window, waiting to be fitted to some lucky fellow, and Pip took a few moments to stare at it longingly. Eventually, he tore his eyes away and considered moving on to the shoemaker's to see what it would cost to have some house slippers made, but he swore under his breath when he suddenly realized he'd forgotten his purse in his haste to leave the cottage. Without it, he couldn't buy anything or even place an order. He supposed he could tell the man to put it on the cottage's account, but he wasn't certain how Mrs. Applethwaite would react to that.

Pip pondered his options for a few moments until a reflection in the shop window caught his attention and his face split into a wide grin, his frustrations forgotten. Agnes Foster, the eldest daughter of the neighboring dairy farmer, was watching him from across the lane, her two little sisters in tow. The girls were all giggling as they fussed with their bonnets and fluttered their eyelashes in his direction. Never one to turn his back on a bit of attention, Pip doffed his cap and gave the girls his most charming, cocksure smile as he strutted across the street and stopped a few paces away from them.

"'Allo, doves. What brings such pretty birds out o' their nests on a fine day like today?" He let a bit of London creep back into his speech because, unlike the older generations in the country, the village chits actually seemed to appreciate a bit of the exotic from him.

"It's Agnes's birthday," the youngest sister, Mary, twittered. "Father let us come into the village to buy new ribbons as a treat."

Pip clapped a hand to his chest. "If only I 'ad known," Pip bemoaned dramatically, making the two younger girls giggle. He winked at Agnes above her sister's heads. "I fear I 'ave no means of wishing you a proper birthday, Agnes."

Agnes smirked back at him, and her eyes raked him boldly from foot to crown. "Another time per'aps?"

Agnes might not be the comeliest chit to be had in Keswick, but she was certainly the most attentive and willing to please. Her apple cheeks were rosy with life. Her plain brown eyes were always full of promises and her plump figure warm and inviting. The first time they met, Pip only had to smile in her direction and she'd all but dragged him to the nearest haystack for a bit of fun. The very few times they'd been able to meet in secret afterward, she doted on his every word and deed, and Pip lapped up her admiration like it was Cobbler's Punch, starved as he was for pleasant company—or any company for that matter—at the cottage.

Other village girls and married ladies had shown an open interest in him of course, but none as brash as Agnes. Most of them wanted to be wooed. And why should he bother with that when Agnes was plenty obliging?

"Yes, per'aps another time, Miss Agnes," he replied. "But alas, I must go now. Old Cooper'll be wondering where I've got to." Pip donned his cap and bowed with a flourish worthy of the gentry before giving the girls another wink and heading back the way he'd come. Their giggles followed him, and Pip couldn't help but smile. Agnes would find her way to him soon enough, if *her* smile were any indication. All Pip need do was wait.

The waiting wouldn't be difficult.

The thought made Pip uneasy, but he refused to examine why. His steps faltered and his smile faded. He shook his head, as if to rid himself of a bothersome insect, and strode with purpose back to Mr. Cooper's shop. He left the village at as quick a pace as he could manage, dragging the loaded cart behind him. He felt eyes on him as he headed down the lane toward home, but he didn't turn to look. The allure of the village had paled for him that day for some reason, and he was suddenly feeling out of sorts.

When he returned to the cottage, Mrs. Applethwaite was waiting impatiently for him, as he'd expected. After a few choice words regarding Pip's slothfulness, she set him to work again, gathering more wood for the kitchen fire, washing the seemingly endless stream of bowls, buckets, and pots she'd dirtied scrubbing the house and cooking what appeared to be a great feast in honor of their master's arrival.

By the time he'd finished the last bowl, Pip's hands ached and his skin was raw, but at least he was no longer uneasy. He was too tired to feel anything but exhaustion. When all was finally to Mrs. Applethwaite's satisfaction, she allowed them to sit down to a bowl of stew and more of yesterday's bread, even though the feast she'd prepared sat in covered dishes by the fire, taunting Pip with the richness of its aromas.

The sun set and darkness fell while Pip fidgeted in his chair after he'd finished eating. All he wanted to do was go to his bed, but the housekeeper insisted they wait to welcome the master when he finally arrived. Pip passed the time by gazing hungrily back and forth between the covered dishes and Mr. Applethwaite's bottle of gin, although more often at the bottle as the long hours passed.

No sound disturbed the quiet of the cottage beyond the crackling of the kitchen fire, the occasional snore from Mr. Applethwaite, and the rustling of cloth as Mrs. Applethwaite worked on her mending. No carriage rattled into the yard, no messenger knocked on the door, and by the time the large clock in the hall chimed eleven, Pip was certain their master would not arrive that night. Perhaps he had fallen ill on his journey or his carriage had needed repairs. Pip was anxious to meet his new master. They all were. But he'd had a very long day and now no longer cared if the man ever showed up as long as the interminable waiting was over and he was allowed to go to his bed.

Eventually, even Mrs. Applethwaite admitted defeat, allowing them a few choice bits of the feast that wouldn't keep until the next day and ordering Pip to his bed. Pip didn't need any further encouragement. He was out of his chair and down the hall before she finished speaking, and he fell asleep before his head even hit the pillow.

Chapter Two

THE HOUSE was completely quiet when he woke the next morning. Despite his exhaustion, his sleep had not been restful. Strange dreams he couldn't recall after waking plagued him for most of the night and forced him out of bed long before the sun rose above the fells. He dressed in the dark and padded to the kitchen, but was surprised to find it empty, even at this early hour. Not questioning his good fortune, Pip snatched a couple of pastries from a crock on the hearth and gobbled them down after stirring up the kitchen fire to warm himself. He dallied by the fire, unwilling to leave its warmth, until he heard sounds coming from the Applethwaites' bedchamber. Before the housekeeper could catch him, he quickly downed the rest of his stolen breakfast and hurried outside.

The yard was draped in mist, and the sun still hadn't crested the hills, but Pip knew the way, even in the dark. If he set to work now, he might be done early enough to sneak away for a long ride on the horse before their master arrived. He battled his fatigue and the cold by attacking his chores with an enthusiasm he did not feel until both at last surrendered the field and he was actually feeling like himself again.

Soon enough, Pip finished tending the animals, and he grabbed a couple of empty pails to fetch water from the well, but a noise at the back of the barn caught his attention and he froze. Heart racing, Pip turned and set the pails down as quietly as he could. The rattle came again as Pip crept slowly down the aisle toward Molly. The old cow stood placidly chewing on her fresh pile of hay, completely unaware of anything amiss. Pip put a hand on her back and waited. He was on the verge of dismissing the noise as a trick of the wind, when the shutters at the back of the barn suddenly swung outward and a darkly cloaked figure began to climb through the opening.

Pip dropped into a crouch and hid behind Molly. He struggled to control his breathing as he searched nearby for a rake or a shovel to wield as a weapon. He'd just spotted an old broom, almost within reach, when a muffled oath drew his eyes back to the intruder—in time to see the figure fall arse over teakettle into a pile of straw beneath the opening. At which point Pip snorted out a laugh in both amusement and relief and hurried to help Agnes with her plight.

"All right, dove?" Pip asked, fighting hard to conceal his amusement as he helped her right her skirts and then picked bits of straw out of her hair.

Agnes pouted for a moment, the pink of her cheeks visible even in the poor light, before she recovered herself and leered at him. "Father don' know I'm gone. I don' 'ave long an' I want me birthday present," she said. And then she started fumbling with the placket of Pip's trousers without so much as a by your leave.

She shoved him back into the pile of straw, and Pip didn't bother to resist. His body was already responding to the attention, if not the girl in particular, and Pip could think of worse ways to spend his morning. The way Agnes was looking at him, as if he was the most delectable morsel she'd ever seen, made his blood flow to all the appropriate places. And soon, after her strong hands set to work on him a bit, Pip was ready to give her the present she'd come for.

Pip pushed his trousers and his drawers to his knees as Agnes lifted her skirts and climbed onto his lap. She rode him like that for a time, muffling her cries with her fist, until Pip decided he needed to finish their encounter soon or they might be discovered. He wrapped an arm around her waist, cupped her arse with his other hand, and flipped her onto her back in the straw. With practiced ease, Pip lifted one of her thighs over his arm, pressed the thumb of his other hand on the place that gave her the most pleasure, and thrust into her, over and over, as her muffled cries grew louder.

Sweat was dripping down his face by the time Agnes appeared to be nearing completion. Pip's thighs were cramping and his thumb was getting tired, but he didn't stop. It was a matter of pride to him that he never finished before his partner. To own the truth, Pip never actually finished *at all* inside a woman, but they always assumed he was simply being considerate—careful to avoid unwanted pregnancy—and Pip thought that was as good a reason as any.

Unfortunately for both of them, he was panting and Agnes was mewling so loud Pip didn't hear the barn door open until too late. Just as Agnes let out a cry and stiffened beneath him, Pip heard uneven footsteps behind him and a voice he didn't recognize shouted, "What the devil?"

Caught bare-arsed in the barn with a milkmaid beneath him, all Pip could do was pant breathlessly as he stared up at the finely dressed gentleman who had to be none other than his new master. Pip should have been scrambling to cover himself and Agnes, making excuses, or begging for forgiveness, but a pair of shocked and angry silver eyes held him rooted to the spot.

Eventually, Agnes shoved him away and got to her feet, blushing furiously and mumbling apologies to the floor. When the man's pale gaze dropped to where Pip's trousers should have been but weren't, Pip finally gathered his wits enough to cover himself and climbed to his feet.

"Sir, I—" Pip had no idea what he would've said beyond that, but the man didn't give him the opportunity. He simply turned his back on the two of them and limped from the barn, moving slowly and leaning heavily on the walking stick Pip could now see clearly. Pip stared in that direction until long after the man had disappeared through the thick dark wood door to the house. He was barely aware Agnes was speaking to him until she shook his arm.

"Ye don' think he'll tell me father do ye?"

Mrs. Applethwaite came rushing out of the kitchen door then, and Pip winced. "Ye'd best go, Agnes, afore she sees yer face," Pip said as he shooed Agnes toward the opening she'd climbed in and hurried to waylay Mrs. Applethwaite in the yard.

"Pip… I don't…. How could you?" The housekeeper was beside herself, so flustered she couldn't seem to form a complete sentence. She clutched at her bony breast with a skeletal hand while the other knotted in her apron, and Pip felt a stab of guilt for the first time since he'd come to Keswick.

He hung his head and whispered, "Forgive me, Missus."

He looked up at the woman from beneath his thick eyelashes, making his brown eyes go soft in a way that Maud, and almost any other woman he'd ever known, couldn't resist. But Mrs. Applethwaite was as immune as ever to his charms. Her face hardened, and her lips drew down into a thin, wrinkled line.

"I thought it peculiar that the housekeeper at your previous place of employment inquired as to whether I had any daughters or whether there would be any serving maids at the cottage. But I expected better of you, Pip." She sniffed and lifted her head, apparently having regained some of her composure as well as her tongue. She looked away from him as she continued. "The master's first day here and already you've shamed not only yourself but me as well. I would send you packing this instant, but the master has sent for you. Go quickly. I will have your wages ready to take with you when he's finished."

As she turned and headed for the kitchen, Pip sighed and tugged to straighten his clothes a little more, brushing the last few bits of straw from his trousers and jacket. This would not be the first time he'd been sacked over a girl, but usually it was an angry father, brother, or husband who sent him packing.

The sun was still low enough in the sky that the interior of the house was dark but for the glow of candlelight coming from the library. Pip paused in the doorway and considered taking off his boots to spare the carpets but eventually decided against it. If he was to receive a dressing down by his soon-to-be former master, he'd rather do it with his boots on, although he did take a moment to use the scraper by the door.

When Pip entered the library, Major Astley McNalty was seated in a stuffed leather high-back chair in front of the hearth. A glass of amber liquid rested on the table next to him, and the man had one booted leg propped on a small padded stool. Pip was pleased to note bits of mud caked the man's boot, so Pip wouldn't be the only one to blame for any damage to the carpets—though he supposed that hardly mattered now.

The major didn't rise or speak as Pip doffed his cap and stood nervously in the doorway. He simply watched Pip with those unnerving silver eyes as the silence stretched between them.

"What is your name?" the major finally asked, his voice quiet and rough, as though he didn't use it often.

"Pip, sir," he answered, caught off guard by the question. Surely the man knew that already.

"Your family name is Pip?" The major frowned at him, his dark gold eyebrows drawing down, shadowing the paleness of his eyes enough that Pip was finally released from their spell and could think more clearly.

"No, sir. Stubbs, Phillip Stubbs, sir. People call me Pip." Stubbs was not actually his family name either, but since he hadn't any other, and he barely remembered his mother, he'd taken Maud and Stubbs's name as his own.

The major took a sip from his glass as he seemed to ponder this, and Pip squirmed, wishing he had a glass or a whole bottle of his own.

"I prefer Phillip to Stubbs," the major said finally. "Pip is simply ridiculous, however."

Pip's own eyebrows drew down in confusion at that. What was the man on about? Why didn't he simply sack Pip and get it over and done?

The major studied Pip for a while longer before he took another drink from his glass and then set it aside. "I understand from Mrs. Applethwaite's letters that you have been under my employ for two months and you have proved to be an able worker. That this is the first time anything of the sort of behavior I witnessed in the barn has happened. Is that correct?"

It wasn't, but Pip was hardly going to admit it.

"Yes, sir," he lied meekly, dropping his gaze to the floor before lifting it cautiously again. He let his eyes go soft and piteous as he had with Mrs. Applethwaite, more out of habit than any expectation the look would gain him anything. But for the briefest of moments, Pip was certain he saw something flash in the major's eyes. Between one blink and the next, it was gone, not enough time for Pip to put a name to what he saw.

The major cleared his throat and looked away as he reached for his glass again and downed a large swallow before he spoke. "I'm willing to overlook what happened in the barn but only once. Nothing like that is to ever happen again. Am I understood?"

"I'm not sacked?" Pip was so surprised he blurted out the first thing that came into his head.

The major's lip twitched for a moment, but Pip wasn't certain whether it was an attempt at a smile or a grimace. "Not *this* time," the major replied, the warning implicit in his tone.

Pip was stunned more than relieved. He didn't understand why the man would bother keeping him on when surely Mrs. Applethwaite hadn't come to his defense. But at least he wouldn't have to go crawling home to Maud just yet. "Thank you, sir."

The major grunted and waved his hand in dismissal without looking up from the coals. "Go. See to the rest of your duties. I wish to hear no more complaints about you."

"Yes, sir. Thank you, sir." Pip ducked his head and hurried out of the room before the man could change his mind.

When Pip returned to the kitchen, the housekeeper was waiting with a pitifully small pile of coins in her hand and an ugly frown on her face.

"I'm not dismissed, Missus," Pip said, and his own surprise and confusion were mirrored in the housekeeper's countenance.

"Are you certain?" she asked.

"Aye. 'e said so 'imself," Pip replied with a shrug.

She continued to look flustered for a moment before straightening to her full height and sniffing. "If that is what the master wishes, then you may remain. But if I hear even so much as a hint of impropriety about you, that will be the end. Am I understood?"

"Yes, Missus," Pip said, giving her his most contrite look.

"Go. See to your duties. I do not wish to set eyes on you until after tea. I will have plenty of work for you to do when you return."

Pip left the kitchen as fast as his feet would carry him. When he'd finished the last of his duties in the yard, he saddled the horse and led it through the gate. He'd received no orders to the contrary, and after the uproar of the morning, Pip needed his escape more than ever.

He let the horse have its head once he mounted. It galloped down the road and across the fells, following their usual track, seeming as eager as Pip to be free of the yard. But once they stopped and Pip gazed down at the village and the water, he didn't feel his usual happiness steal over him. He was strangely agitated, and he didn't know why. True, being caught quite literally with his trousers down wouldn't have been his first choice of ways to meet his new master. But the major had forgiven him and allowed him to stay. He should have been relieved.

Pip pursed his lips and thought back on the meeting in the library and on the man himself. The major was nothing like what Pip had expected. He was tall, probably the same height as Pip. He was broad-shouldered though he appeared somewhat lean and frail. For some reason Pip had envisioned a man past the prime of his life, but despite being a bit drawn and pale, the major looked to be in his midthirties at the most. Pip was foolish not to remember a man might have reasons other than old age for retiring his commission. Whatever had caused that limp must have ended the major's career early, that's all.

Pip closed his eyes and lifted his face to the sun, enjoying its warmth on his skin as the brisk wind toyed with his hair and clothes and whistled past his ears. He took several deep breaths, trying to ease the tightness in his chest as the horse shifted impatiently beneath him. But when it appeared that neither he nor the horse were going to settle, Pip gave in and goaded the horse into a gallop again. If he couldn't breathe the unease away, he'd run it out instead.

They flew across the fells until Pip's face and hands were red with cold and his thighs burned. Only when he was breathless and the horse was spouting great plumes of steam into the air did Pip climb down and walk the animal back along the road to the cottage. Once they were back in the barn, he took extra care in wiping the horse down, making sure it hadn't suffered any injuries from their wild ride, before giving it a thorough brushing and an extra bit of grain as a treat. Then he draped a blanket over its back and left it in its stall. After that, he brought Molly in from the small fenced area where she was allowed to graze and closed the barn for the night.

Both the housekeeper and her husband were gone when he finally came inside. Pip assumed they were seeing to their master, and he gladly crept back to his room to wash up a little before returning to warm himself by the kitchen fire. He was tempted to hide in his room for the rest of the night, but he was in enough trouble as it was, so he thought he'd better not make the housekeeper come find him when she wanted him. Once his hands had warmed, Pip went in search of a bit of food and Mr. Applethwaite's gin bottle. He found some bread and a simple stew in a crock by the fire, but the housekeeper's husband had hidden his bottle well as always, and Pip still hadn't found it by the time the couple returned to the kitchen.

"Pip, the master needs more coal. Go and fill the buckets again," Mrs. Applethwaite ordered without even bothering to look at him.

"So soon?" The question slipped out before he could bite it back. He was tired, and he really didn't want to go out into the cold again.

She frowned at him. "It isn't your place to question. It is the master's wish." Her sharp features softened a little with what Pip could only assume was pity as she looked toward the door that led to the rest of the house. "I think he feels the cold most acutely. He is but a few months back from the Cape, after all. They say it's so very hot in Africa. I'm sure it is a great change for him and with his injury.... Well, we will simply have to order more coal, and you will have to fetch it more often. That is all."

Pip shrugged and bit back any further complaints. She was right. It wasn't his place to question, especially after this morning. And if the man could afford to keep his rooms like a hothouse, why shouldn't he? In the major's place, Pip would probably do the same.

And the Cape? The master had been to the Cape?

Pip had heard stories of Africa—its savagery and the riches to be found there. What must a place like that be like? What stories could the man tell? Pip couldn't even imagine, though he tried to dream of a place that warm as he stepped out into the frigid night.

Pip carried the scuttles to the front of the house and left them inside the door, as Mrs. Applethwaite instructed so her husband wouldn't have to carry them farther than necessary in his "frail" condition. The woman was probably more afraid the old sod would lose his balance and dump the mess on the master's carpets than that he would expire from the effort of carrying them from the kitchen, but either way it made no difference to Pip.

The house was dark as Pip peeked curiously inside the front door. He didn't see any sign of the major, and he felt an odd pang of disappointment at that. They would not likely have much interaction in future, given Pip's place in the household, and Pip was even more curious about the man now than before.

A sudden image of pale silver eyes came into his head, and Pip felt his chest tighten strangely. He backed out of the house and closed the door before he was caught. The Applethwaites could deal with the gentleman. Pip would be more than happy to spend his days with the horse instead.

Chapter *Three*

OVER THE next several days, things at the cottage settled again. The housekeeper fretted and fussed about feeding the major and seeing to his washing, but her hysteria seemed to have ebbed now that they all knew what to expect from him. The major wasn't actually much trouble at all, from what Pip could tell. He kept to himself and only rang for the Applethwaites once or twice beyond his regular meal times. Mr. Applethwaite still grumbled endlessly about the "extra" work he had to do. But Pip's own duties no longer seemed so overwhelming, and he was able to stop slinking about the place and rejoin the other two servants at most of their meals—his little incident with Agnes for all intents and purposes forgotten.

As Pip expected, he had almost no interaction with his new master beyond their disastrous first meeting. He saw the major often at his library window, and every once in a while Pip would receive a nod of the head as he crossed the yard attending to his duties. But if the man ever came out to the barn again to inspect his brother's present—the very reason Pip's services had been retained in the first place—Pip never saw him, nor did he speak directly with him again.

That first week, in addition to the deliveries of the post and feed for the animals, a few of the village notables paid calls to the major. Pip didn't know any of them by name, nor did they deign to introduce themselves to someone as lowly as Pip, but he could tell their status by the fine cut of their clothes. The visits were never long and the major never sent for a carriage or his horse to return any of the calls, so soon enough the visitors stopped coming. In fact, the only time Pip ever saw the major outside the cottage at all was when the man went for a short walk each evening before dinner. He would limp slowly across the yard as the sun set behind the fells, stop on a small rise not far from the house, and simply stand there, his back stiff and his shoulders straight, gazing off into the distance as the world darkened around him. Then, after his lonely vigil, he would return the way he'd come and disappear into the house again.

For reasons he didn't understand, Pip began lingering over the horse during those times. At first, he hadn't realized he was doing it. And when he did, Pip told himself he was only concerned for his master's health. The major was obviously impaired in some way. If he fell or needed assistance, Pip would know it straight away and the poor man wouldn't be left to cry for help until someone discovered him. But as the days passed, and the major appeared to recover some of his strength, moving more easily across the uneven ground, Pip continued to watch, despite the promise of a warm fire and a hearty dinner of his own awaiting him in kitchen.

The way the major stood each night, wrapped in solitude and gazing at nothing, struck Pip as so very melancholy and tragic. Pip had no place intruding on the man's privacy, and the major certainly wouldn't thank him for it, so Pip simply waited, shivering in the shadows of the barn, until the major slowly made his way back to the yard and safely into the cottage again before he too went inside.

The day the major did finally come out to the barn again, Pip was caught so completely off guard, he managed to make an ass of himself the second he opened his mouth. Late that morning, the sky clear and the sun warm despite the November chill, Pip eagerly looked forward to taking the horse out. He had just put the saddle on the horse's back when a noise from the open doorway made him turn. The major limped toward the stall and stopped a short distance from them. His eyes were even more unnerving in the bright light of day, and the fact that he simply stood there watching only increased Pip's unease.

Pip fidgeted nervously under the weight of his stare, uncertain of what he should do. Should he go back to saddling the horse or wait until his master gave him some sort of instruction? The major's expression was unreadable, and when the silence finally became too much to bear, Pip broke down and blurted out the first question that popped into his head. "Do ye want to ride 'im, sir?"

The major's jaw tightened, and his eyes narrowed to slits. Without a word, he spun around and limped out the way he'd come, leaving Pip to kick himself for his own stupidity. Of course the man didn't wish to go riding. Pip still knew nothing of the injury he'd had suffered, but he was obviously lame. What kind of an idiot asks a lame man if he wants to ride? Pip just *had* to go and open his giant gob and plant his boot directly in the middle of it.

Pip fought the urge to run after the major and apologize. He had a feeling that would only add insult to injury. Instead, Pip laid his head on the horse's neck and groaned.

"Daft bugger, ain't I?"

The horse snorted his agreement, and Pip smiled despite himself. He patted the beast's neck and let his eyes close for a time. When the horse began to shift restlessly beneath him, Pip finally shook off his mortification and finished saddling it. But as they rode out, Pip knew at once that his ride was already spoiled.

It hadn't taken him long to realize that the only reason he was allowed to continue his favorite duty was that the master was unable to perform it himself. A gentleman of the major's birth wouldn't forgo the pleasure of such a fine animal unless he had to. Never one to take pleasure in another's pain, that fact had put a bit of a pall on Pip's afternoon rides already. Now, after having seen the man's pain for himself, Pip couldn't get the image out of his head, and he urged the horse into a run, trying to escape his thoughts.

In the end, his guilt turned to irritation, the longer he thought about it. Why should he care if his new master was lame? What difference did it make? If their roles were reversed, the man wouldn't shed a tear for him. Pip knew that for certain. The gent had enough money to sit on his arse in comfort for the rest of his days and pay people like Pip and the Applethwaites to wait on his every need. That wasn't much of a hardship from Pip's way of thinking. Why on earth should Pip feel sorry for him?

Eventually the horse slowed to a stop at their usual place, and Pip sat back in the saddle, indulging in a solitary vigil of his own. He was purposefully trying to distract himself with the beauty all around him when a shout from nearby startled him out of his gloom.

"Oi, Pip!" Agnes waved as she crested the hill.

Pip forced a smile and climbed down from the horse. "Agnes, m' dove. Did yer father unlock the tower or did ye' climb down on yer own?" he teased.

Agnes huffed and giggled a little breathlessly. Her father's dairy farm might be the closest habitation to Greer cottage, but it was still a fair climb over rough hills, and she must have hurried for she was clearly out of breath—her ample bosom heaving beneath her knitted shawl.

"I were out in the barn when I saw ye on the hill. Father don' know I'm gone. But I 'ad to speak with ye," she panted. "I thought for sure ye'd be sacked after what 'appened. But I've 'eard not a word in the village."

Pip shrugged. "The master was forgiving. But I 'ave to be on me best from now on."

She snorted and Pip grinned, forgetting some of his earlier disquiet. Being with Agnes was always like that, always so easy. He should have sought her out long before now. He had no idea why he hadn't.

"Come sit wi' me." Pip reached for her hand and led her and the horse over to a small outcropping of rocks.

Agnes sat on a large flat stone, attempting to tame her wild brown curls beneath her bonnet and tugging her tan shawl more tightly around her shoulders while Pip secured the horse's reins. She'd apparently recovered her breath by the time Pip returned to sit beside her because she immediately began peppering him with questions. "What's 'e like? Everyone's all agog in the village. Is 'is brother truly a *baronet*? Is it true 'e were at Waterloo? An' that 'e's a surgeon? An' 'e's just back from the Cape where 'e were cut down by savages?"

All except for the bit about coming back from the Cape was news to Pip, so he held his tongue until she wound down a little. Pip was almost jealous that Agnes seemed to know so much more than he did, but he certainly wasn't going to admit it.

"That's what I 'eard," Pip lied. "But what else are they sayin'?"

Agnes's plain brown eyes were wide with excitement as she pressed herself close to his side, the warmth of her breast seeping through to Pip's skin despite the layers of wool and linen. "Only that 'e 'asn't been back to England more'n a couple o' times since Waterloo, travellin' the world over. Mary Trent said that Doctor Fields paid a call on 'im but stayed barely 'alf an hour. Is that true?"

Pip shrugged. "'E's 'ad a few callers, but I don' know who they were. We weren't exactly introduced. I saw to a few 'orses. I don' think none of them stayed long."

"Mary says 'e's been invited to at least two dinners in the village already, but 'e's accepted nary a one."

Her tone was scandalized, and Pip felt compelled to come to his master's defense for some strange reason. "'E's only just settled in, Agnes. An' I don't think 'e's recovered from his travels yet. 'is leg pains 'im, I'm sure."

"I suppose so." She shrugged and then looked coyly at Pip through her eyelashes. "'E is a 'andsome gentleman, though, ain't 'e? I only saw 'im that once, but I wouldn't mind bringing that one 'is breakfast every morning."

"Aye," Pip replied, too distracted by all he'd learned to fully understand her question until he looked up to find her watching him with a strange expression on her face. "What?"

She frowned at him, and it took a few seconds for Pip to realize his mistake. Instead of jealously objecting to her speaking that way about another man, he'd simply agreed with her without thinking. Before he could devise a means of smoothing Agnes's feathers, she huffed and jumped to her feet.

"Father'll be wonderin' where I've gone," she said tersely before turning her nose up and stalking away.

"Agnes!" Pip tried to call her back, but his efforts were halfhearted at best. And when she didn't stop or turn around, he let her go. She'd calm down after a space, and he'd try to talk to her again later… perhaps.

Chapter Four

THAT NIGHT at dinner, Pip wanted to ask Mrs. Applethwaite about all that he'd heard from Agnes but changed his mind when he saw what a temper she was in after she returned from seeing to their master. The woman even snapped at her drunkard of a husband twice in the space of a few minutes, more than she had in all the time Pip had been at the cottage, and Pip decided he would do best to remain invisible. Hopefully he'd find her in a better humor the next day so he could wheedle some of the story from her and satisfy his rampant curiosity.

As soon as he was finished eating, Pip hurried off to bed before she remembered he was there. The moon was full and the sky clear, so instead of risking drawing attention to himself by lighting a candle, Pip read by moonlight until he fell asleep.

He was dreaming about watching the major ride the horse in circles around him, smiling happily, when pounding on his door and Mrs. Applethwaite's harried voice startled him awake. "Pip! Pip, wake up. Come at once!"

Pip stumbled out of bed and opened his door a crack. "What is it?"

"The master! I need your help!"

In the light of the single candle she held, the housekeeper's eyes were wide and frightened beneath her nightcap. Without waiting for a reply, she spun around and hurried down the hall, her steel gray braid swaying down her back and the sleeves of her gown fluttering in the candlelight like the wings of a great moth.

Pip shook his head to clear it of the strange fancy and quickly pulled on his trousers before following her down the hall.

Too much poetry before bed.

As he passed through the kitchen on the way to the rest of the house, he spotted Mr. Applethwaite snoring in his chair by the fire, his mouth open wide and an empty bottle on the floor by his feet. Pip spared a moment to frown at the man and curse him under his breath before he hurried to catch up to the housekeeper's rapidly receding candle. Pip found her in the library, where she stood clutching a handkerchief to her mouth with one boney blue-veined hand as she looked down at the prone form of their master lying on his side on the floor.

"I tried to wake him, but I couldn't," she said shakily.

Pip crouched down next to the man's body and felt his cheek. The skin was still warm, and when Pip put his fingers under the major's nose, he could feel his breath. Pip rolled him onto his back, and the major let out a groan as the smell of whisky filled the air. A glance in the direction of the sideboard showed Pip that the crystal decanter was almost empty, and Pip had seen Mrs. Applethwaite fill it only that afternoon from the bottles she kept locked in a cabinet near her bedchamber.

"C'mon, master. Let's get ye t' bed," Pip said with only a hint of the annoyance he was feeling. He draped one of the man's arms over his shoulders and tried to lift him onto his feet.

Together, Pip and Mrs. Applethwaite managed to pull their master upright. Supporting the major on the side he usually held his cane, Pip followed Mrs. Applethwaite as she lit the way upstairs. Pip was sweating and panting by the time they made it to the master's bedchamber, where he dumped the man rather unceremoniously onto his bed, because he didn't have the strength for anything else.

Mrs. Applethwaite hovered in the doorway, not yet recovered enough from her fright to take charge as she usually did. Pip had to wonder at that, since he assumed she'd had to do this with her husband at least once a fortnight, but he made no comment. Instead, he took pity on the woman, lifted the candle from her shaking hand to light the lamp next to their master's bed, and said, "I'll 'andle things from 'ere, Missus. I'll stir up the coals and get 'im tucked in so 'e don' catch chill."

"Thank you, Pip," Mrs. Applethwaite said and gave him a rare smile. She cast one last concerned look toward their master before taking the candle and heading back the way they'd come.

Pip went to tend the fire first, poured on more coals, and then stirred it up until the heat coming off it soaked into his chilled limbs through the damp linen of his shirt. Now that he'd recovered a bit from lugging the wretch up the stairs, he was regretting not grabbing his jacket before leaving his room. He allowed himself the luxury of resting in front of the coals until his shirt dried and his muscles relaxed.

A groan from the bed reminded him that he had a task to finish before he could return to the warmth of his blankets. He sighed, walked to the bed, and stood staring down at his foxed master. This was the first opportunity Pip had to study the man without those unnerving silver eyes boring into him, and he had to admit Agnes was right. The major was a handsome gentleman. He looked younger in his sleep. The lines of strain around his eyes and mouth had eased, and the silver in the thick waves of his dark blond hair were harder to see in the lamplight. He had a strong chin, framed by carefully trimmed sideburns, a patrician nose, and lips that were neither too full nor too thin. They seemed to have a natural upward curve to them in repose, and Pip had to wonder what made him force them downward so often.

Was it his injury, or was there something else that tortured him?

When Pip realized he was still staring at his master's mouth, he shook his head to clear it and set to work finishing what he'd begun. He shoved the major over, none too gently, eliciting another moan, and then he drew the heavy blankets back. Pip was about to drag him into the spot he'd cleared, when he realized the major still had his boots on. It struck Pip as rather odd that a man who could most certainly afford house slippers would wear his boots indoors when he rarely went out. He found it equally strange that the man would wear loose trousers over his boots rather than a tighter fitting pair of breeches tucked into them, as most country gentlemen did.

But who was Pip to question the ways and wants of the gentry? Perhaps it pained the major to take his shoes on and off, so he kept to the same pair all day. Pip shrugged and set to removing them so Mrs. Applethwaite wouldn't have a fit when she discovered the dirty linens.

The first boot came off without too much of a struggle, and he set it on the floor next to the bed, but when Pip tugged on the other, it didn't budge. Pip grabbed the heel and gave it another good pull. The major moaned louder this time, but nothing yielded beneath Pip's hands. In fact, the heel and leg inside the boot felt strangely hard. Pip pushed the trouser leg up and up until it passed the top of the boot and that's when he realized the leg wasn't real. Pip stared at the contraption of wood, leather, and metal for a few moments in morbid curiosity before quickly pulling the trouser leg back into place. He had no idea how to remove the thing without removing the man's trousers, and Pip was fairly certain any attempts to do that without leave would surely get him sacked this time. He was no valet, and he wouldn't risk the master taking offense.

Feeling strangely unsettled, Pip simply dragged the major across the mattress, pulled the blankets over him, grabbed one of the warming bricks from the hearth, and placed it at the man's feet—*foot*—before taking the lamp and hurrying from the room.

Pip slept fitfully the rest of the night, uncertain why the whole affair had him so flustered. It wasn't as if he'd never seen a man who was missing a leg or an arm before. The battle at Waterloo occurred only a little more than a decade ago, and Pip well remembered the hundreds of wounded soldiers who had flooded London's streets afterward. But for some reason, the thought of the major suffering that, and still so obviously in pain, kept Pip tossing and turning in his bed, and he was next to useless when Mrs. Applethwaite roused him for his duties the following morning.

Chapter *Five*

THE MAJOR didn't leave his bedchamber at all that day. Pip was made well aware of this fact by the endless stream of complaints issuing from the housekeeper and her husband as he came and went, attending to his duties. Both of them were forced to climb the stairs many times throughout the afternoon and into the evening, seeing to their master's needs, so Pip decided it would be in his best interest to stay out of their way and let his curiosity remain unsatisfied.

After taking the horse out for his afternoon exercise, Pip felt a little better than he had upon waking that morning. He'd let the wind blow through him and the quiet soothe him and clear his head. The master probably wouldn't remember how he'd made it to bed, and Pip would simply pretend the night before had never happened, like any good servant. The major could keep his secret, and Pip could keep his job—quite simple really.

At dinner, the Applethwaites seemed in better spirits as well. Apparently the master had decided he didn't want to be disturbed for the rest of the night, so Mr. Applethwaite was able to return to his favored place by the fire—and his gin—and Mrs. Applethwaite was able to take up her usual place beside him while she worked on her sewing.

Pip retired to his room early again. The news that their master intended to remain in his bedchamber had started him thinking that tonight would be the perfect opportunity to return the book he'd borrowed. He'd already read it three times through, memorizing several poems, and he really shouldn't risk it being discovered missing by keeping it any longer. The moon was bright enough to light his way without a candle, and the

Applethwaites would be tired from their busy day, so this was probably the best opportunity he'd have to sneak into the library without being discovered.

To pass the time, Pip reread his favorite passages until he heard Mrs. Applethwaite attempting to rouse her husband so they could go to bed. When the house finally grew quiet again, he crept from his room, down the dark hall, and through the kitchen, skillfully avoiding every creaky floorboard that might betray him. As he made his way through the hall to the library, he carefully placed one stocking foot in front of the other, easing his weight down until he was sure the wood beneath him would make no sound before taking another step. Thankfully, the door opened quietly on well-oiled hinges, and Pip slipped inside.

He'd only been in the library twice since the books had been unpacked, and both times he'd been a little too preoccupied to note how they'd been arranged. In the bands of moonlight coming through the windows, it took him some time to locate where the small poetry volume should go. But eventually he was able to slide it into its proper place.

He was trying to decide on the next book he should borrow, when a thump from upstairs froze him in his tracks. His heart thundered in his chest as he strained his ears and waited. The thump was followed by what sounded like muffled cursing, and then the house went quiet again. Pip held his breath and tensed, ready to run if he heard anyone coming, but nothing happened. He gave up on the idea of taking another book and hurried out of the library as fast as he could. He'd almost made it to the door to the kitchen again, when the sound of muffled sobs reached him and then abruptly cut off.

Pip's frantically beating heart squeezed painfully in his chest as those sobs echoed in the silence they left behind, and part of him ached to rush up the stairs to check on the master, but he didn't dare. The man would not thank him for the intrusion. And how would he explain his being in the house?

And when had he become so bloody softhearted?

Disgusted with himself, Pip crept quietly back to his bed and crawled beneath the blankets. His own life had been hard enough without borrowing another man's troubles. He didn't understand why the major's quiet, solitary suffering clawed at him the way it did, but he resolved to ignore it from then on.

UNFORTUNATELY, PIP'S resolve did nothing to improve his humor the following day. His spirits didn't lift, even when Mrs. Applethwaite ordered him to take the cart to the village. They actually fell further when he read the first item on her list: four bottles of whisky, wine, or brandy, or whatever Mr. Cooper had in stock. Mr. Applethwaite only drank gin, the major never had any guests, and Mrs. Applethwaite certainly wasn't getting the whisky for Pip, so he knew who'd requested it. But *four*? He went to the village at least once a week. Tongues would wag. That was a certainty. Not that Pip gave a damn what the gossips said. But the major might someday. And Mrs. Applethwaite, though loyal to her master, would feel the sting of it too, the next time she ventured that far.

Pip took the slip of paper and put it in his pocket, not allowing his face to reveal a thing. He'd known plenty a drunkard in his life. Gin was like mother's milk to any child raised in the rookeries. Pip had always aspired to become a true drunkard someday himself, when he could afford it. But the major didn't have the look of a longtime sot. This was new to the man. Pip knew it in his bones. And he felt unaccountably saddened to see the major wasting his days and his health like this when he'd seemed to be getting better.

Pip trudged to the village as ordered. He stayed with the cart and didn't bother to look in the shop windows. He ignored Mr. Cooper's warning glares, and he didn't even notice if the shopkeeper's pretty daughter was behind the counter. Pip returned to the cottage as soon as the order was filled and completed his duties with little enthusiasm.

As usual, his afternoon ride lifted his spirits a little, only because he didn't allow himself to think on much of anything but the horse beneath him and the land they crossed. The strange melancholy that had plagued him since the night before even fled for a time until he saw the major watching him from the library window as he led the horse through the gate on his return.

Strangely irritated, Pip quickly put the horse in its stall and set about giving it a vigorous rubdown. He lingered over the work, hoping the major would be gone by the time he was finished. And as he brushed the horse's coat until it gleamed, Pip decided he would under no circumstances stand vigil over the major's evening walk any longer. If the man chose to do it, he would be on his own. When Pip was finished in the barn, he would go to the kitchen, eat his supper, go to bed early, and forget all about affairs that were none of his concern.

Decision made, Pip gave the horse one last pat and set the brush aside. He picked up the saddle from where he'd left it and turned to leave the stall, only to let out a decidedly unmanly shriek when a shadowy figure in midnight blue, with ghastly pale clawlike hands and black eyes, blocked his path.

"What have you done now?" Mrs. Applethwaite asked as she stepped into the light, and Pip could only look at her in confusion as he tried to convince his heart that the specter of death had not indeed come for him.

"What?"

She frowned at him. "The master has sent for you again. You must have done *something*."

Pip felt a sudden fluttering in his stomach that had nothing to do with the panicked beating of his heart. He shook his head. "I don't know, Missus."

She harrumphed. "Well, hurry up. He's waiting in the library."

Pip closed the door to the stall, set the saddle down, and reluctantly followed her to the house. Despite his objections, she made him remove his boots before she would let him into the kitchen and then merely pointed imperiously toward the door that led to the rest of the house. Once in the hall outside the library, Pip paused, giving himself a moment for his eyes to adjust and to calm his nerves. For some strange reason his heartbeat hadn't slowed from his fright, and his hand shook a little as he reached out to knock on the door.

When the major called "Come," Pip entered nervously. Despite the darkness of the hall, the windows in the room provided plenty of light from the late-afternoon sun, but the major still sat in shadow, his high-backed chair turned away from the light and close to the fire as before. The man's pale eyes seemed to glow in the darkness as he regarded Pip silently, and Pip squirmed, wracking his brain for any misdeed. He'd only been following orders the night before. The major couldn't find fault with him on that score. But Pip couldn't think of anything else he might have done wrong recently... until he spied the small slender volume of poetry resting on the major's knee.

Pip's stomach dropped, and he began to sweat in earnest now. He watched the major nervously through his eyelashes as he pretended to study the carpet at his feet. But when the silence stretched too long, he couldn't stand the waiting any longer, and he asked as meekly as possible, "Ye sent for me, master?"

The man remained silent, his elegant fingers tapping lightly on the book until he finally seemed to take pity on Pip and asked, "Do you like poetry, Phillip?"

How to answer that?

Pip shrugged and decided to play the country simpleton. "Don' 'ave much chance to 'ear it, sir. But I s'pose so."

The major pursed his lips, but Pip couldn't tell if that meant he was angered or amused by his response. "I like poetry quite a bit myself, prose as well. I fear reading is one of the few amusements left to me these days, so you can imagine my distress when I believed one of my favorite books had been lost... and my happiness at its sudden reappearance on my shelves today. Quite the miracle, don't you think?"

Pip knew he was caught but decided it was worth another go. "Per'aps it were only misplaced, sir."

The major frowned at him then, his pale gray eyes turning frosty. Pip wasn't sure how the man managed it in the warm glow from the coals, but he hoped to never see it again. Pip swallowed thickly, blew out a breath, and decided on a different tack. He ducked his head and gave his master a guilty quirk of the lips as he said, "Or, per'aps someone foolish might've borrowed it when 'e shouldna' and returned it 'oping no one would notice the short time it were away." Pip steeled himself then and met the major's gaze straight on, trying to look as contrite as he possibly could.

As before, something flickered in the man's eyes before disappearing again, and he grunted. "Perhaps so." The major dropped his gaze to the book in his lap, and Pip slumped a little in relief now that he no longer had to fight to hold it.

The major lifted the book from his knee and toyed with it for a few moments before sighing wearily, closing his eyes, and allowing his head to drop against the back of his chair. "Perhaps I wouldn't mind if other books disappeared from my collection, from time to time, if they were returned in the same manner," he said quietly, "And if, *perhaps*, someone were to come and read them to me when my head aches and my eyes have grown weary."

The major hadn't opened his eyes, so he missed the look of incredulity that was surely on Pip's face in that moment. In the silence that followed, Pip was able to get hold of himself, and when the major lifted his head and opened his eyes again, Pip dredged up a tentative smile. "The master need only ask, and any servant worth 'is salt would be 'appy to read to 'im of a night."

For the first time since Pip had met the man, the major actually smiled. His smile wasn't the broadest Pip had ever seen, merely a quirk of his lips, but for some strange reason Pip felt as if he'd been given a present, and his own smile widened in response.

The major quickly looked away and cleared his throat. "Good. Then we have an understanding. You may come this evening, after you've finished your duties."

"Yes, sir. Thank you, sir." Pip ducked his head and backed out of the room, clearly dismissed but not unhappy about it… very puzzled, but not unhappy.

The major was a queer sort, with his brooding silences and unsettling eyes, but he might be all right after all. Any other gent would have sacked Pip twice over by now, and Pip counted his blessings as he went back to the kitchen, all of his earlier irritation gone.

When he got over the worst of his confusion, he was actually quite pleased with how the interview had gone. Not only had he been given permission to read whatever he liked, but the major wanted him to come and sit with him of an evening. Even if his presence rattled Pip's nerves a bit, Pip could ignore that for a chance at company other than his own or the Applethwaites. And who knows, he might not only get a chance to satisfy his curiosity about the major but, if he played his cards right, he could spend his winter in front of a warm fire and maybe coax a bit of that whisky out of him in the bargain.

When Pip told her the news, Mrs. Applethwaite couldn't quite hide her astonishment and disapproval. Pip took a bit more pleasure in her *dis*pleasure than he should have, but he didn't let it show in his expression.

"Well," she said, all affronted dignity, "If that is the master's wish, then of course you must do it. But you will wash your hands before you go and you will mind your station when you are with him. You will also see to the fire and the lamps, fetch and carry whatever he needs. If you're going to be in the house, you should at least make yourself useful while you're there."

Pip stared at his threadbare stockings and kept his face blank while she prattled on. He hadn't expected anything less from the woman, and he was too happy to let her ruin it for him. A quick glance at Mr. Applethwaite showed him that the man was definitely more pleased with the turn of events than his wife. The old sod grinned toothlessly at him and raised his bottle in salute before downing a swig. The bastard was probably ecstatic that he wouldn't have to tend to the master after dinner on the nights Pip was sent for. And now that he'd been given the master's permission to enter the rest of the house, Pip had a feeling he'd be called on to take over more of Mr. Applethwaite's duties there whenever the man became *unwell* again. But hopefully the benefits would make up for an extra work. At least he'd be warm and dry.

Chapter Six

SUPPER THAT night dragged on interminably now that Pip had something to look forward to. Mrs. Applethwaite wouldn't let him leave the table until she was certain the master had had plenty of time to enjoy his own meal, and Pip was positively bouncing in his chair by the time she excused him. The master hadn't actually said when he should arrive or if he should wait until he was sent for. "After he finished his duties" was not very specific.

Before he went to the library, Pip returned to his bedchamber and changed clothes quickly, putting on his best shirt, waistcoat, and jacket after giving himself a good wash. He even cleaned his boots of every speck of mud and muck so he wouldn't have to go to the major in his stockings again. Mrs. Applethwaite hadn't said anything about how he should dress, probably because she disapproved of the whole arrangement altogether and wanted him to fail, so Pip just did what he felt he should. He wanted to look his best.

Lamplight spilled onto the rich red hall carpet from the open library door as Pip passed through the doorway into the main part of the house. He took a few nervous steps toward it but stopped in front of the looking glass mounted on the wall, straightening his waistcoat and combing his fingers nervously through his hair. He was a vain thing, he knew. The major probably wouldn't even notice the effort he'd gone to, but Pip did it anyway. Perhaps the street wretch in him was still anxious to show his betters that he wasn't dirt beneath their feet. Pip lifted his chin proudly and took the last few steps to the opening.

When he entered the room, the major was sitting in the same place he'd been earlier, with his leg propped on the stool, his head tipped back

44

against the chair, and his eyes closed. In the light from the lamps, the lines on his forehead and around his eyes and mouth were more pronounced than they'd been that afternoon and a surge of pity made Pip stop just inside the door, waiting quietly to be acknowledged, in case the man was asleep.

"Don't hover, Phillip. Come in and sit down," the major said tiredly, without opening his eyes.

A sweep of his hand indicated the chair directly across from him, and Pip gingerly sat on the cushioned surface after picking up the book that rested there.

"*Melmoth the Wanderer*," Pip read the title aloud, and the major nodded.

"Have you read it?"

"No, sir."

"Then I hope this will prove to be a treat for the both of us. You may begin when you're ready." The major picked up his glass from the small table next to him, took a drink of his whisky, and set it down again, still without opening his eyes.

Pip began to read quietly at first, uncertain what was expected of him. But soon he was so engrossed in the tale he nearly forgot he had an audience. So much happened in such a short span of pages that Pip was literally on the edge of his seat, anxious to learn what came next. He didn't realize how long he'd read until his throat began to protest his treatment of it. When he looked up in embarrassment at having become so carried away, he found the major staring at him intently, and he felt his cheeks grow hot.

A hint of amused curiosity appeared in the arch of the major's brows and the slight curve of his lips when he finally broke the silence. "Where did you learn to speak like that?"

Pip looked at the major in confusion for a moment until he realized his mistake. He'd been so immersed in his reading that he'd slipped into the proper English Vicar Halford had drummed into his nob from the first day he started schooling. When he read, Vicar Halford's carefully controlled voice was what he heard in his head, and so he'd read the words aloud the same way.

Pip cleared his throat nervously. "The man who taught me t' read, sir. Vicar 'alford."

The major's eyebrow quirked higher at Pip's attempt to return to a northern accent, and he seemed even more amused. "You are certainly full of surprises, young Phillip. I wonder how you'll surprise me next."

Pip had the uncomfortable feeling the major was having a laugh at his expense, even if he didn't know what the joke was, and it got his back up. He shrugged sullenly and said a bit defensively, "I can ape me betters, sir, but I know me place."

The amusement in his pale eyes faded. He turned his face to the fire and waved a hand dismissively. "When we are here, you may speak however you are most comfortable, Phillip. I won't make a fuss either way. I was only curious."

Mollified, Phillip studied his master's profile for a few moments, trying to discern if he was sincere. But when the major shifted in his chair and clenched his jaw in what had to be pain, Pip decided it didn't really matter. He'd take the man at his word. And if that meant he ended up out on his arse for getting above himself, well, at least he'd have the satisfaction of having done his best to carry with him on his journey back to Penrith.

Pip read for another hour while the major remained silent and still across from him. Pip was almost certain he had fallen asleep, but when he finally reached a stopping point, the major surprised him by saying, "Thank you, Phillip. That was well read."

Pip preened under the compliment, and he was almost disappointed when the major dismissed him for the night. But the hour was late, and Mrs. Applethwaite would be banging on his door very early the next day, so he simply said, "Good night, sir," and rose to leave.

"Good night, Phillip."

Pip was halfway to the kitchen when it occurred to him that he should have offered to bank the fire and put out the lamps. He turned back and poked his head through the door. The major had his head thrown back against the chair, his eyes tightly closed, and his face contorted in a grimace of pain as he rubbed the top of his damaged thigh. Pip hesitated, thinking he shouldn't intrude, but he also didn't want Mrs. Applethwaite angry with him for not seeing to his duties, so he knocked quietly.

"Excuse me, sir. Should I see to the fire and the lamps afore I leave?"

The major dropped his hand from his thigh immediately and sat up straighter in his chair. "No need. I will see to it."

Pip continued to hesitate. He didn't want to insult the man, but Pip would obviously have an easier time of it than the major would. And it was his job after all, wasn't it?

For this reason, Pip had never tried for a position inside a house, keeping to the heavy work despite the fact that he had a better education than many a man in service. He loved the outdoors, and he didn't relish spending his days inside. But mostly the gentry were such a touchy lot he never knew when they'd take offense.

"Good night, Phillip," the major said again, more firmly, and Pip ducked his head and retreated without another word. He didn't want their sessions to end after they'd only just begun.

Chapter Seven

THE MAJOR sent for him three more times that week, all much like the first. Pip read from a volume the major selected and the man remained a quiet audience, only interrupting if Pip seemed to be struggling with a word or phrase he was unfamiliar with. The major encouraged no intimacies and shared no stories of his own, so Pip's curiosity remained unsatisfied. But when Pip arrived on the third night, he was surprised to find a pair of finely embroidered velvet house slippers waiting for him on his chair, in addition to the novel they'd begun the night before.

"Sir?" Pip lifted the slippers carefully and turned to the man with his eyebrows raised.

"I have no need of them, and I thought you might be more comfortable in those than your boots," the major said gruffly. "I assume Mrs. Applethwaite would also prefer them for the sake of her carpets."

Pip ran the tip of his finger over the intricately patterned embroidery, his rough skin catching on the fine threads. They were beautiful, a rich burgundy velvet, the embroidery exotic in design and the colors vibrant. They must have cost a pretty piece. "Thank you, sir," he said, his voice catching a little at the end.

The major nodded tersely and turned his face to the fire. "You may begin when you're ready," he said.

Obviously he had said all he wished to on the matter, and Pip was no fool. He pushed the strange surge of emotion away and simply smiled happily to himself as he set the slippers aside, picked up the book, and took up where he'd left off.

He received more gifts over the course of the following weeks—a pair of warm mittens and a thick knitted scarf, a pencil box and paper for writing his weekly letters to Maud, a lap blanket for him to keep warm under while he read. They were all delivered in the same manner, waiting for him in his chair. And the major dismissed any attempts at gratitude with the same gruffness he had shown from the start. But out of the corner of his eye, Pip caught the man smiling at him every now and again, and despite the carefully maintained distance between them, Pip began to feel a certain intimacy form as they shared their evenings in front of the library fire.

He never spoke of it aloud to anyone, but Pip felt as if he was coming to know the major little by little, despite the pains his master took to the contrary. He had a generous nature he didn't want the world to know about, but also a wry wit that would reveal itself only rarely in the slight curve of his lips or a small crinkling at the corner of his eyes when Pip read something humorous. And he was incredibly clever as well. Pip sometimes got the impression his master didn't actually need Pip to read many of the pages aloud, because he already had them memorized.

That realization, when it struck, led Pip to wonder a bit why the major would bother having him there at all. If he were simply lonely, plenty of people in the village would have made more proper company for a gentleman, and much more interesting conversation than Pip could provide. But wonder though he might, Pip wasn't fool enough to call attention to it, not when he was enjoying himself so much and appeared to actually be doing his master some good—as evidenced by the fact that, during those weeks, the major didn't drink to excess even once.

Pip took a certain amount of pride in that. He liked to think his care and attention had lifted the man's spirits and aided him in some way. The major seemed to brood less and less as time went on, and every so often, he even began short conversations with Pip instead of simply dismissing him when he was done reading for the night. They only discussed the text, of course, nothing of a personal nature. But Pip was encouraged and flattered by it just the same.

By the end of the third week, Pip was feeling particularly proud of himself. Not only had the major been out for his walk every day that week but Pip had also spotted him going into the barn at least twice during that time. The major never went when Pip was working there, but he stayed for quite some time on both occasions. Rather than dreading the prospect of having his favorite pastime taken away, Pip began to hope for a time when he could share his afternoons with his master as well, helping him achieve whatever it was that took him out there.

Pip was in fact feeling so pleased with himself, he couldn't help the smug grin that split his face when the bell rang for him that night, nor the swagger in his step as he entered the library.

"Good evening, sir," he said cheerily after the major bid him enter.

The man raised a single gold eyebrow at him, but his lips curved slightly in response. "Good evening, Phillip."

Pip went directly to his chair, but no book awaited him.

"I thought perhaps you should choose tonight," the major said in response to Pip's questioning look.

Pip's face split into an even broader grin, and he sauntered over to the shelves, inordinately pleased that the major was allowing him his choice. He decided his spirits were too high for anything too weighty so he settled on a small printing of Shakespeare's *The Comedy of Errors*. The major actually chuckled when Pip sat down with it, and Pip had to hide his pleasure in so simple a sound behind the pages he held.

He began reading slowly to give him time to familiarize himself with the characters. But soon enough he was fully immersed in the farce, inventing comical voices for all as he went. By the time he reached the second act, Pip was on his feet, playing out the parts, emboldened because the major had actually begun to laugh quietly at his antics, and Pip didn't want him to ever stop.

When he reached halfway through the part where Dromio and Antipholus of Syracuse were determining the placement of countries on the globe-like body of the kitchen maid, the major snorted, and Pip had to stop reading because he was laughing too hard to speak. His own foolishness and the major's mirth were too much. Pip fell into his chair, holding his belly as tears fell from his eyes. Every time he thought he'd managed to regain control, the major would start chuckling again and that would set Pip off as well.

Eventually, they both wound down and Pip was grinning like a fool at the major, feeling as if they'd broken more of the barrier between them. But as quickly as it had started, the major's merriment fled, his expression turned grave, and his gaze almost pained. The man turned away from Pip, staring resolutely into the fire and missing the hurt that had to be written plainly on Pip's face.

"I think perhaps I've had enough for tonight. Thank you, Phillip. You may go," the major said, his voice cold with all the stiffness of their first encounters.

Why? What have I done wrong?

Pip wanted to object, to reach out and shake the man until he showed some human feeling again. But his throat hurt from more than overuse, and he feared what he might say when he regained his voice. He rose to leave and set the small volume on his chair before making his way back to his empty bedchamber in sullen silence.

After that night, things between them changed for the worse again, and Pip couldn't understand why. As the days grew shorter and the nights turned colder, the atmosphere in the library chilled as well. No more presents waited for him on his chair. The major went back to staring pensively into the fire and drinking more heavily. He chose all the readings, most of them heavy treatises on medicine and philosophy that defied Pip's understanding and dragged the minutes into hours. The few times Pip caught the major watching him, the man's expression was no longer indulgent or amused but pained or unreadable. If Pip asked him whether he'd read something wrong or he wished to be done for the night, the major would only shake his head, ask for another glass of whisky, and wave for Pip to continue after he'd fetched it.

Before long the major began sending for him less and less, a turn of events that Mrs. Applethwaite was quite pleased with even if it left Pip hurt, confused, and concerned for his master's welfare. Try as he might, Pip couldn't understand what had happened.

Perhaps as a means of self-preservation, Pip's hurt eventually transformed into resentment and anger. After all, Pip had tried his best to please the man and what did he get for his pains—only coldness.

Why had he allowed himself to care?

Before he'd given up completely, Pip tried once to express his concerns to Mrs. Applethwaite, not about his treatment of course, she'd have no sympathy for that, but about their master's well-being.

"I think, 'e might be ill. Shouldn't we do *somethin'* at least?"

She'd frowned down her hawk nose at him and shook her head. "Do I have to continually remind you of your place, Pip? The younger generation has no sense of propriety. I knew his encouragement of such familiarity would give you airs."

Pip ground his teeth in frustration. "We're in the middle of bleedin' nowhere. Who else is 'e goin' to be *familiar* with but us? Isn't it our Christian duty to—"

She sliced her hand through the air to cut him off. "He is a grown man, a gentleman, and fully capable of determining his own needs without the help of one such as you. As long as he is able to speak for himself, it is only for you to do as you are bid and remember your proper place."

Pip didn't give a damn about propriety. The major was a man who'd been places and done things Pip couldn't even imagine. It didn't make any sense for someone like that to shut himself away from everyone and drink himself into ruin and despair.

But Pip was no martyr either. From his earliest days, he was a survivor. If his help and concern were truly unwanted and unappreciated, as they appeared to be, then the lot of them could go get stuffed for all he cared. He'd do the job for which he'd been hired and nothing beyond. He'd eat his meals in silence with the Applethwaites. He'd take the horse out for his daily ride, and he'd spend the rest of the winter trying to remember why he'd left the comfort and acceptance of Maud and the rest of his people on the sheep farm in Penrith.

Chapter *Eight*

Pip KEPT his promise to himself. He remained aloof and silent about his concerns, and the days passed at the cottage, chilly but uneventful until one night in early November, when a fierce storm blew in from the sea. It rattled the shutters and pelted Pip with icy needles each time he was forced outside to check on the animals or to fetch more coal or wood, leaving him in a foul temper all day. He was already tired from another sleepless night he couldn't explain and unable to take the horse out for his afternoon ride because of the weather.

After a very long day, Pip ate his supper in gloomy silence by the kitchen fire while the wind howled and the cottage creaked around them. He eyed Mr. Applethwaite's bottle of gin longingly as he rubbed his chilled hands together and wiggled his toes within the dubious protection of the beautifully crafted, but not particularly warm, velvet house slippers. He was pondering the likelihood that he would receive a cuff to the head for his pains if he asked the man for a tiny dribble from his bottle—and whether he'd return the blow in kind if he did—when the bell rang from the library, twice, the major's signal for him.

Pip was still in the muddy and slightly damp clothes he'd worn all day because his only other set of work clothes was still damp from the rains leading up to the storm the day before. But when the signal was rung again, only a few moments after the first and louder this time, Pip leapt to answer the summons, not bothering to take the time to dig out his best clothes from the chest where he'd buried them. The major would have to take him as he was.

He grumbled a little under his breath, but he hurried just the same, glad to be given something to think about other than the chill in his bones or the fierceness of the storm. But when he reached the library, his relief was short-lived. The major did not appear to be in any better humor than Pip. Instead of relaxing in his chair, the man was pacing in front of the coals, his hands white-knuckled on his cane and his face tight. When the major spotted him, he waved impatiently toward Pip's usual chair.

"Sit. Read to me. I don't care what," the major ordered through gritted teeth before reaching for his glass on the mantel and downing half the amber liquid it contained in one swallow.

Pip felt the tension in the room like a living thing, and he edged nervously around the major to pull a book of poetry off the shelf, hoping it would ease both of their minds.

Pip read for a time as ice pelted the shutters, and the major continued to pace in front of the coals. Pip was halfway through the second love poem when a particularly sharp blast of wind howled past the cottage, banging the shutters against the window frames, and the major slammed his fist on the mantel. "Enough!" he barked. "Choose something else."

Pip clenched his jaw against the first words that came to mind, closed the book, and carefully set it aside so he wouldn't chuck it at his master's head.

What did he have to be so surly over?

Pip was the one who'd been out in that storm all day, freezing his ballocks off so everyone else could stay warm and dry. His nose was red and sore from wiping it. He was tired and cold. But he'd still come to do his duty by his master. And though he was a little ashamed to admit it, he'd actually felt a surge of relief and excitement when the bell had rung, happy that the master deigned to give him the opportunity to share an evening with him again. And now he felt like a fool. He wasn't a dog to come running back even when he was kicked, and he wouldn't stand for being shouted at when he was only trying to help.

"Per'aps the master would prefer to be left alone," Pip gritted out.

"No. The master would not." The major's pale eyes speared Pip where he sat as he continued through clenched teeth, "The *master* would like for you to read. Only. Choose. Something. Else."

54

Pip stood up, raised his chin, and met his gaze, allowing a bit of his own temper to show. "Per'aps the master should choose the book for 'imself, since 'is servant 'as chosen so poorly."

The major growled and took one menacing step toward Pip, his eyes blazing. Pip held his ground and was grateful he had a moment later, because the major misjudged his footing and would have fallen if Pip hadn't leapt to steady him.

The major shook him off at once. "Get out! Leave me!"

Pip hovered for a moment in indecision until the major shouted at him again. "Get out!"

Pip stormed out of the room and through the door to the kitchen, passing under the astonished gazes of the housekeeper and her husband, and not stopping until he was in his own room with the door slammed shut behind him.

He paced the confines of his tiny bedchamber in agitation for a long time, fuming and cursing under his breath. Why should he give a rat's arse if the bastard rotted in his bloody library? The major could drink himself into an early grave, and it wouldn't make one bit of difference to Pip. Maybe he should just pack his things now and go back to Penrith as soon as the storm passed. He hadn't needed to buy house slippers, and he'd given up on the russet waistcoat, so he still had enough put by to pay his way home... although the roads would probably be impassible for some time.

When he finally stopped pacing, a sudden tide of exhaustion and melancholy swamped him. But despite his fatigue, Pip couldn't bring himself to crawl into his cold, empty bed yet, so he decided to risk a trip to the kitchen for a heel of bread and perhaps a stone to warm his feet. He listened at the door, but all seemed quiet apart from the storm. The Applethwaites were gone when he ventured out, and Pip stirred up the kitchen fire and ate his bread and butter while he waited for his stone to warm. He was resting against the hearth, his eyelids drooping, when a loud thump and a clatter of wood on wood startled him awake. Pip was still angry enough that he considered ignoring the sound, but when a piteous moan followed it, he sighed and went to investigate.

He found the major in a heap halfway up the stairs. The man's cane lay at the bottom, and Pip picked it up before climbing to his master's aid. The major's breath was heavy with whisky as he mumbled and cursed at

Pip, but eventually Pip was able to get him upright, and he half carried, half dragged him the rest of the way to his bedchamber.

Once inside, Pip dumped him on his bed and went to stir up the coals before lighting a lamp. He could feel the major's gaze on his back as he fussed about the room, and when he finally turned to face him, a strange heaviness hung in the air between them. Pip shook his head at his own fancy and frowned disapprovingly at his master. "Do ye need me to tuck ye in, or can ye manage that yerself?"

Instead of the rage Pip expected, the major's face crumbled. His earlier temper had vanished, the fire in his pale eyes gone, leaving nothing but sorrow in its wake. "Forgive me, Phillip. Please forgive me. Don't leave me alone," the major mumbled brokenly as he swayed on the bed.

Pip sighed, his own temper and irritation fading quickly. He stepped forward and attempted to help his master out of his jacket so he could tuck him into bed, but the major grabbed his wrists, stopping him. "Tell me you won't leave me alone."

Pip looked at him in confusion. "I won't be goin' anywhere in this storm, sir. C'mon now. Let's get ye inta bed."

He didn't wait for a response, he shook free of the major's grip and went back to trying to get him out of his jacket, a task that was proving uncommonly difficult. Once the offending article was removed, the major quit flopping about enough for Pip to reach for the knot of his cravat. It wouldn't do to have his master choke in his sleep. The major stilled beneath his hands, and when Pip looked up, the man was watching him intently with something in his eyes that made the blood pound in Pip's ears.

"Forgive me, Phillip. Beautiful Phillip," the major slurred, searching Pip's face intently in the lamplight. "Stubbs is such an ugly name for someone so beautiful."

If Pip was surprised by his words, he was stunned into immobility when the major fisted a hand in his shirt and pulled him down for a kiss. The lips that touched Pip's were soft and warm at first, gently coaxing. Pip opened his mouth to object, but anything he might have said was cut off when the major's tongue invaded his mouth. He tasted of the rosemary and garlic from his dinner but mostly of whisky, and Pip felt himself melting into the warmth and wetness of his kiss. Pip's body responded, heat pooling in his belly, as an unexpected surge of desire threatened to overcome any rational thought he possessed.

He didn't know how far he might have gone if the major's kisses had remained gentle. But when the man's lips became hard and demanding, and a strong hand circled his neck, forcing him closer, something evil, buried deep inside Pip's memories, writhed and tried to break free of its bonds.

Pip fancied he actually heard the crack form in the walls he'd placed around that darkness. The sound was terrible, like the splitting of the ice on the Thames the spring he'd been released from Newgate, after that long terrible winter. He was eleven years old again, cowering in the cold and the dark of his cell as heavy footfalls and the jingle of keys drew nearer.

Suddenly, the unaccustomed scrape of stubble across his chin and the strength of that vise around his neck became unbearable. It awoke a fear he hadn't felt in more than a decade, and he panicked.

Choking off a cry, Pip threw up his arms, breaking the major's hold on him. When the man reached for him again, Pip shoved back hard, knocking the major to the side in his desperation to get away. He heard a crash behind him, followed by a cry of pain, but Pip didn't stop to look. He flew from the room, down the stairs, and out the front door into the storm. He was a fool to run blindly into the darkness and the ice and wind, but Pip was fleeing from memories of far worse, and he feared if he stopped, even for a moment, they would catch him.

Pip ran until his lungs burned, slipping on icy rocks and tripping over unseen hazards in the dark. He didn't know where he was going, but by the time he reached Agnes's father's farm, he was frozen with cold, his clothes soaked through, and his pretty house slippers ruined beyond repair. When Pip reached the shelter of their barn, he finally stopped, taking in great lungfuls of air and shivering so hard his teeth clacked together like some ghastly wooden puppet in a street player's show.

With a shaking hand, Pip wiped the water from his eyes and stared at the looming shadow of the farmhouse through the sheets of sleet and rain, but he didn't go to it. He'd regained some of his reason now that he'd stopped, and the panic had ebbed into exhaustion. What would he say when they asked him why he was there? How would he explain his mad dash across the fells in the middle of the night, during the worst storm in years?

He shivered hard and retreated farther into the barn as a great gust of wind buffeted him. His feet and hands were numb with cold, and his mind was going numb as well. The dairy cows were all huddled together against the chill, as near as they could get to the stone wall of the barn that afforded them the most protection. Pip pushed his way between them until he found a small pile of straw to fall onto. Pressed against that wall, surrounded by what warmth the animals could provide, Pip surrendered to darkness and oblivion.

Chapter *Nine*

AN EAR splitting shriek woke him the following morning. When he cracked open one eye, a shaft of sunlight pierced his skull, and he quickly shut it again, groaning. He tried to move, but he was weak as a kitten, and every part of him ached. He desperately wanted to go back to sleep, but when he heard the voices of several people surrounding him with concerned murmurs, Pip thought perhaps he should do something to let them know he wasn't dead—at least he didn't think he was.

He lifted his head and pried open both eyes to find Agnes, her sisters, and three men Pip assumed were her father and brothers staring down at him.

"Oi, lad, are ye injured?" the man Pip assumed was Agnes's father asked.

Pip steeled himself against what was certain to be a significantly unpleasant experience and forced his body to sit up. His head throbbed fiercely, but he managed to stay upright. "I don' think so, sir."

"Lads, help 'im up."

Agnes's brothers each took an arm and pulled Pip to his feet, where he swayed for a moment and might have fallen again if they hadn't rushed to support him. They mostly carried him into the farmhouse and set him down by the fire, where he finally began to shiver as blood flowed painfully back into his frozen limbs.

An older version of Agnes draped a blanket across his shoulders and fussed over him until Pip had a steaming cup of broth warming his hands and his bare feet were resting in a tub of hot water. At first, it felt as if a thousand needles were piercing the soles of his feet, and he had to stifle a whimper of pain, but soon the warmth was soothing on his battered flesh, and he began to doze off.

When he woke for the second time that day, he was alone in the kitchen except for Agnes and the woman he assumed was her mother.

Agnes rushed over to him as soon as she saw he was awake. She handed him another cup of broth. "'Ere, drink this."

Her mother looked up from her cooking and gave Pip an encouraging smile, but she must have thought he was sufficiently seen to, because she returned to her work.

When the older woman had turned away, Agnes leaned in close to him and hissed, "What on earth were ye' doin', ye damned fool? Ye scared the wits out o' Mary this morn."

When Pip didn't answer right away, she pinched him on the arm, *hard*, and Pip yelped.

"Are ye all right, lad?" Agnes's mother called from her place by the table.

"Yes, ma'am." He gave Agnes a wounded look. "Ye didn't 'ave to pinch me," he whispered sullenly, rubbing his arm.

"Me father'll be back soon, so if ye 'ave summat to say, ye should say it now," Agnes hissed under her breath as she reached for the kettle on the hook by the fire and poured more hot water into the tub at his feet.

Pip could only shake his head. He was exhausted and feeling a little light-headed. The fire, the blanket, the mug of broth in his hands, and the steaming tub were almost too warm now.

"I should go 'ome," he managed weakly.

"Muther," Agnes called worriedly.

A moment later, a cool hand touched his brow, and the woman said, "'E 'as a fever. Go and get yer father."

Pip remembered only snippets from then on, worried voices that sounded as if they were underwater, a blast of cool air, being bumped about in a cart, and then nothing until he woke to find himself in his own bed at the cottage. The sun was high in the sky outside his window. He was tucked tightly beneath a mound of blankets, and his head felt as if it were full of goose feathers.

Pip was trying to determine whether or not his limbs would support him enough to sit up in bed when his door opened and Mrs. Applethwaite came in with a tray. He braced himself for the tongue-lashing he would receive, but the woman surprised him with what seemed like a genuinely relieved smile. "You're awake at last. How are you feeling?"

The first word that came to mind was "puzzled," but he assumed she meant his health, so he said, "Better. I think."

She nodded. "Good. I shall run and tell the master after you've had a bit of this."

She set the tray by the bed, and to Pip's utter shock actually helped him to sit upright so he could drink broth from the bowl she handed him. The woman was being far too solicitous, and Pip was finding the change in her rather alarming.

"How long were I asleep?" he asked in between sips of broth.

"Three days! We were all terribly frightened you wouldn't wake up again. The master stayed with you every night until I feared for his health as well and convinced him to go to his bed."

Pip nearly choked on his broth. "The master... was here? Why?" he gasped in between coughing fits.

Mrs. Applethwaite took the bowl from him and handed him a linen to wipe his face. "We were all in such a state when that farmer brought you here in his cart. We were going to send for the doctor, but we feared the roads after the storm would make it impossible. The master took charge at once, and we didn't need the doctor after all. Did you know he studied for *two years* at Guy's Hospital in London?"

Pip shook his head and regretted it immediately as his temples began to throb.

"Oh yes, he was studying to become a physician before he bought a commission and went off to the wars as a surgeon instead. According to his brother's housekeeper in London—she's an old school friend and the one who recommended me for this position—no one knew why he chose to go, brave man, but *everyone* expected him to return to the school when he came home. Then... well, with his injury and all, I suppose things changed. But he certainly knew what to do with you."

Pip was having enough trouble trying to absorb the fact that Mrs. Applethwaite was actually sharing gossip with him, so the rest didn't sink in straight away.

She fussed with Pip's blankets until she seemed to remember herself and frowned at him. "You should be properly grateful to him when he comes to check on you. I don't know what you were thinking going out in the storm like that, but we've had enough trouble out of you for a lifetime. Mr. Applethwaite is like to catch a fever himself with all the extra work he's had to do since you've been ill. And the master has actually been looking after the horse in your stead. Can you imagine? Such a kind man."

When Pip simply stared blankly at her, she harrumphed and bustled out of the room, leaving him to try and make some sense of all she'd said with a head that seemed determined to remain muddled. Try as he might, Pip kept coming back to what she'd said about the master staying with him, watching over him, and caring for him while he slept.

Pip wanted to be angry for what had happened in the man's bedchamber. He wanted to be disgusted. But he couldn't seem to manage it. He searched his mind for the fear that had taken over him, but it was gone too. The evil memories had slithered back beneath the rock he'd buried them under. He was strangely numb, bereft of any feeling at all other than confusion. He felt lost. And not for the first time in recent weeks, he wished Maud were there to comfort him. She was the only person in his life whose presence brought nothing but peace and joy. He longed for the simplicity of that connection when everything else seemed so complicated and unsettling.

Pip set his bowl of broth aside and closed his eyes, then pulled his blankets over his head and snuggled down into the mattress. He couldn't think. He didn't *want* to think. Perhaps after he'd slept, things would be clearer or he'd wake to find the past few days had been a dream.

WHEN PIP woke for the second time, Mrs. Applethwaite was standing over him again with another tray and the sun was disappearing behind the fells. This time the tray held a meat pie instead of a bowl of weak broth, and Pip's stomach growled in appreciation. He was suddenly famished.

After a brief word of thanks to the housekeeper, Pip dug in to the pie with relish and did not stop until he had licked his plate clean.

When he was finished, Mrs. Applethwaite took the plate and nodded her approval. "You must be feeling better, now your appetite has returned. I spoke to the master and told him you were awake, but he was too tired to come himself. He said to let you eat your fill, now that the fever has passed, and to order you to stay in bed for a couple days more, until your strength has returned. We'll hire a boy from the village to come and look after Molly and the horse until you're well enough to venture out again, if need be."

Pip shook his head and tried to rise. The very last thing he wanted was to be stuck in bed for days with only his thoughts for company. He'd go mad. "A few more pies like that and I'll be right as rain, Missus."

The housekeeper pushed him back down with one boney hand, her strength an embarrassingly easy match for him in his current state. "You'll do as the master says. I won't have him think I haven't done my duty by you. If he says you need your rest, then abed you will stay. He's even offered you your choice of books from his library to pass the time, though I'm not sure you deserve such generosity. You will not insult the man by refusing his instructions."

Pip sighed and dropped his head in defeat. It appeared he had no choice.

"You haven't yet told anyone what you were doing out in that storm in the first place," she said as she fussed with his blankets and collected his plate.

His wince was purely internal, but her eyes narrowed on him just the same. "Don't remember, Missus. The fever an' all. Perhaps I 'ad the fever afore I left, or I 'eard summat or walked in me sleep. I don't know."

Her lips twisted, not at all improving her appearance. "Hmph. As long as it didn't have anything to do with the dairymaids on that farm. Remember my warning. The master may have allowed you more license of late, but he will not tolerate any more trouble from you, ill or no. Mark my words."

She swept out of the room in a great rustling of soot gray bombazine, and Pip slumped back into his pillows, drawing the blankets over his head in hopes the world would forget him for a time.

Chapter *Ten*

OVER THE next two days, Pip did little but read, eat, and sleep. He was more exhausted than he realized, unable to stay awake for more than an hour or so at a stretch. But even with plenty of rest and his choice of novels from the major's library, he couldn't completely distract himself from the turmoil in his head.

At least the major never did come to check on him. Pip was thankful for that because he had no earthly idea what he would say the next time they met. The mere thought made his head ache and his stomach threaten to return whatever of Mrs. Applethwaite's fine cooking it possessed. Part of him hoped the major would simply ignore him from then on, and Pip could pretend nothing had happened between them. He could go back to his duties, and it would be as if the past few days had never happened. Another part... well, he refused to let that part have any say in the matter whatsoever.

Selective memory and outright denial seemed like the best course for all concerned and by the third day of his convalescence, Pip had almost convinced himself that was the truth—nothing *had* happened. Unfortunately for him, the lie shattered the first time he stumbled outside for a bit of fresh air and came across the major brushing the horse in the barn. Pip's stomach flipped at the mere sight of him, and he cursed himself under his breath for his weakness.

He stood frozen outside the stall, watching as the major whispered gentle words to the horse while one of the man's elegant hands ran the brush over its back. The major's deep voice and assured movements made the hairs on Pip's neck stand on end, and he shivered. He would have slunk back the way he came, but the major noticed him before he could make his escape.

The major cleared his throat uncomfortably into the heavy silence between them. "I see you're back on your feet at last, Phillip. How are you feeling?"

Pip shuffled from foot to foot, staring anywhere but at the man's unnerving eyes. "I'm well enough, sir, thanks. I can return to me duties. There's no need for ye to do that," he replied, nodding toward the brush still in his hand.

"Yes, well, you should perhaps not tax yourself too greatly until you are fully recovered. I've actually enjoyed having something to fill my days. It was wrong of me not to show more appreciation for my brother's gift before this." The major paused for a moment before he straightened his shoulders and lifted his chin. After drawing in a long breath he said, "I have perhaps overindulged in a great many things I shouldn't of late. I, ah, regret any… *discomfort* I may have caused you, Phillip. I know I am fully to blame for what happened. You have my assurance that nothing of the kind will *ever* happen again, and I would take it as a great favor if you would not speak of it to anyone."

The major's posture was all pride and noble bearing, but Pip knew him well enough to see the cracks around the edges. He could have made the man suffer a bit for what he'd put Pip through, but he didn't. He was anxious to be done with the whole affair. He didn't like the thoughts and feelings it stirred up, and he wanted to forget it as much, if not more than, the major did. "Of course, sir."

The major eyed him warily, as if he expected Pip to say more. But Pip couldn't think of anything else, and eventually the man nodded curtly. "Thank you." He set the brush on top of the gate to the stall, grabbed his walking stick, and left the barn, his back stiff and his shoulders straight. When he finally disappeared inside the house, Pip let out a relieved breath he hadn't even realized he was holding. He slumped against the wall of the barn, suddenly exhausted, and a long time passed before he dredged up the energy to finish seeing to the horse and return to his bed.

OVER THE following week, Pip's strength returned slowly. Despite the major's words about appreciating his brother's gift, Pip didn't see him in the barn again after his first day out of bed. In fact, Pip didn't see him at all. The major didn't go out even for his evening walks, and Pip wasn't called once to the library to read.

He hadn't truly expected to be, and he should have been relieved that he wouldn't have to be alone with the man, but instead, he was strangely saddened by it. It seemed unfair that he should be deprived of something he enjoyed when he had done nothing wrong.

As it usually did, his hurt turned to anger fairly quickly. Pip hated being ignored above all things, even if the rational part of him argued that he didn't want the gentleman's company anyway. It didn't help matters that he couldn't get that night out of his mind, no matter how hard he tried.

And the kiss.

Despite all of his denials and his efforts to the contrary, Pip thought about that kiss often. He even dreamt of it once or twice, but he couldn't bring himself to face those dreams in the bright light of day. For the life of him, he didn't understand why he couldn't just let what happened between them go. He didn't dwell on... well, *anything* really, and it was only a bloody kiss.

Why did it matter if Pip had enjoyed it at the start? There was no shame in that. A kiss was meant to be a pleasant thing, and men's lips were not so different from women's. Such intercourse was next door to a mortal sin, of course, but Pip was hardly one to cast stones in that regard. He was well acquainted with sin and did not hold out much hope for the fate of his immortal soul. And besides, Master Carey and Master Carruthers were *that way* with each another, even if Pip had never seen the proof of it himself, and he didn't honestly believe them damned for the way they were.

The major had promised to never do it again. Pip believed him. The matter should have been settled. But he found no comfort in that as he shuffled through his duties each day and sat in front of the kitchen fire each night, part of him hoping for the bell to ring for him and part of him dreading it.

When Pip did finally get a glimpse of the major again, he was dismayed by what he saw. Mrs. Applethwaite's husband was asleep by the fire as usual when the housekeeper was summoned by the master's bell—a single ring, not two. After she left, Pip decided to retire, but before he took a step, the housekeeper came hurrying back into the kitchen obviously troubled. She went to her husband first but seemed to think better of it when she saw Pip standing in the hall that led to his room.

"Oh Pip, the master is… unwell again. I need your help to get him to his bed before he catches a chill. Are you recovered enough from your illness?"

Pip nodded despite the sudden twist in his belly. He followed her to the library where he found the major slumped awkwardly in his chair, a nearly empty tumbler dangling from his fingers. His face was haggard, pale and sallow in the lamplight. His normally well-trimmed sideburns were uneven, his chin and upper lip dark with whiskers. His cheeks looked hollow beneath the dark rings that shadowed his eyes. Feeling a sudden surge of sadness, Pip gently took the glass from his hand and set it on the table before draping the man's arm over his shoulders and helping him to his feet. The major stirred a little and mumbled, but Pip couldn't understand him.

Despite Pip's brave words to the housekeeper, he was utterly exhausted by the time they got the man to his bed. Pip had barely been able to manage the task when he was hale and healthy. He couldn't imagine what made him think he could do it now. But he managed, if only just.

As before, he told Mrs. Applethwaite to leave and when he'd recovered a little, he set to work getting his master out of his jacket and cravat, keeping his mind utterly blank as he worked. When that was finished, Pip knelt and reached for the major's boot with hands that shook despite his efforts to control them. He pulled the one boot off the major's good leg and was fighting with himself over whether to try to remove the false leg this time when one of his wrists was caught in a painful grip. "Don't."

Startled, Pip looked up to find the major watching him, the man's bloodshot silver eyes filled with anguish. "Go. Please, just go," the major whispered, his jaw clenched so tight Pip could see the muscle jumping.

"I were only trying to 'elp, sir."

The major closed his eyes and turned his face away, allowing Pip's wrist to drop from his grip. "I know. But I don't want you to see me like this. I don't want… you to see."

Shame was written plainly across the major's face despite the fact that he tried to hide it, and Pip ached for him. "You've no reason to be ashamed, sir. Aren't many who can say they've done what you 'ave and lived to tell about it after. Let me 'elp ye."

Pip reached out only to have his hand knocked away when the major tried to stand up. The man clutched the foot of the bed as he swayed on his feet, but Pip dared not reach for him again. Fury blazed in his eyes now, and Pip actually took a step back from it. "Don't patronize me. I don't need your help. Can't you see you only make it worse... looking at you and knowing... knowing what I'll never have, what I'll never *be* again. Having perfection so close...." The major slumped back down onto the bed and buried his face in his hands, all the fight gone out of him.

Pip stayed where he was, hurt and confused by all the emotions roiling inside him. "Tell me what to do," Pip whispered.

The major sighed and shook his head. "Nothing, Phillip. There's nothing."

Pip took a few steps forward then and stopped in front of him, unable to leave him as he was. He stood like that for a long time, laboring to breathe against the bands that were squeezing his chest. The major made no move to meet his gaze, and Pip found himself staring at the man's bent head, following the waves of dark blond hair to the thick muscle of his neck and then down to where it disappeared beneath his shirt. Time seemed to stop, and Pip had no idea how long he stood there like that before the major finally lifted his head and stared back, searching Pip's face. Whatever he saw there erased some of the lines of anguish from around his eyes and he sat up straighter on the bed, letting his hands fall to his lap.

"Why are you still here, Phillip?" the major asked quietly.

"I don't know." He felt lost, as if he were being carried away and he had nothing to hold on to. He stared back at the major, silently begging him to help.

The major closed his eyes for the briefest moments before locking gazes with Pip again. Ever so slowly, he reached out a trembling hand until his fingertips brushed the hem of Pip's waistcoat. Pip took one shaky breath in and held it, but didn't back away, even when he felt one of the major's fingers push beneath the wool and hook in the waist of his trousers, then gently draw him forward.

"If you won't leave, then there must be a reason you want to stay," the major murmured, his deep voice resonating low in Pip's belly.

Pip swallowed and expelled the breath he'd been holding. His heart raced, but he didn't know whether from fear or something else. A gentle tug was all it took to bring Pip forward another step, until he was standing between the major's thighs. Then the major unhooked his finger and dragged it ever so slowly down the placket of Pip's trousers, tracing the outline of Pip's hardening cock through the coarse wool. Pip jerked as sensation shot up his spine like lightning and his breath caught. The major froze, watching and waiting for Pip to make the next move. But somehow, knowing he could walk away made it impossible for Pip to leave, and when the major reached up to undo the buttons of his placket, Pip did nothing to stop him.

As each button was undone, Pip's cock throbbed in anticipation and after an eternity, the major reached inside, lifting Pip's shirt out of the way, and pulled Pip's cock through the opening in his drawers. Pip gasped as the warmth of the man's hand contrasted sharply with the cold air in the bedchamber, and he moaned when the major leaned forward and engulfed his crown in his hot, wet mouth.

Pip stared, transfixed, unwilling and unable to look away, as his cock disappeared, sliding deeper into that moist cavern. The major's tongue swirled around his length, painting patterns on his skin, and Pip had to grab the foot of the bed when his knees threatened to give out. The major's strong hand gripped his hip, but Pip felt it only distantly. Nearly all of his attention was taken up by what the man was doing with his mouth and the warm palm that slipped beneath to cup and roll his ballocks.

The major was no inexperienced maid. He took Pip all the way to the root before pulling back and starting the whole agonizingly perfect journey over again. Too soon, Pip was trembling with need, fighting every instinct to thrust his hips in time with the rhythm of that mouth. When Pip could hold still no longer, he cupped the back of the man's head, threading his fingers through the soft waves of blond hair, and thrust his hips gently, hoping the major would understand his need and work his prick harder and faster.

The major surprised him then by letting go of his ballocks and gripping Pip's other hip, drawing him closer and encouraging him to thrust, to fuck his mouth. When Pip hesitated, the major's hands slid back and gripped his buttocks hard, no longer encouraging but demanding Pip take over his own pleasure. As the major stared up at him with those striking eyes, Pip thrust with increasing force. The major took all he had, gazing up at him with his mouth stretched wide around Pip's prick, enough heat in his eyes to set Pip's entire body aflame. A tingling began at the base of Pip's spine that he was helpless to fight, and for the first time he could ever remember, he lost command of his body, jerking madly and arching his back, spilling his seed down the major's throat as he stifled a cry with his fist.

When Pip had spent his last drop, the major released his punishing grip on Pip's arse and drew off his softening cock. Pip could only pant and tremble in the aftermath of his release. While Pip watched dazedly, the major swiped a hand across his swollen lips and slumped back onto his bed, bracing himself on his elbows as he too panted from exertion. They stayed like that for several moments, staring at one another and trying to regain their breath. But once he had, Pip didn't know what to do next. So many thoughts and feelings ran through his head he couldn't make sense of any of them, and his body was still vibrating with the strongest release he could ever remember, muddling his thoughts even more.

Eventually the major must have read some of what Pip was feeling for he stopped searching Pip's face, and his eyes softened. He gave Pip a small, sad smile and said, "I think you should go to your bed now, Phillip. Go on. It's all right."

Pip's wits may have been a bit addled but that still seemed wrong somehow.

"What about you, sir?" he asked without thinking.

The major's smile fell a little. "I can manage from here. No need to worry."

Pip shook his head. "No. I meant…." Pip flushed, unable to finish his sentence, and the major's smile returned.

"Ah. That. No need to worry there either. I spent when you did, just from watching you."

The look he gave Pip then, as if he couldn't take his eyes off him, made Pip's stomach flip and his body tingle anew. Pip shifted uncomfortably, at a loss as to what he should do. He knew he should leave. He needed to think about what he was doing. But he didn't want to think. He wanted the major to take over, as he had before, and make it so that Pip couldn't think for the rest of the night.

In for a penny….

"Go on, Phillip. You'll catch another chill if you stay like that much longer." The major's voice pulled Pip back to the present, forcing him to remember that his cock was damp and exposed to the air. He shivered and set himself to rights before turning and numbly making his way to the door.

"Good night, Phillip," the major called to him as Pip stepped into the hall.

"Night, sir." Pip turned and started down the dark corridor but stopped when the major called to him again.

"If you still wish it, I would like for you to come and read to me tomorrow after dinner," the major paused then and continued in a quieter voice, "If you don't come, I will understand and I won't impose on you again."

"Yes, sir," Pip whispered automatically before continuing to make his way to the emptiness and quiet of his room.

Pip undressed and climbed beneath the blankets, feeling drained in more ways than one.

Chapter *Eleven*

HE SLEPT deeply that night, despite his fears that the uproar in his head wouldn't allow it. But in the morning, he was no less troubled than he'd been before and for most of the day he wandered through his duties in a daze, unsure how to face what he'd allowed to happen—what he'd wanted to happen.

The work helped. Mrs. Applethwaite's strident commands were familiar and oddly comforting. Because of her and the fact that he still tired easily, Pip was able to avoid thinking unduly much about anything up until his afternoon ride. But when he was finally alone with his thoughts, sitting astride the horse, looking down on Keswick, he could no longer hide from the enormity of what he'd done.

He'd had relations with another man.

He'd enjoyed it.

And then afterward he'd slunk off to bed like a frightened child.

Pip climbed down from the saddle and buried his face in the horse's shoulder, feeling mortified and strangely exhilarated at the same time. He took one shuddering breath and then another as he stroked the long neck beneath his cheek to keep the animal—and himself—calm. Despite his efforts, the horse snorted and shifted, restless in the chill wind, so Pip pulled himself together enough to turn him around and begin the walk back to the cottage. It would give them both something to do while Pip fretted.

As they walked, Pip thought back on all the women he'd ever bedded. He couldn't remember all of their faces, let alone their names, but a few memorable women had done more than lie back and allow Pip to see to their pleasure before taking his own. He'd cared for some of them, enjoyed their company, been charmed and flattered by their attention and admiration. But he couldn't remember ever feeling anything like the fire in his veins when the major had taken him into his mouth. Pip's whole body ached with the memory of it, and he suddenly felt like an ass for all the years he'd wasted believing he knew what true desire was.

Back when he'd first learned of Master Carey's affection for Mr. Carruthers, Pip had thought the man all kinds of fool for choosing to be with another man—and all the danger that entailed—when so many women would gladly offer up everything they had for a chance with the wealthy and handsome gentleman. Pip hadn't understood at all. And now he thought perhaps those two men had something together that Pip had never experienced before and never realized he was missing.

Who is the fool now?

Pip closed his eyes and an image of the major sitting on his bed with Pip's cock in his mouth and those eyes staring up at him flashed across his mind. He shivered in the cold wind even as his cock stirred. He wanted more. His body didn't lie. So what was stopping him from taking what the major offered?

The church? Propriety?

Pip laughed out loud, startling a snort out of the horse. *Not hardly.*

The law?

While Pip certainly had no wish to ride the three-legged mare, he didn't think he needed to fear over much for his neck. Who would betray them? The major certainly wouldn't. That left only the housekeeper and her husband in their lonely little cottage, and Pip could be careful.

Even if the couple did suspect something, they'd be unlikely to risk their comfortable positions by kicking up a fuss. Wouldn't they?

A small ripple in the darkest part of his memories gave Pip a moment's pause, but he shoved it down again before it could break free. The present circumstances were nothing like what had happened to him at Newgate. The fear hadn't risen in him again. He was a grown man now, and the major wasn't some fat, foul-smelling child rapist buying a bit of arse in the middle of the night. The major was a gentleman, and though a little proud, high-handed, and cold at times, the man had dignity and morals... and in his present state, Pip was fairly certain he could best the major if it came to actual physical blows. He had no need to be afraid on that score.

Pip paused on top of the ridge above the cottage and took a deep breath… and then another. He could do this. With the promise of pleasures like he'd experienced the night before, he could set aside his fears and reservations. It didn't have to last forever, none of his dalliances ever had before, and once he'd fulfilled this strange aching need inside him, he'd move on like he had before, with no one the wiser.

Back in the barn, Pip rubbed the horse down and settled him in, feeling much lighter of heart than when he'd departed. His nerves threatened to get the better of him twice more during the afternoon and once while he changed clothes before dinner. But when his plate was emptied and the bell rang for more coal for the master's fire, Pip didn't hesitate to offer his services. "I've got it."

Mrs. Applethwaite frowned at him while her husband grinned and settled back into his chair. Pip cleared his throat. "The master asked me t' read to 'im tonight. I can take the coal with me. No need for Mr. Applethwaite to trouble 'imself."

Her eyes widened a little in surprise, and her disapproving frown grew deeper, but she didn't stop him when he reached for the scuttle and headed for the door to the rest of the house.

By the time he made it to the library door, Pip's heart was racing so he could barely draw breath. He knocked once and let himself in when the major called "Come."

The major turned his brooding gaze from the fire as Pip stepped inside, and his eyes widened when he saw who it was. Pip's hand shook and threatened to drop the pail he carried as he walked to the grate. But he managed to hold himself together enough to stir up the coals and add more without looking too foolish. He stayed in front of the fire with his back to the major until the heat began to soothe him, loosening the tenseness in his muscles despite the fact that he could feel the major's eyes on him as he worked.

When he'd delayed as long as he could, Pip rose and turned, lifting his gaze until he could meet the major's eyes. He looked as stern and aloof as ever, but beneath that appeared the barest hint of vulnerability and uncertainty. That tiny glimpse into his soul soothed Pip enough for some of his natural confidence and bluster to return, and he grinned. It wasn't as cocksure as it would've been if the major had been a woman, but Pip managed the best he could under the circumstances. Wrapping his bluff of confidence around him, Pip closed the distance between them and bent down to pick up the book that rested on the major's knee, allowing his fingertips to graze the man's thigh in the process.

"*Confessions of an English Opium-Eater*," Pip read the title aloud and clicked his tongue. "Don't sound particularly pleasant, do it? Per'aps we should find somethin' else."

Pip leaned close to the major as he set the book on the small table next to his chair, pushing aside the man's mostly full whisky glass. The major didn't move, but a small hitch in his breathing betrayed him. He was not unaffected by Pip's closeness, and Pip felt his nerves settle a bit more, replaced by anticipation. He'd done this dance before. Even if the partner was different, he wasn't a complete innocent.

Pip moved away and casually perused the bookshelves on the other side of the library, knowing the major's gaze followed his every move.

"Per'aps somethin' from the Bard would be better," Pip mused idly as he slid a finger across the spines of the books. "Or poetry?" Pip looked over his shoulder coyly, and the major swallowed and shook his head.

"You choose," the man said gruffly.

Pip strolled back to him and crouched down next to his chair. "There must be somethin' ye want other than that dreary book."

The major's cheeks flushed, but his face hardened at Pip's words. "I want not to be toyed with, Phillip."

Pip's grin faded, and his nerves returned in a rush. He blew out a nervous breath. "I'm not toying with ye, truly sir. I don't know what it is I am doing, but it's not that."

The major closed his eyes and sighed. "I want no games. I only want the truth from you. Did you come here only to read to me tonight, or did you want something else?"

"Somethin' else."

The major made to rise, and Pip reached for him automatically, only to have his hands knocked away. "I don't require your assistance. I am not so crippled as all that," the man snapped.

Pip must have looked as wounded as he felt, because the major sighed and lowered his head. "Forgive me, Phillip. I do not mean to be cruel. But I can manage well enough when I'm not in my cups. I don't want you to see me as any less a man than I already am. Allow me to retain some of my dignity, even if it is a pale shadow of what it once was."

Pip swallowed around the tightness in his throat. "I don' think of ye as less a man than any other, sir. I only wanted to 'elp."

The major reached out tentatively and cupped Pip's jaw. He caressed Pip's cheek with his thumb as his sad eyes searched Pip's face. "Is that why you're here now? To help? Is this pity?"

The question cost the major, Pip could see it in the ticking of his jaw muscles, the pain and mortification written plainly across his face. "No, sir. I wouldn't. I'm 'ere because I want t' be."

The major blew out a long breath and closed his eyes. "Thank you."

Pip grimaced and shook his head, out of patience with both of them and their mincing about. Flirtation and kindness had only earned him anger and a rebuff. He needed to try something else. "Don't thank me," he said harshly, "Get yer arse up those stairs an' show me the man ye are afore I think both of us 'as turned into a couple o' faintin' flowers."

That did the trick. The major let out a bark of laughter, and his eyes lit in a way that took Pip's breath away, as much as the hand that cupped his cheek firmly, drawing him in for a kiss. The major's lips were tentative at first, barely a whisper across Pip's own. But when Pip didn't pull away, the major pressed on, teasing a wet tongue along the seam of his mouth until Pip's ventured out to play. Pip closed his eyes then and sank into that kiss, every inch of his skin tingling and alive with it. His breath stuttered in his chest as the major devoured him, and only came rushing back when the man pushed him back on his heels.

"Come on," Pip gasped impatiently.

Pip turned and grabbed a lamp, then quickly led the way out of the room before he could change his mind. He only slowed when he remembered the major's impairment. Pip waited at the bottom of the stairs for him to catch up and then took to the steps a great deal slower than he really wanted to. But the major was even slower still, and when Pip looked back in concern, he found the man staring hotly at his arse through the split in the back of his jacket. Pip's stomach fluttered with a combination of lust and sudden trepidation as he began to regret his brashness. He turned back to finish the climb, but his earlier boldness was gone, and along with it some of his arousal.

What had he been thinking? Of course the man would want to bugger him. Fucking is what a man did. He'd learned that early enough. Pip shuddered and determinedly pushed the memories away, refusing to be swallowed by them. His heart sped for an entirely different reason. He started to feel a little sick as they continued down the hall, and his erection faded to softness in his trousers.

Once at the door, Pip hurried into the room and busied himself with the fire so the major couldn't see his hands shake. When the coals were stirred up as much as they could be, Pip had no choice but to rise and go to the man waiting patiently with an arm braced on the footboard of the bed. As Pip drew near, the major reached for him, and Pip did his best not to flinch away. But his best wasn't good enough.

"Second thoughts?" the major asked. His voice sounded much too indifferent about the answer for Pip's liking, but at least it held no judgment or anger.

"No, I…." Pip shook his head and clenched his jaw.

"Phillip, you don't have to—"

"I *want* to," Pip interrupted fiercely. He'd thought about nothing else since last night. His body ached for it. But some things he simply could not do.

Pip closed his eyes and concentrated on the way the major's hands had felt on him the night before, and the vise around his chest eased. He opened his eyes, reached out, and cupped the major's face in both hands, this time taking pleasure in the roughness of the man's whiskers against his palms. "I want to," he repeated, breathing the words against his master's lips. "There are some things I just canna' do. Do ye understand?"

The major's breath had quickened with Pip's closeness, feathering across Pip's lips and cheek as he searched Pip's face. "Not fully. But you have my word I would do nothing you didn't want. I would never force you, Phillip. You may leave or stay as you choose."

Pip blew out a breath and rolled his shoulders to ease the tension that had built there. He leaned forward and pressed his forehead against the major's, closing his eyes again and willing the darkness inside him away.

After a few moments, the major stepped back and took one of Pip's hands, drew it away from his face, and led him to the bed. The major sat on the mattress and pulled Pip closer, as he had the night before. But when he began to unbutton the placket of Pip's trousers again, Pip stopped him.

"I want to touch this time," Pip whispered.

The major held his gaze for a long moment before letting his hands fall to the bed, palms upward, silently giving Pip permission to do as he wished.

Pip's own hands trembled as he helped the major out of his jacket and untied his cravat. He carefully draped both over the foot of the sturdy wooden bed before reaching to undo the buttons at the major's throat and expose the strong column of the man's neck. Through it all, the major remained passive, waiting for Pip to lead, and a surge of lust followed closely behind the wave of gratitude that crashed through Pip.

On impulse, Pip leaned forward and buried his face where the major's neck and shoulder met, breathing in his scent, nuzzling and nibbling a little, reveling in the strangeness of it. The man was all salt and musk and spice—exotic but not sweet or flowery—like the bits of fabric and ornament strewn about the cottage from his travels.

As Pip continued to sample him, the major drew in an unsteady breath and a moan rumbled deep in his chest. He cupped Pip's skull and threaded his fingers through Pip's curls, gently holding him in place. His touch held only tenderness, no force, and the fear did not rise in Pip. He felt cherished rather than controlled, like something worthy of being handled with care, and his cock throbbed with renewed interest.

The major slid his hands to Pip's shoulders and tugged at the coarse wool of his jacket, and Pip helped him push it off. Pip's neck cloth soon followed, joining his jacket on the floor. He paid little attention to where they fell. His clothes were nowhere near as fine as the major's and had seen far worse than the elegant Persian rug beside the bed.

They both reached for the buttons on the other's waistcoat at the same time, their arms tangling in their haste, and Pip laughed, swatting the major's hands away. "Let me."

Pip hastily removed his own waistcoat and tossed it aside before seeing to the major's.

"It's been a long time since I had a true valet," the major mused as Pip undid the buttons. "Perhaps I should give you a promotion."

Pip rolled his eyes and snorted. He tugged the waistcoat off and tossed it carelessly over his shoulder to demonstrate what he thought of that idea. "Sure cove. If ye want Mrs. Applethwaite t' think ye've lost yer bleedin' mind more'n she already does. Lie back now."

"Yes, sir," the major quipped with a wry smirk and a teasing glint to his eyes Pip had never seen before.

The major stretched out, propping himself up on his elbows, and Pip dropped to his knees beside the bed. He pulled the boot off the major's good leg. Then climbed onto the bed and stretched out alongside him. They were both down to only their shirts, trousers, and undergarments now—except for the major's false leg—and Pip thought perhaps he needed to spend a little time distracting them both before he went any further.

When Pip was settled, he reached for the major who rolled to face him. One of the major's brows was raised in question, and the smirk was still in place, but his eyes were no longer laughing. They'd gone dark and heavy-lidded, the silver only a pale ring around deepest black, and Pip's breathing sped in response.

While the major gripped Pip's upper arms loosely, smoothing the fabric of his shirt and tracing the line of muscle with his thumbs, Pip slid a trembling hand up the flat plains of the major's chest, ghosting over each ridge and valley he found. The major's injury and lengthy recovery must have taken some of the meat from his bones, but Pip could still feel the definition there, all masculine hardness, no softness beyond the fine texture of the linen.

A small patch of dark blond hair peeking through the opening in the major's shirt tickled Pip's palm as he moved further up, until he reached the smooth, almost delicate skin along his collarbones. Pip trailed his fingers lightly over that softness, enjoying the contrast and the major's answering shiver. Then he curled his fingers around the man's neck.

The muscles flexed beneath his hands as Pip tightened his grip. He pulled, and the major's lips were soon pressed to his. They were just as warm and soft as Pip remembered, and he spent some time teasing and sucking on them before pushing his tongue between them again.

As with the major's scent, the kiss was an intoxicating combination of the familiar and the strange, and Pip continued to draw it out so he might fully appreciate the experience. Once or twice, the major attempted to deepen it, but when Pip only retreated under each advance, the major eventually relaxed and allowed Pip to set the pace.

The major's hands drifted lower, caressing Pip's flanks as he pressed their bodies closer. Pip could feel the heat radiating from the man's skin and the evidence of his desire but he hesitated to go any further until the major broke away and whispered, "Please. Please touch me, Phillip."

The need in his voice and the way he looked at Pip hit Pip like a punch to the stomach. His cock throbbed and suddenly he was desperate to have more. Pip tore at the ties of his own shirt, dragged it over his head, and tossed it aside. He didn't even pause to see the admiration in the major's eyes before tugging *his* shirt out of his trousers and running his hands over the hot skin he found beneath. Pip shoved the shirt up under the major's arms and pushed him back on the bed. He had no breasts to fondle, only hard muscle and bone, but Pip liked a good tickle of his nipples from time to time, so he bent and suckled on one of the major's experimentally. The major gasped and arched his back, and Pip smiled in triumph.

Perhaps pleasuring the man would be easier than he thought.

Pip lavished attention on the nipple beneath his lips before moving to the other. All the while, the major writhed beneath him, mussing Pip's hair and stroking Pip's face and shoulders with restless hands.

Soon enough the major was reduced to panting the word "please" over and over, and Pip's cock ached so much he felt it would burst if he didn't move on. Pip slid off the mattress and undid the buttons of the major's trousers first. The major propped himself up on his elbows again, watching Pip's every move. His face was flushed, his lips swollen with Pip's kisses, and the heat in his pale eyes was enough to keep Pip from thinking too much over what he was about to do.

Safe and warm in his house, the major wore no drawers beneath the fine wool, and his cock sprung free as soon as Pip released it. The prick was long and slender, not as thick as Pip's but beautiful if such a thing could be called beautiful. The head was purple and swollen, already peeking out from its foreskin and wet with excitement. To Pip's utter amazement he felt his mouth water just gazing at it as it curled up from the thatch of dark blond hair at its base.

Pip refused to examine the feeling and let his hunger rule as he reached for the waistband and began to tug the trousers the rest of the way off.

"You don't have to do that," the major said, putting his hands over Pips to stop him and drawing Pip's attention back to his face.

"'Ow else am I going to get ye undressed?" Pip said in confusion, fighting the hands holding him still.

"I only meant you don't have to look at it. You can leave the trousers most of the way on if you don't wish to see—" The major stopped abruptly and clenched his jaw. Some of the heat had faded from his eyes, and Pip did not want that.

"Don't be daft. Lift yer 'ips," he commanded brusquely, and after a moment's pause, the major complied.

The false leg was laced to the major's thigh much like a corset, and Pip smiled in relief. He had plenty of experience with those. "Can I?" he asked as he placed his hands lightly over the strings and looked up into the major's eyes.

When the major blew out a breath and nodded, Pip untied the laces as gently as he could. The thigh beneath looked bruised and swollen even in the dim light of the lamp, so Pip was careful not to jar it as he pulled the whole contrivance off and propped it against the night table. The major watched him closely with shame written plainly across his face, forestalling any of the questions that sprang to Pip's mind. Pip didn't really want to talk at the moment anyway. He simply shucked off his own trousers and drawers in an effort to distract the man.

It worked.

Heat immediately flared back into his eyes and he reached for Pip. Being careful of his leg, Pip stretched out on top of him, pressing the lengths of their bodies together. They were of a height, so their pricks lined up perfectly, and both of them groaned as Pip flexed his hips a few times. The major slid his palms around Pip's back, urging him to continue as Pip took most of his weight on his elbows and leaned in to claim his mouth.

They stayed like that, kissing and gently rocking against one another until the major's movements became more urgent and he grabbed two fistfuls of Pip's arse, holding Pip in place as he thrust up into him and panted against Pip's cheek. Heat built in Pip's belly, and his blood pounded in his ears. Their cocks dripped a steady stream between them, and Pip hardly noticed that he'd lost control of their coupling until the major's fingers slipped between the globes of his arse and the tips teased Pip's back entrance.

Pure instinct took over then, and Pip's entire body tensed. He shoved himself off the man and sprang to his feet. "Don't!" Pip's breathing was ragged from more than passion now, and he shivered in the sudden chill of the room.

81

The major sat up quickly, his eyes wide with confusion and concern. "What did I do?"

Pip took a breath and then another to calm himself. "I can't. I'm sorry... but I can't."

The major pulled himself to the edge of the bed. Pip moved further away, eliciting a sigh from him. "Phillip, I can hardly run after you," he said, sweeping a hand to indicate his missing leg. "Please, forgive me. I was only carried away by the moment, by how you made me feel. Don't go. Tell me what I did wrong."

The quiet pleading in his voice as well as the regret and sorrow in his eyes calmed Pip enough that reason returned, and he nodded stiffly and walked back to the bed. He couldn't find the words to tell the major what was going on inside him, but he stood still between the major's legs as the man tentatively reached out and slid warm, soothing hands down Pip's flanks.

Watching Pip intently, the major leaned forward and nuzzled Pip's flagging cock back to life, plying it with gentle kisses until Pip's heart was racing for the right reasons again.

"Would you allow me to pleasure you as I did last night?"

Pip sighed and threaded his fingers through the soft waves of the major's hair, mussing it further. He'd wanted to do more than that. Sometime during their kissing and petting, an image had formed in his mind of the major in the throes of release, with all the pain and sadness gone from his countenance, replaced by peace and more of the adoration Pip thrived on. The picture was so beautiful, he'd desperately wanted to see it become reality, and yet his demons had betrayed him, keeping him from it.

When Pip still didn't speak, the major said, "Perhaps you'd like something else? It has been some time—years actually—but I am not averse to being taken, if you wish it."

Pip's head shot up in surprise, and the major grinned back at him as he began stroking Pip's cock in his fist. He leaned forward and kissed Pip's crown. "This is magnificent. T'would be a shame to see it go to waste."

Pip's knees trembled and his cock twitched in the major's grip even as he frowned in confusion. "Is the master sayin' he'd like to be buggered?"

The major's grin grew. "As I said, it *has* been a long time. But I think it might be something we would both enjoy."

"Ye'd like it?" Pip asked, disbelieving.

"Oh yes."

When Pip only stared at him, the major put his hands on Pip's hips, turned him around, and gave him a light shove toward the far side of the room. "In the trunk there, you'll find a case with several glass vials. Bring me the one marked 'Elysium.'"

Still confused but willing to follow the major's lead, Pip padded across the room. The floorboards were cold beyond the carpet, so he moved quickly. He opened the lid of the small wooden trunk and peered into the shadows inside. He could just make out the shapes of books and loose papers, a rolled leather case with some sort of metal instruments peeking out the end, some small pots and jars, and a latched wooden case. He opened the case and lifted the vials into the lamplight until he found the one he was sent for.

"Elysium?" Pip asked as he hurried back to the bed.

The major's answering smile was a little sad. "Another time."

As soon as Pip was close enough, the major wrapped a hand around his wrist and drew him gently back. He took the vial from Pip's grasp, unstoppered it, and poured a small amount of oil into Pip's palm. "Your fingers. First one, then two… three if you're feeling generous. And then your cock."

Pip stared at the oil in his hand and then at the major as the man lay back on the bed and propped the foot of his good leg on the edge of the mattress, opening himself up to Pip's gaze. Pip's hand shook a little as he dipped his fingers in the oil and knelt beside the bed. The major began to stroke his cock, watching Pip between his thighs, and some of Pip's nerves abated. The major appeared to want this—his desire plain in the hardness of his cock and the heat in his gaze.

Pip leaned forward and teased a finger around his back entrance, familiarizing himself with the texture. He'd never buggered anyone before. None of the women he ever bedded had asked him to. The opening twitched, and the major drew in a shaky breath as Pip continued to touch it. Emboldened, Pip pressed inside, up to the first knuckle. The channel was warm and smooth, soft as silk, and it squeezed his finger so tightly Pip's cock throbbed in response. Pip pumped in and out a few times, and when the major moaned and spread his thighs wider, Pip added a second finger.

The major groaned. "That's it. Stretch me, make me ready for you."

Pip shivered as he felt a bead of moisture form on the crown of his cock. The major's channel was quivering around his fingers, begging him to do more, and Pip wasn't sure how much longer he could stand to be out in the cold when such heat awaited him. He added a third finger and flexed and twisted them until the major gasped and pressed down hard upon them. "That's enough, Phillip. Now you."

Pip stroked his own cock with the oil remaining in his palm and stood up. His stomach fluttered nervously as he lifted the major's injured thigh over his arm and guided his cock to the entrance with his other hand. He pressed against the opening for a few agonizing seconds before it relaxed and allowed him inside. The major gasped, and Pip froze in place until the strain eased on the man's face and Pip was able to push in further.

When Pip was fully seated, the major cried, "Wait!" and Pip stilled again, panting with the effort of holding back. The need to thrust into that heaven was nearly overwhelming.

"All right," the major panted. "Move."

Pip lifted the major's other leg as well, wrapping his arms around the major's thighs for leverage as he began to thrust, carefully at first, watching his face closely. The major arched beneath him, moaning and bracing his arms on the bed, meeting Pip's thrusts with equal force, and Pip succumbed to his baser nature as pleasure exploded across his senses. He was lost in it for a time, thrusting his hips and riding a wave of bliss… until something evil crept in alongside it. A sudden surge of anger took him so completely by surprise that he had no defense against it. One moment he was in the throes of a pleasure so intense he knew he'd never experienced anything like it before, and the next, rage filled him as memories of pain and fear long buried struggled to the surface.

Pip closed his eyes, fighting against it as he pounded the body beneath him, but his hands convulsed, digging into the flesh he held, and his pace only increased. He no longer remembered who was beneath him, only that he was the one in control now. He wasn't a child anymore. He wasn't defenseless. He felt dizzy and sick even as the pressure built at the base of his spine. The body beneath him grunted and thrashed, but Pip held on, pounding into it until his vision went white and his release consumed his entire being.

In the aftermath, Pip's anger fled as quickly as it had come, leaving him suddenly hollow and utterly horrified. He released his hold on the major's thighs and stumbled backward, grabbing the foot of the bed for support before he collapsed.

As Pip watched in shock, the major groaned and rolled onto his side exposing to the lamplight the livid marks Pip had left on his flesh. Pip wanted to weep, but no tears came to his eyes. They both stayed as they were, panting into the sudden stillness. Eventually the major seemed to recover himself. He dragged his body to the top of the bed and collapsed onto the pillows, grimacing in pain as he rubbed the thigh of his damaged leg.

Pip swallowed twice before his throat eased enough for him to speak.

"I'm so sorry. Did I hurt you? Are you in pain?"

The major closed his eyes and chuckled as he collapsed onto his back with a sigh. "Always. But not from anything you did. Don't worry."

Pip remained where he was, shaking and disgusted with himself, and the major finally seemed to realize something was amiss.

He sat up again and stared at Pip. "Phillip? It's all right. You didn't do anything wrong." The major's lips quirked. "You were a little rougher than I expected, but that wasn't necessarily a bad thing."

Pip could only stare at him in confusion.

How could the man jest about such a thing?

"I don't know what came over me," Pip whispered. His voice shook, sounding small and lost even to his ears.

The major's eyebrows drew down. "It really is all right, Phillip. You didn't do me any harm." The major reached out to him, and Pip fell into his arms, shivering. "Bloody hell, but you're freezing," the major complained as he drew the blankets over them. He held Pip gingerly, as if he didn't know quite what to do with him.

Pip let his head fall to the major's breast and closed his eyes. "Forgive me."

The major's chest rose and fell beneath his cheek, and he patted Pip's back somewhat awkwardly. "There's truly nothing to forgive. I don't understand why you believe there is."

Pip could only shake his head. He wanted to believe what the major was saying, but too many emotions were grappling in his breast, guilt chief among them.

"If you won't tell me what's wrong, I cannot help you," the major said, a hint of irritation in his voice.

Pip drew away from him, swung his legs over the side of the bed, and sat up. "You were in pain… after. I thought…." Pip couldn't finish.

"I told you. I'm fine. I may have let you bugger me, Phillip, but I'm not a maid. I don't need your concern, nor do I want it." The major's irritation was much plainer now. He blew out a loud breath before continuing. "Look. My leg was badly broken, nearly crushed. They took the lower half, but I refused to allow them to take it all. What is left pains me along with my hip and my back because of that damned contraption I have to use in order to walk. That is all. I enjoyed what just happened between us, and I'd enjoy it more if you stop being so bloody foolish about the whole thing."

Pip turned to face him in surprise. The major's cheeks were flushed, his eyes blazing in temper, and his mouth set in a hard line. Some of the tightness in Pip's chest eased, and he felt his lips turn up in a wry smile. The major was almost as handsome when he was in a temper as he was in the throes of passion. Pip felt his skin heat despite the chill of the room.

"Yes, sir," Pip said only partly in jest.

The major frowned and his eyes narrowed for a moment, as if he were trying to determine if Pip were making fun of him, before he nodded and his lips eased into a hesitant smile of his own. "Good. Then we're done with that. And for God's sake, don't call me 'sir' when we're alone like this. It feels wrong somehow after you've only just finished rogering me."

Pip coughed and flushed for a moment before he fell back on old habits and gave the man his cocksure grin and winked. "What should I call ye, then?"

"My Christian name is Astley. You may call me that when it's only the two of us."

Feeling a little more like himself, Pip pursed his lips, frowning in his best imitation of the major the first time he'd spoken to him in the library. "I don't know." Pip tapped his chin with a finger. "I suppose I prefer it to master or sir, and McNalty would be *simply ridiculous*."

The major's eyebrows drew down again until he seemed to realize Pip was mocking him with his own words, and he chuckled. "Call me what you like, then. Anything but Major or McNalty."

Pip leaned over and kissed him gently. "Astley doesn't suit you, I think."

The major rolled his eyes. "I have other names, a whole string of them between the first and the last. Shall I rattle them off to see if any of them suit me better?"

Pip pursed his lips again, showing every appearance of giving the matter great thought before he shook his head. "No. I think I shall call you Ash, like your hair." Pip combed his fingers through the sweat-dampened waves as he said it, and Ash closed his eyes.

After allowing Pip to pet him for only a short time, Ash grabbed his wrist to stop him. The warmth and playfulness that had been there only a moment before was gone as he said, "I think you should find your bed now, Phillip."

Pip hid his disappointment at being dismissed so coldly with a careless shrug and climbed to his feet. He had a lot to think on anyway, and he hadn't truly expected Ash to ask him to spend the night.

He quickly pulled on his clothes, feeling Ash's eyes on him as he dressed. Pip turned and faced the man while he slowly buttoned his waistcoat hoping he might be tempted to change his mind, but Ash only looked away.

"Good night, Phillip."

Pip's sigh was purely internal. "Good night, Ash."

Pip crept out of the room and down the stairs. He briefly went to the library to bank the coals and put out the other lamp after lighting a candle to take with him. He paused in front of the looking glass in the hall and took some time to set his clothes to rights before making his way back to the kitchen.

Mr. and Mrs. Applethwaite were still sitting by the kitchen fire and seemed surprised to see him. Pip shrugged a little uncomfortably under their questioning stares and said, "The master was feeling tired so 'e went to bed early. I put out the lamps and took care of the fires."

The housekeeper nodded and went back to her mending. Her husband shrugged and took another drink from his bottle, both seeming satisfied with his excuse. "I'm feeling a bit tired m'self, so I think I'll turn in as well," Pip added.

Mrs. Applethwaite looked up at that and frowned. "You're not feeling ill again, are you?"

"No, Missus. A bit tired is all."

"Then you should most certainly go to bed. Good night."

"Good night."

Pip turned and walked the short distance to his room. As he was shutting his door, he heard the woman call out, "And don't waste that candle sitting up with one of the master's books all night."

Pip rolled his eyes and closed the door. He had no thoughts of reading. He was much too unsettled to concentrate on the words.

He stripped down to his shirt and drawers, gave his nether parts a quick wash, and crawled beneath his blankets. He blew out the candle and closed his eyes, but visions of the evening played through his head over and over, making it nearly impossible to sleep. He was exhausted, but the guilt of losing control, the irritation over being dismissed so easily, and the bone-deep satisfaction of the best fuck of his life were waging war inside him.

Eventually, he decided he didn't care who the victor was as long as they would leave him the bloody hell alone. He had work to do in the morning and perhaps another chance to bugger his master come the evening. What did the rest of it matter?

Chapter *Twelve*

ALL THE next day, Pip went about his duties studiously ignoring the niggling doubts and insecurities at the back of his mind. It would have been nice if he could have seen Ash at least once during the day to set his mind at rest on a couple of scores. But no matter how many times he searched for Ash through the windows of the cottage, the man never appeared. And by dusk, Pip was fretting like a mother hen over one chick.

Perhaps he had truly hurt him and Ash was just too stubborn to admit it. Or did he simply not want to see Pip?

Pip's pride shied away from that possibility. Ash had called him beautiful more than once. He'd wanted Pip. He'd said he'd enjoyed their encounter. He had to want more, as Pip did.

At supper that night, Pip desperately wanted to ask Mrs. Applethwaite about their master, but he didn't dare. Not only was she sure to tell him it was none of his concern, but he didn't want to raise any suspicions about their relationship. So instead, Pip sat and stared broodingly into the fire as the minutes ticked past.

He'd worked himself up to a full sulk by the time the clock in the main hall chimed eight, but then Ash's bell rang twice, only a few seconds after, and Pip was on his feet before the second ring had finished.

He tried not to appear too anxious as he forced himself to walk at a sedate pace to the library. Before he knocked, he took a deep breath to settle the butterflies in his stomach and combed his fingers through his hair in front of the looking glass.

"Ye wanted to see me, sir?" Pip said, trying not to sound as petulant as he felt.

Ash frowned at him from his seat by the fire. "I thought we'd agreed you would call me something else when we were alone."

Pip shrugged and pouted, knowing he was behaving like a child but somehow unable to stop himself. He hadn't received a word or even been allowed a glimpse of the man all day. He hated being ignored or forgotten about.

"Phillip, what's wrong?" Ash struggled to his feet and took one hesitant step toward him before seeming to check himself.

Pip shrugged again and stared at the shabby stockings on his feet. "I looked for ye today, *all day*. Never once did ye come to the window. I know it's too cold for ye to venture out, but ye could've at least come to the window. Unless ye didn't want to see me."

Ash sighed and crossed the last few feet that separated them, but he didn't reach for Pip. "Of course I wanted to see you, Phillip. I thought of you all day." He chuckled and shook his head. "I suppose my pride wouldn't allow me to let you see me mooning over you."

Pip harrumphed. "I like to be mooned over."

Ash's smile froze on his face. "It probably happens all the time. Shall I be lumped in with all your other conquests, then?"

Pip frowned, hurt. "I didn't lie to ye. This is all new to me, ye know."

The major blew out a breath and returned to his seat. "I'm sorry, Phillip. Don't listen to my foolishness. Am I forgiven for not coming to the window?"

Pip nodded. He would have felt better if he didn't have the sneaking suspicion Ash was laughing at him behind his usual calm mask.

"Is there anything I can do to make it up to you?"

A slow grin spread across Pip's face. He let his gaze drop and linger on Ash's body. "I can think of a thing or two that might 'elp."

Ash chuckled. "It's a little early for that, don't you think? What will Mrs. Applethwaite think?"

Pip stepped forward and braced himself on the arms of Ash's chair. He leaned down and nuzzled the man's neck as he whispered, "It's never too early for this. And I 'ope the old crow won't be thinkin' anything at all. But if ye'r worried about 'er stirring from 'er warm nest in the kitchen, it's not likely if she don't 'ave to. Even if she does, I'll tell her ye were chilled and ailing and wanted me t' read t' ye in bed."

Pip bit his earlobe and suckled on it, and Ash groaned and fisted a hand in Pip's jacket.

"I suppose you have a point," Ash said breathlessly.

When Pip pulled back, he could see only a pale ring of silver in Ash's eyes, quickly being swallowed by black, and his insecurities from the day faded. Ash most definitely wanted him.

Pip let his eyelids droop suggestively and licked his lips. Ash drew in a sharp breath and mirrored his move, wetting his lips and tightening his hold on Pip's jacket. Pip preened under the admiration in Ash's eyes, soaking it up like warm summer sunlight. He needed that look more than he wanted to admit.

"Does that mean we can go upstairs now?" Pip asked as he drew Ash to his feet.

Ash pulled away a little. "I don't think—"

Ash's words cut off on a moan as Pip palmed him through his trousers. Pip gave the hard prick a good rub and then stepped away. He chuckled throatily as he hurried toward the stairs, knowing Ash would follow. Ash moved more slowly of course, but this time Pip didn't wait for him. He hurried to Ash's bedchamber, quickly stirred up the coals, and shucked off his clothes as fast as he could manage.

By the time the uneven tread of the Ash's boots sounded in the hall, Pip was completely undressed but for his stockings. The air in the room was icy, and he had gooseflesh all over his body, but he was vain enough to wait for Ash to see him before he climbed into bed.

He wasn't disappointed.

"My God, you're beautiful," Ash whispered after he stepped through the door and froze in his tracks. "You make me wish I could draw or paint."

Even in the chill of the room, Pip's cock filled and lengthened at the look of adoration on Ash's face. Pip actually flushed under the weight of it, surprising himself. He'd been called beautiful before, and handsome too many times to count, but the words hadn't ever moved him quite like they did now. He never wanted Ash to stop looking at him like that.

Pip stayed where he was and waited for Ash to come to him. Ash limped across the floor, leaned his walking stick against the footboard, and reached for Pip. He slid his palms over Pip's chest, teasing his already hard nipples with the warmth of his skin before caressing Pip's flanks and then gripping his hips. Ash leaned forward and kissed along Pip's jaw— light and teasing—and Pip shivered from more than cold. When Ash stepped into his embrace, pressing a wool-clad thigh between Pip's legs, Pip moaned and ground his cock into the man's hip.

Ash smelled of whisky and wool, the sweetness of silk, and that spicy musk Pip had discovered the night before. A hint of the oil they'd used still lingered in the air, and Pip's prick hardened even further at the memories the scents conjured. He took Ash's mouth in a hard kiss, pushing his tongue inside and gripping the man's face in his hands to hold him still. Ash released Pip's hip and grabbed the rail at the foot of the bed, perhaps to steady himself as he pushed back into that kiss. The hand on Pip's other hip tightened, but Ash made no move beyond that to take command.

Even in his passion, Pip regretted that he couldn't give Ash the same trust the man had shown him last night. Part of him would have liked to feel Ash's strength unleashed, to experience his passion without restraint, to ease some of Pip's guilt by reaping some of the harshness he'd sown. Pip's heart raced just thinking about feeling the evidence of how much Ash wanted him, of the marks on his body that would act as reminder of Ash's need for him. But he couldn't do it.

Pip groaned into the kiss and clawed at Ash's clothes. Undressing the man took entirely too long, but Pip finally managed it after dragging Ash to the bedside and pushing him down onto the mattress. This time, they both crawled beneath the counterpane before Pip pulled Ash into his arms and kissed him until they were breathless. They writhed on the bed together, kissing and touching until their bodies were slick with sweat. Pip rolled on top of Ash and kissed his way down the man's body, lavishing attention on his nipples before moving lower, only pausing when Ash's cock bumped his chin. Ash's belly quivered beneath him as Pip panted hot breaths against his skin.

Pip closed his eyes and wrapped a fist around the warm, silky column of flesh that bobbed in front of his face. He leaned forward, swiped his tongue over the crown, and then waited, fearing the memories would try to surface again… but nothing happened. Ash tenderly caressed his hair and face as the man looked down at him with only patience and desire in his eyes. Ash was gentle and undemanding, clean and healthy—nothing like what Pip was trying to forget. In a sudden surge of need and gratitude, Pip swallowed Ash's cock as deeply as he could manage, bathing and teasing it with his tongue as he drew back up its length, copying what Ash had done to him. Ash groaned and his body tensed, but he made no move to thrust, and Pip repeated the move over and over, trying to draw as many different sounds and epithets from Ash's throat as he could.

Pip immersed himself in the act, giving it all he had until Ash cried, "Stop!" and the man's hand tightened in Pip's hair.

Pip pulled off and stared up at him questioningly. Ash panted for a moment or two but then began fumbling in the drawer of his night table. With his other hand, Ash tugged on Pip's arm and Pip crawled up the bed until they were face to face.

"Here." Ash handed the vial of oil to Pip and spread his thighs, wrapping his good leg around Pip's hip.

Pip swallowed nervously and shook his head. "I can't."

"Why?"

I'm afraid.

Pip couldn't bring himself to admit it, so he simply said, "Not tonight. Please."

Ash frowned and chewed his lip as he studied Pip's face for a time before he took the vial back and poured a little into his palm. Pip watched him warily as Ash set the vial aside and slid closer to him. Ash cupped his palm around his own member, coating it with oil before he reached out and wrapped his fist around Pip's cock. Pip closed his eyes as Ash's strong grip slicked the oil over his skin, the heat and silkiness of it drawing a moan from him. Ash's hand withdrew, but before Pip could utter a word of protest, the man pressed his body even closer and wrapped his fist around both their cocks, squeezing them together.

Pip cupped the back of Ash's head and buried his face in Ash's neck, sucking and nipping at the skin there while Ash pumped his fist along their lengths. His pace quickened, and soon Pip was thrusting into that grip and fisting his hands in the bed linens.

"Ash, please," Pip whispered against his cheek, so close to the brink, he was shaking with the need to let go.

Ash threw his head back and stifled a cry. His whole body tensed and his fist tightened almost painfully around them. Pip moaned and thrust hard one more time, mingling his seed with Ash's and nearly fainting from the pleasure of it. Before it became too much, Ash let his hand fall away, and Pip rolled onto his back, struggling to breathe.

He must have dozed off after that, because when he woke, Ash already had his shirt back on, and he was propped on an elbow watching Pip thoughtfully. Pip smiled happily up at the man, but the smile was not returned.

"Where did you come from, Phillip?" Ash asked quietly while his fingers traced Pip's lips and cheeks.

His tone was somewhat bemused, and Pip wasn't certain if the man had intended to speak the question aloud, but he answered as he always did, with a flippant "Here and there."

Whether Ash had intended to ask it or not, he didn't appear to like Pip's answer, because his eyebrows drew together. "I've heard a bit of London in your speech from time to time, though your references came from Penrith," he pressed.

Pip shrugged. As much as he liked to spin tales for the village chits, he didn't want to lie to Ash. But he didn't want Ash to know the truth of his sordid past either. Why couldn't the man leave things as they were?

"Determined to remain a man of mystery, then?" Ash's tone was still light, but he put some distance between them.

"Per'aps," Pip said brightly, trying to lighten the mood.

Ash blew out an obviously irritated breath and sat up against the pillows.

The move angered Pip. "And what of you, *Major McNalty?*" he asked defensively. "Village gossip has you a world traveler, an officer, a surgeon, but I've 'eard naught from your own lips, now 'ave I?"

Pip regretted the deflection immediately when a mask dropped over the major's countenance. His eyes were cold and his tone haughty as he said, "Perhaps you should go to your own bed now, Phillip."

Pip was too proud to let go of his pique, so instead of apologizing for snapping at the man, he threw the coverlet back and climbed out of bed. He hurried through the icy room collecting his clothes, only taking the time to pull on his shirt before he headed for the door.

"Wait."

That one word, spoken so quietly shouldn't have held the power to stop him, especially as Pip was a bit tired of taking orders at that particular moment. But Pip froze where he stood, with his trousers dangling from one hand.

Ash drew in a long breath and let it out. "I'm sorry. Of course you would be curious about me, as I am about you."

Pip straightened and turned expectantly, willing to be mollified.

"But, I think perhaps this isn't the time or place for this discussion. May we continue this tomorrow?"

"Per'aps," Pip mumbled petulantly.

When Pip simply stood in the door, frowning at him, the major eventually looked away and said. "Very well. Good night, Phillip."

"Good night, Ash."

Pip closed the door and dressed in the darkened hall before making his way back to his room.

Chapter *Thirteen*

THE NEXT night, a new pair of russet velvet house slippers waited for him when Pip entered the library. He'd collected numerous parcels from the village earlier that day, and now he wondered if the slippers had been among them.

"For me?"

Ash nodded. "I can't have you catching another chill, now can I?"

Feeling slightly placated by the gesture, Pip gave the man a small smile and sat to put them on. "Do ye want me to find somethin' to read, or can we dispense with the niceties and go on upstairs?" he asked with a wink as he wriggled his toes into the plush lining of his slippers.

Ash squirmed in his seat and looked away. After clearing his throat, he said, "I think it would be better if we stayed down here tonight."

Pip raised his eyebrows. They had a greater risk of being caught down there than in the man's rooms, but he shrugged. He wasn't exactly against the idea of them having a go at each another in the library. Pip grinned and closed the distance between them. "If that's what ye want…."

He sank to his knees in front of Ash's chair and reached for the placket of the man's trousers only to be stopped by Ash's hands on his wrists.

"I didn't mean that. Not here, Phillip."

Pip growled and stood up. "What do ye want, then?"

Ash closed his eyes and rubbed at the bridge of his nose. He sighed heavily and took a large swallow from his whisky glass before he said, "I want peace in my house. I want you to no longer be angry with me. That's what I want."

"Then come upstairs," Pip said and walked out the door without looking back. If the man insisted on being so bloody high-handed all the time, then Pip would give him a little of his own medicine, see how he liked it.

Ash made him wait. Pip didn't hear the man's limping footsteps in the hall until he'd been buried beneath the blankets for a good five minutes. When he did arrive, he was silent while Pip undressed him, the passion in his eyes muted compared to their other encounters, and Pip began to feel guilty for pushing him.

In an attempt to make amends, Pip asked, "If I were to answer yer questions from last night, would it be fair to expect a return in kind, then?"

Without waiting for an answer, Pip pushed Ash down on the bed, began nibbling his neck, just below the ear, and rolling the man's nipples between his thumbs and forefingers.

Ash swallowed and took a shuddering breath. "Quid pro quo? I... suppose that would be fair."

Pip wrapped his hand around Ash's rapidly filling prick. "I'm from London... originally."

Ash moaned and thrust into his grip. "Devon. The—the family seat is in Devon," he panted as Pip gave his cock a few pumps and bent to suck one of Ash's nipples.

Pip released the swollen nub and grinned against the man's chest. "That weren't me question, but glad to 'ear it."

Ash growled and Pip chuckled.

"Then ask me one, brat," Ash demanded impatiently.

Pip grinned and bent to suck the other nipple before he said, "For that affront, I think I deserve a big question. Hmmmmm. 'ow 'bout, why on earth would a fine, intelligent gentleman like yerself ship 'imself off to war as a surgeon when 'e coulda' stayed 'ome, safe and comfortable in 'is own bed?"

The question had been plaguing Pip since Mrs. Applethwaite told him of it. Coming from a life of abject poverty and strife, it always seemed beyond madness that anyone would leave behind all that privilege and prestige to throw their lives away for God and country.

But it was the wrong thing to ask.

Ash's entire body tensed beneath Pip, and his chest bumped Pip's chin as the man struggled to sit up. Pip put a hand on his arm to stop him from going any further. "Wait. Forget I asked."

The story had to have more to it than a simple desire to do his patriotic duty and all that rubbish. Pip was even more curious now, but he let it go in favor of better things.

He crawled on top of Ash, resting his hands on Ash's shoulders and straddling his hips so he couldn't get away. "Touchy," Pip admonished as he pressed his chest to Ash's and ground their cocks together to soothe the man.

Ash closed his eyes and allowed Pip to push him back into the pillows. And when Pip felt Ash's hips arching upward, meeting Pip's thrusts, he tried again. "All right. Let's see. The gossips said ye didn't come 'ome after old Boney surrendered. Would ye tell me where ye went after?"

Ash's expression was still guarded, but his cheeks were flushed and his eyes dark as he rocked against Pip. "Nepal and the East Indies," he panted, "and then the Cape."

Pip smiled and bent to kiss him in reward.

Ash reached up and cupped Pip's jaw. He pressed their foreheads together and held Pip there as he said, "My turn." He took a few panting breaths before asking, "Why did you leave London?"

Pip groaned. The blood pumping in his ears and the throbbing in his cock as he thrust it against Ash's was not quite enough to stop the sudden twist in his belly. His rhythm faltered a little. "Which time?" he asked evasively.

"The first," Ash breathed back as he thrust harder and faster against Pip.

Instead of answering, Pip surrendered to the pleasure building between them, closed his eyes, and cried out his release, painting Ash's stomach and cock with his spend. Ash gripped the back of Pip's neck hard and pumped against Pip's sensitive prick until jets of his own spend joined Pip's.

Pip collapsed beside him and they both lay panting on the bed. Ash obviously recovered more quickly—*again*—for he rolled onto his side facing Pip and lifted an eyebrow in question, obviously waiting for Pip for fulfill their bargain.

Pip sighed. "I left because Master Carey took an interest in me and sent me away to school with Vicar 'alford."

He didn't lie. Ash simply didn't need to know the rest—how broken Pip had been, how in need of the salvation Mr. Carey and the vicar had offered him.

The sweat and other fluids on his body were cooling quickly, so Pip hopped out of bed to grab a flannel from the washstand, avoiding Ash's gaze as he did. The water from the ewer was icy, and Pip only did a cursory wipe down before hurrying back to the bed and handing the flannel to Ash. Ash didn't complain as he wiped the remnants of their coupling from his belly and handed the flannel back to Pip, but his nipples tightened prettily and gooseflesh spread over his pale skin. Pip tossed the flannel in the general direction of the washstand and pulled the blankets over them both as fast as he could.

When Pip was settled against his side again, Ash said, "I remember Mr. Carey's name from the references Mrs. Applethwaite forwarded to me. But who is he to you that he would take such an interest?"

Pip kept his grin to himself as he toyed with one of Ash's nipples. Was that a hint of jealousy in his master's voice?

"It isn't your turn to ask the question," he said smugly.

Ash harrumphed. "Well then ask yours so you can answer mine," he said petulantly.

Pip had planned to tease the man some more, but when Ash dropped a hand to his injured thigh and began rubbing it beneath the covers, Pip's playful mood dissipated. "What was it like in the East Indies?" he asked, instead of the myriad more personal questions he wanted answered.

"Hot."

Pip stopped toying with Ash's nipple and flicked it hard with a fingernail. Ash yelped, writhing away from Pip until Pip pinned him to the mattress. "Oh, all right. It was strange, beautiful… frightening. The air was redolent with spices and exotic flowers. There was so much color and ornament all around I was overwhelmed when I first experienced it. There's no subtlety in anything there, not the food, nor the decoration or clothing. And yet all that richness is contrasted sharply with the filth and abject poverty of the lower castes. But I suppose the same could be said about London, now that I'm thinking about it." Ash sighed and put a hand over the one Pip still had on his chest. "I fear I did not much enjoy my time there. I didn't always agree with the choices and policies of my superiors, particularly with regards to their treatment of the local peoples. But my duties in the surgery kept me quite busy… although I was more often called upon for my skills in medicine than with the knife due the various fevers and cholera outbreaks."

Pip was silent as he tried to imagine what it must have been like. The best he could manage was a vision of an ornamental garden he'd seen once, but where the flowers were actually exotic birds, animals, and people all mashed together and noisy like in the London markets.

"Will you answer my question about your Mr. Carey now?" Ash asked grumpily. His eyes were closed, and he seemed only moments away from falling asleep.

Pip leaned over him and kissed his brow. "Tomorrow," he whispered.

Ash's brow furrowed and he grumbled a little more, but soon enough his quiet snores filled the room. Pip stayed, watching over the man in his sleep until he could barely keep his own eyes open. As carefully as he could, he slid out of bed and pulled on his clothes. Then he poured another shovelful of coal on the fire and crept out of the room.

Chapter *Fourteen*

THE FOLLOWING day Pip was in much better spirits than he'd been the day before. He'd managed to pull another few stones from the wall around Ash, and he was looking forward to having another crack at it after supper. When he'd finished with all the tasks Mrs. Applethwaite set for him, Pip happily went back to the barn to get the horse ready for his afternoon ride. But he had a surprise waiting for him when he got there. Ash stood in the horse's stall, and instead of the brush, he held a crop.

"Ash?" Pip asked uncertainly.

"Not a word, Phillip. Just help me determine how I'm going to get on the blasted thing before I lose my nerve."

Pip wanted to argue. It should have made him happy that Ash finally wanted to try, but his gut clenched just thinking about Ash so far off the ground, without both legs to use for balance and control. The look on Ash's face was determined, however, and Pip had neither the heart nor the right to tell him he couldn't do it. The connection they'd made was much too fragile for Pip to presume upon it like that, and Pip was fairly certain he wouldn't like the outcome if he tried.

The horse was sweet-tempered enough, but it would have been better if Ash had given Pip some warning of his intent so he could prepare the creature or find someone to train him.

"Are you going to help me or not?" Ash demanded impatiently, all traces of the man he'd lain with the night before gone, replaced with the haughtiness and coldness Pip had come to expect from the gentry.

"Of course, *sir*. Certainly, *sir*. Beggin' yer pardon, *sir*," Pip said as he stomped to the back of the stable in search of something for Ash to use as a mounting block.

He found the crates Ash's books came packed in, piled in a corner, and dragged them to the aisle outside of the horse's stall. Without a word or even a glance in Ash's direction, he stacked one on top of the other two, up against a wall, and went to collect the horse's saddle.

As the heavy silence stretched between them, Pip saddled the horse and led it past Ash to where he'd left the crates. Once there, he stood at the horse's head, held him steady, and waited like any proper groom.

After only a few moments pause, he heard Ash sigh and begin to make his way to the horse's side. But when Ash made no move to climb onto the crates, Pip felt a sudden pang of guilt despite his anger. He could only imagine how hard this must be for the man.

With only a tiny bit of sullenness creeping into his tone, Pip asked, "Would you like me to fetch Mr. Applethwaite to 'elp, sir?"

"No." Ash bit out that one word, and Pip clenched his jaw and held his tongue.

Several long minutes ticked past as Pip held the horse's lead and Ash stood next to the crates. When the waiting became too much, Pip peered around the horse. Ash's shoulders were slumped. He was staring disconsolately at the crates while a muscle ticked in his jaw.

"Ash?"

Ash straightened suddenly and shook his head. "Forget it. It's not going to work."

Before Pip could think of something to say, Ash limped past him, moving faster than Pip had ever seen before. Pip quickly tied the reins so the horse wouldn't get into trouble and ran after him. But Mrs. Applethwaite was standing on the stoop outside the kitchen door, so Pip could do nothing but watch Ash make his way into the house.

"What is it, Pip?" Mrs. Applethwaite called to him.

"Nothing, Missus. I think the master is tired, is all."

Mrs. Applethwaite didn't appear much satisfied with his answer, but Pip didn't really care. He desperately wanted to go after Ash, to talk to him, or hold him, or whatever the man would allow, but he hadn't been sent for, and he had no reason to be in the house otherwise. He ground his teeth in frustration, spun around, and stalked back to the stable. He didn't want to go out riding anymore, but the horse was saddled now, and the beast would be in a miff if Pip didn't give him some exercise before putting him away for the night.

With a heavy heart, Pip walked the horse through the gate, climbed on its back, and gave the gelding his head. The horse had obviously picked up on the tension in the air because it took off like a shot, racing across the fells until Pip's hands were numb on the reins and his face and head ached with the cold. He took no joy in the ride, and he headed straight back for the cottage as soon as the horse slowed, rather than lingering on the slopes, as was his wont.

He put the horse away quickly and went to find Mrs. Applethwaite, for once hoping that her husband was too ill to accomplish any tasks she might have in the rest of the house. The housekeeper was busy preparing their suppers and shooed him away when he asked. But when he peered through the door into the entry hall, he found Mr. Applethwaite lifting one of the scuttles Pip left by the front door.

"Oi, let me do that," Pip said as he rushed to help the man.

Mr. Applethwaite frowned at him for only a second before he shrugged. "Suit yerself. 'e's in the library." He handed over the scuttle and hurried back to the kitchen, quick on his feet for a man with so many ailments.

Pip grabbed the scuttle and took a breath to steady himself before heading for the door. A quick glance in the looking glass showed that his hair was a windblown rat's nest and his cheeks were still red with cold, but for once he didn't care how he looked. He needed to know Ash was all right.

"Come," Ash called in response to his knock.

When he saw Pip instead of Mr. Applethwaite, Ash's jaw tightened and he turned his face away. Pip carried the scuttle to the hearth and stirred up the fire. Without turning around, he said, "Mr. Carey is me benefactor. That's all. 'e's a good man, who took me under 'is protection because a friend asked 'im to."

He turned to look at the man then, and Ash was watching him with a slight smile on his face, his eyes no longer so anguished as they'd been in the stable. "I suppose it's your turn to ask a question now, is it?"

Ash followed his every move as Pip went to close the door and then returned to kneel by his chair. "I only 'ave one question for ye right now. How can I make ye 'appy?"

Ash closed his eyes, took Pip's head in his hands, and bent forward until his face was buried in Pip's hair. "Don't leave me."

Pip wrapped his arms around Ash's waist and they clung to one another. The warmth of the fire and the steady rhythm of Ash's breathing wove a spell over him until Pip forgot the rest of the world existed. But all too soon, the chiming of the clock on the mantel forced him to remember.

"Mrs. Applethwaite'll be bringing yer supper soon. I suppose it'd be bad if she found us like this." Pip drew away, and Ash released him with obvious reluctance.

"I suppose you're right." Ash drew in a deep lungful of air and expelled it noisily. "I'm sorry, Phillip. I'm sorry I snapped at you in the barn. It was a bloody foolish idea in the first place. I simply didn't want to admit it."

Pip stood and put some distance between them, before he was tempted to fling himself at the man again. He wanted the two of them back in Ash's bed. Ash was so much easier to talk to when he wasn't wearing anything.

"It weren't all that foolish, Ash. But maybe give me some time to work with the 'orse an' think on 'ow best to do it."

Ash shook his head. "Even if I can get on the bloody thing, there's no way I could stay on him in a real ride. I could tolerate the pain, but I'd have no balance, no control."

"You don' know that," Pip said with more conviction than he felt. Even if the thought of Ash on a horse made his stomach twist with worry, that didn't mean he liked hearing the man sound so defeated. "I'll build ye a proper mounting block, an' then we'll give it another go. Just in the yard so ye can get a feel for it. No one t' see but me an' the chickens."

Ash's smile didn't quite reach his eyes, but it seemed genuine nonetheless. "You're good for me, Phillip."

"I'm better'n good, sir," he replied with a wink, and Ash chuckled as Pip hoped he would. "I'd best go afore she boxes me ears for disturbin' the master."

Ash nodded. "All right. After dinner, then?"

"Aye."

ASH RANG for him early that night. Mrs. Applethwaite compressed her lips in disapproval, but she didn't say anything when Pip leapt to his feet and hurried through the door. Ash was in his chair by the fire. He looked unhappy, and the whisky glass by his side was already almost empty. He nodded when Pip entered but made no move to rise, and Pip crossed the room and looked at him worriedly.

"I think it best if we stay here and read for a while tonight," Ash said quietly.

Pip's smile immediately fell away and he pouted. That was not at all what he'd been hoping for. What had changed in only a few hours?

Ash turned to face the fire and said, "Mrs. Applethwaite will become suspicious if we continually disappear upstairs when you're supposed to be reading to me. My bedchamber may be the furthest room from the kitchen, but sound carries, Phillip. She's bound to have heard us on the stairs, and she may decide to investigate eventually, if we aren't more careful."

Pip bit his lip and stared at Ash's profile as he spoke. Ash wasn't telling him everything. But Pip wouldn't spoil their time together by arguing. He shrugged off his disappointment and bent to retrieve the book Ash had left on his chair.

"*The Life and Exploits of the Ingenious Gentleman Don Quixote de la Mancha*," Pip read aloud. He knew the story, had read it more than once. He looked up at Ash and sighed. "Sure ye don't want me to read somethin' else?"

Ash glanced sideways at him and twisted his lip into what Pip assumed was supposed to be a smile. "I thought you enjoyed farce."

Pip rolled his eyes heavenward in a plea for patience and decided to let the man have his way. If Ash wanted to brood and sulk into the coals while Pip read aloud the adventures of a daft bugger on a horse and his equally foolish but loyal servant, then Pip would oblige him. But Pip would get something for himself out of the bargain as well.

He filled Ash's glass from the decanter on the sideboard before plopping himself down on the carpet at Ash's feet. He took a healthy swallow from the glass, waiting for it to burn a path down his throat and into his belly before resting his head against Ash's knee and beginning to read.

105

The muscle beneath Pip's cheek tensed at first, and Pip smirked to himself as he continued to read. Eventually though, Ash's body seemed to relax again, and not long after Pip felt fingers combing through his hair.

Despite his earlier disappointment, Pip rather enjoyed his evening in the library. He even wanted to object when Ash suddenly called a halt to his reading, until Ash fisted a hand in Pip's shirt and dragged him up for a fierce kiss.

"I would say the housekeeper should probably be in bed by now. Wouldn't you?" Ash panted against Pip's now damp and swollen lips.

Pip could only nod in response. He climbed the rest of the way to his feet quickly and offered his hand to Ash. Ash's chin jutted stubbornly for only a moment before he sighed and accepted Pip's help. Pip drew Ash into his arms and kissed him some more as a reward—and because he'd become addicted to his lips.

Remembering Ash's words of concern earlier, Pip took more care on the stairs. But knowing Ash was behind him and feeling the man's hungry gaze on his body was distracting. All he could think of was the aching hardness between his legs and Ash's naked body beneath him on Ash's bed.

As before, Pip reached the bedchamber first and undressed before Ash could get there. Ash's pale eyes painted fire across every inch of Pip's skin they touched, and Pip was trembling with want by the time he stripped the man and tossed his false limb aside. They grappled on the bed, kissing and caressing every bit they could reach.

Ash hooked his leg over Pip's hip. "I want you, Phillip."

"You 'ave me, Ash," Pip chuckled breathlessly.

When Pip would have lunged back in to taste more of Ash's skin, Ash gripped Pip's face in both hands to stop him. "I meant I want you inside me again."

Pip's stomach twisted and he drew in a shaky breath. He stared at Ash, unable to think of what he should say.

"Do you not want to? Did you not enjoy it, before?"

"No. I enjoyed it plenty."

"Then why?"

If he told the truth, that he was afraid of hurting Ash, it would only make the man angry and defensive. But anything was better than the wounded look he was giving him now. "I don't want to hurt ye."

Predictably, Ash's jaw tightened, and he drew away from Pip. "How many times must I tell you that you didn't harm me? What must I say to convince you I'm not as weak as you seem to believe?"

Pip threw an arm over him to keep Ash from getting out of the bed. "I don't think ye'r weak. I never said that. Ye'r already in so much pain, I just don't want to give ye any more."

The frown Ash gave him conveyed his disbelief and confusion more clearly than words. "You gave me pleasure, Phillip, not pain. I don't understand why you can't believe that."

Now Pip pulled away. He couldn't meet Ash's eyes, so he stared at the foot of the bed as silence descended between them. Eventually, Ash sighed and pressed himself along Pip's flank. He laid his forehead against Pip's temple and cupped his other cheek. "I don't know what happened to you that made you believe as you do. But I wish you would trust me when I tell you you're wrong." Ash pulled back, kissed Pip's cheek and waited for Pip to turn to him before continuing. "Beautiful Phillip, you have done more for me than you know. I would show you the pleasure such coupling can bring the recipient if you would let me. But for now, you only have my word that the men I have taken in that way only ever enjoyed it, as I enjoyed you."

"Ye promise I didn't 'urt ye? Ye swear?"

Ash's smile was pure sin. "I wouldn't have asked for it again if you had."

This time, Pip didn't need the words. The smile was enough. He pulled Ash on top of him and kissed him until the fear was silenced by the pounding of his heart.

Pip ground his throbbing cock against Ash's hip while he fumbled in the night table. His hands shook so much Ash had to unstopper the vial for him, but soon enough they were kissing again, breast to breast, while Pip struggled blindly to reach around to prepare Ash's nether entrance. As soon as Pip breached his opening with oiled fingers, Ash stilled and groaned into his mouth. Pip's cock throbbed painfully between them as Ash threw his head back, pushed himself up on his arms and ground his arse down onto Pip's hand.

"There. God, right there," Ash moaned.

While Pip watched in wonderment and need, Ash twisted his hips and rode the fingers penetrating him until Pip's belly and cock were bathed in a steady drip of the man's seed. Unable to take any more, Pip withdrew his fingers from that clinging heat and rolled Ash onto his back. He immediately wrapped his arms around Ash's thighs and dragged that tempting arse into his lap.

"Yes," Ash demanded.

Pip breached his opening slowly at first, but Ash was having none of it. He gripped Pip's thighs hard, those elegant hands much stronger than they appeared, and lifted his good leg over Pip's shoulder, forcing Pip all the way inside him in one quick thrust.

They both grunted at the impact, and then Pip moaned as pleasure flooded his body. Ash's steely grip on his thighs eased and Pip wrapped an arm around the leg by his shoulder as he began rocking into Ash's tight passage with increasing force. Soon after, Ash let go of Pip's legs entirely and braced his arms against the bed frame while the sound of flesh slapping against flesh filled the air.

Still a little afraid of losing control again, Pip refused to close his eyes, and in the end, he was rewarded with the vision of Ash as the man surrendered to oblivion. Ash threw his head back and arched his spine as much as he could with Pip nearly folding him in half. The muscles in Ash's arms and neck drew taut, trembling and straining as ropes of his spend painted his belly. The sight was too much for Pip, and he only managed a few more ragged thrusts before his own release seized him.

Afterward, Pip collapsed next to Ash's heaving body and struggled to calm his breathing as a sweet euphoria stole over him. This was how he was meant to feel. Anything he'd ever done before was a pale shadow in comparison to what he felt now. He cuddled against Ash's side, grinning like a fool as his eyes grew heavy. He could spend the rest of his life just like this.

Unfortunately, Ash didn't seem to share that feeling. Pip's joy was short-lived when Ash yawned, patted the arm Pip had thrown across him, and said, "You should go before you fall asleep."

Pip lifted his head and stared at Ash while the bastard merely blinked calmly back him. The face that had been so stunning in the throes of passion only a few short moments before was now devoid of any warmth of feeling.

"I don't 'ave to leave yet. It'll be hours afore anyone comes to check on ye."

108

"Nevertheless, I think it best not to chance it. Good night, Phillip."

The change from lover back to master happened so suddenly, Pip had difficulty feeling anything but shock. He climbed out of the bed and gathered his clothes, and then quickly set himself to rights.

He paused in the doorway and turned back to Ash, hoping the man would say something, anything to ease Pip's mind. But Ash had already turned away from him and drawn the blankets over his head. Pip clenched his jaw against the insults he wanted to hurl at him and hurried down the stairs. He went to the library and put out the lamps and banked the coals so he wouldn't have to endure a lecture from Mrs. Applethwaite in the morning, heaping insult upon injury.

Before he left the room, Pip refilled Ash's glass and downed some more of Ash's fine whisky in a single gulp. His eyes watered from more than the fiery liquid, so Pip poured himself another, downing that as quickly as the first.

"He can bloody well bugger 'imself next time," Pip said aloud before he took one last swig directly from the decanter and returned it to the sideboard.

He grabbed the candle he'd lit before dousing the lamps and set off for his room. The whisky settled warmly in his belly as he crawled beneath his blankets. One advantage of not being able to visit the village pub easily was that the drink went further when he did manage to sneak a bit. He settled beneath the blankets while the palliative worked its magic, and soon the sharper edges of his hurt were softened in a haze of inebriation. He fell asleep with only a vague sense of discontent.

Chapter Fifteen

DESPITE HIS lingering pique over the abruptness of his dismissal the night before, Pip still found time to work on a mounting block the following day. They could have hired a stonemason from the village, but it seemed a waste for something so simple, and besides that, Pip wanted to build it. A full and exhausting day of lugging rocks back to the yard in his cart and venting his frustrations with a hammer and chisel sounded much better than brooding over his hurt pride, even if the day was wet and the air unpleasantly cold.

He found a likely spot against the stone wall that surrounded the yard and set to work not long after exercising the horse. By the time the sun set, he had a good start on it and nearly every muscle in his body ached from his exertions. He ate his supper in sullen silence and then excused himself early.

"If the master rings, give 'im me regrets. I'm done in."

"Certainly," Mrs. Applethwaite replied. "You worked quite hard today. I'm sure the master will understand." Her words were gentle and her mien concerned, but Pip could see that she was secretly pleased. She hated that the master had chosen to spend his time with someone so lowly instead of inviting any of his peers from the village or even hiring someone more appropriate to act as his companion. And perhaps that was what he should have done instead of raising Pip's hopes only to smash them again at the end of each night they had together.

Pip feared the sourness of his mood would make it hard for him to fall asleep that night. But he needn't have worried. Working himself into exhaustion did the trick, and he was asleep almost the moment his head hit the pillow.

He woke only once, in the middle of the night, judging by the position of the moon. An eerie cry had him bolting upright in bed, his heart hammering in his chest. He was almost certain it had come from the other end of the cottage, Ash's bedchamber, and he held his breath, straining to hear if it was repeated.

Nothing but the wind and the everyday creaks and rattles of the cottage came back to him, and after several minutes ticked past, Pip settled beneath his blankets again and tried to go back to sleep. Ash had nightmares. Pip knew that after the first time he'd heard the man cry out in the night. But if he wanted Pip's help beyond a quick fuck every now and again, he had an odd way of showing it.

"Don't leave me."

Ash's words rang in Pip's head only to be followed by a harsh and dismissive *"Good night, Phillip."*

So which was it, then?

THE NEXT day Pip was as stiff as a plank when Mrs. Applethwaite roused him from his troubled sleep, and not in a pleasant way. He had to push himself through several hours of misery before his body limbered up enough that every move wasn't a hardship.

Upon seeing what he'd accomplished in the yard, Mrs. Applethwaite took pity on him and did not add overmuch to his regular duties, but a part of Pip wished she had. It would have given him something to do instead of wandering about the place useless for anything but sulking and looking longingly toward the library window.

Pip was hauling scuttles of coal back to the cottage, sighing despondently for the hundredth time that day, when he caught his reflection in one of the kitchen windows and stopped in his tracks. Mournful brown eyes underscored by dark rings looked back at him from above a set of full, downcast lips. His cheeks looked hollow, and he'd missed several spots shaving. His hair was in disarray and his neck cloth looked as if a child had tied it. In short, he looked awful.

And why was that?

Because he was mooning over his master like a bloody maid, that's why.

The realization hit him like a punch to the stomach, and all his pathetic melancholy fled, chased away by a wave of anger and mortification. For weeks now, he'd been following Ash like a puppy, begging for scraps.

Where was the Pip who'd wooed and bedded dozens of women across the length and breadth of the countryside?

Now *he* was the bloody woman, reading more into a couple of tumbles than he ever should, expecting more than was ever offered. Ash had made no promises, confessed no feelings beyond a desire for Pip to remain at the cottage and to warm his bed from time to time.

Pip was disgusted with himself. If Master Carey, Maud, or Stubbs had been there to see it, they would have laughed themselves silly by now, and Pip would have well deserved their ridicule. Living in the country had made him soft.

Ash was an opportunity to fill his lonely nights with good company, in warmth and comfort. Pip could sate his lusts without having to put much effort into it at all and without having to worry about any angry relatives or husbands coming after him. Pip had absolutely nothing to complain about. So what if Ash got a bit high-and-mighty? He was a gent. What did Pip expect?

Pip turned back to his reflection and lifted his chin high. He straightened his shoulders and set off to finish his task with renewed vigor. The time for mooning about and self-recriminations was done. He silently vowed to accept only what was offered from that moment on, without any further histrionics on his part. And when Ash's bell rang for him after supper that night, Pip answered without any hesitation at all, holding firmly to his new resolve so no other feeling could creep in and undermine it.

"Yes, sir?"

Ash frowned at him from his seat by the fire. "Am I 'sir' again, then?"

Pip shrugged against the tension in his shoulders, closed the door behind him, and strode across the room. He plastered a grin across his face that was not entirely genuine and winked at the man. "Depends on what I'm 'ere for, I s'pose."

No leather-bound volume lay on his chair. A wrapped parcel waited for him instead. Pip avoided looking at it, though curiosity and hope clamored for his attention. Instead, Pip resolutely kept his eyes on Ash. The sooner they got to the fun part of the evening, the less time he would have to think about anything else.

"Mrs. Applethwaite said you were unwell last evening when I sent for you. I hope that you are better now," Ash said, watching Pip closely.

"Right as rain, sir—*Ash*," he corrected.

Ash studied him with his forehead creased and those damned beautiful eyes appearing almost hurt. Impatient to do away with the polite, and pointless, conversation, Pip crossed the final distance between them, brazenly took a swallow from Ash's whisky glass, and then bent to claim his lips. He had no interest in reading that night or whatever gift Ash wished to bestow. He wanted to fuck until he couldn't think and then go to his bed, alone but sated.

Ash's lips stiffened in surprise but soon parted, and Pip's tongue swept inside. Pip fisted his hands in Ash's fine wool jacket and drew the man to his feet, uncaring the damage he did to the cloth. Ash clutched at Pip's upper arms while Pip slid his hands around the smooth silk of Ash's cravat, imprisoning his neck and preventing any escape. He plundered Ash's mouth, swallowing the man's moan as he pressed his thigh forward against the hardness of Ash's prick.

After rubbing Ash's cock a bit, Pip let go of Ash's neck and tore at his cravat until it fell away, exposing the flesh underneath. Then Pip fumbled between them until Ash's cock sprang free of his trousers. Pip bit and suckled the smooth salty skin beneath the coarseness of the man's whiskers while he pumped his fist along Ash's length until Ash was struggling to remain upright.

When Pip was certain Ash's need was at its peak, he dragged him nearer the hearth and awkwardly lowered him to the Persian rug. Ash gazed up at him in confusion with eyes that had gone nearly black with desire, but Pip wasted no time with explanations or asking for leave. Tonight he would take what he wanted, and if Ash truly wished to stop him or complain, he would have to do so with conviction before Pip would hear him.

Pip knelt beside him and smashed their mouths together again as he pulled Ash's jacket off his shoulders and cast it aside. Ash struggled in his arms, tearing his mouth away and gripping Pip's wrists to stop him. "Not here," he said breathlessly.

Pip grinned back at him and then captured Ash's earlobe between his teeth, nibbling and sucking on it by turns. Ash's grip on his wrists relaxed, and Pip dropped a hand down to fondle Ash's prick again while the other squeezed his arse.

"This way we don' make noise on the stairs," Pip whispered, his hot breath in Ash's ear and his other ministrations making the man shiver and melt beneath his hands.

Catching Ash by surprise, Pip pressed his advantage and had Ash draped on his belly over his padded leather stool before the man could draw breath to protest. Pip yanked Ash's trousers down and lifted his shirt out of the way, exposing the taut, pale orbs of his arse to the lamplight.

"Phillip—" Ash hissed, but Pip didn't allow him to finish. He dove in and bit one delectable mound while he swirled a thumb over Ash's nether opening and fondled his sack with the other hand.

Ash gasped and moaned loudly, and Pip chuckled against his flesh.

"Shhhhh," Pip admonished gleefully. "Ye don' want Mrs. Applethwaite to come runnin', do ye?"

Ash swore under his breath and flung out an arm, narrowly missing Pip's head as he ducked out of the way. Still chuckling, Pip dove between the man's cheeks and licked Ash's entrance, ending any further protests or attempts at violence against him. Pip liberally wetted the man's hole and Ash let out a guttural sound Pip hadn't heard before. Encouraged, Pip toyed with Ash's opening, experimenting with sucking and nibbling on the tender flesh before penetrating it with his tongue. He'd only begun this because he knew the oil was out of reach and he had no other means of easing his passage. But the strength of Ash's reaction to his ministrations emboldened him.

By the time Pip drew away and clawed desperately at his clothes to free his own weeping cock, Ash was trembling and begging beneath him. Pip's crown was so slick he hardly needed to bother, but he spat in his hand and rubbed it on his prick for good measure anyway. He pressed forward, and Ash arched beneath him, sending his arse higher in the air to meet Pip's thrust. They came together hard. Pip withdrew and rammed home again, over and over, their muted grunts and the slapping of flesh their only accompaniment beyond the ticking of the mantel clock.

Ash lost the battle first, stiffening beneath him, his channel rippling around Pip's cock. Pip shuddered through his own release soon after and collapsed against Ash's back, his face pressed into the softness of Ash's damp linen shirt.

Ash's body rose and fell with each labored breath, but he was still the first to recover. He pushed up on his arms, forcing Pip to withdraw. They both hissed as Pip's cock slid free of Ash's channel, and he dropped back against the leather chair. Ash righted his trousers as best he could, pushed the stool aside, and dragged himself over to sit on the hearth, closing his eyes and letting his head drop back against the stone.

Pip watched him warily, unsure of his reaction and ready to leap back if the man took another swing at him. But Ash didn't react at all. He simply sat there with his eyes closed until the clock began to chime. After the last bell faded, Ash turned to him with an unreadable expression and inhaled deeply, preparing to speak. Pip was fairly certain he was about to be dismissed again, and he decided not to give Ash the chance. He stood up quickly and turned away, tucking his cock back into his trousers and setting the rest of his clothes to rights.

Instead of speaking, Ash blew the breath out noisily and began to stir as well. Without thinking, Pip reached for him, but Ash shook his head.

"I can manage."

"Yes, sir. Of course. Will that be all?" Pip asked through gritted teeth.

Ash didn't answer until he was fully upright, leaning against the mantel. He looked pale, and Pip began to regret his rough treatment of the man, but the feeling evaporated as soon as Ash spoke. "Yes, thank you. You may go."

Calm and collected as ever a gentleman should be.

"Yes, sir."

He turned to go but stopped when Ash called after him. "Don't forget that." Pip turned back and only then remembered the parcel on the chair. When he hesitated, Ash said, "Take it. Please."

Pip snatched it up and left as fast as his feet would carry him, narrowly avoiding slamming the door behind him. When he reached the kitchen, Mrs. Applethwaite looked up from her needlework with a puzzled frown.

"You're back early."

"Yes, Missus. The master decided he didn't wish my company this evening after all," he answered, keeping the parcel tucked under his arm and his expression bland.

He could tell she was pleased, but all she said was, "He must be tired, poor man. The turn in the weather must pain him. I would think, he probably won't wish to stay up late often when winter is fully upon us."

Pip nodded sullenly and returned to his room. Once there, he sat on his bed and stared at the package in his hands for a long while. Eventually, curiosity won out, and he untied the string. When he pulled the paper aside, a stunning waistcoat in russet and brown brocade was revealed, much finer than the plain one he'd been lusting after in the tailor's shop window.

Pip stared at it for a long time before lifting it to his face, breathing in the sweetness of the silk and smoothing the fine cloth across his cheek. Ash really needed to stop giving him presents like this, because they made remaining unattached to the man very difficult.

Pip pulled the waistcoat away from his face and tucked it at the bottom of one of his dresser drawers, resisting the impulse to try it on. It was a silly present anyway. He would never be able to wear something so fine where the housekeeper or her husband could see him. If they or anyone else ever caught him with it, they'd only assume he'd stolen it from the master. Pip should just give it back to the man… but he knew he wouldn't.

Instead, Pip pushed it from his mind and readied himself for bed. He still had a few novels he'd taken from Ash's library, so he lit a candle and tried to distract himself with one until he grew tired enough to fall asleep. The books were poor bedfellows, but they were all he had.

Chapter Sixteen

MRS. APPLETHWAITE'S words to him that night proved prophetic over the next two weeks. Ash did indeed call for him, but rarely. As the weather grew colder, so did their relationship. And despite all his vows to the contrary—and a thorough disgust for himself—Pip mourned the loss of what he hadn't even had to begin with, a depth of feeling that he was now completely certain Ash didn't share.

"Who does 'e think 'e is? Mr. High-n-Mighty. I ought t' pack me things and be on me way," Pip grumbled to the horse after a particularly cold and miserable afternoon ride.

He hadn't seen nor heard from Ash in days. The horse was the only set of ears Pip dared vent his spleen to, the only friendly ears he had at the cottage, so the poor creature got more than its fair share of Pip's griping. Of course, it also got a lengthy grooming session in the bargain, so Pip thought it a fair trade.

"Only talks to me when 'e wants somethin', 'e does. Won't tell me nothin' about 'imself. I bet Mr. Cooper in the village knows more about 'im than me," Pip continued as he vigorously brushed the horse's thickening winter coat. "I should leave. Find someone else. That would show 'im." The horse whickered in what Pip assumed was agreement. "Too right. I *should* go. Who needs 'im anyway? 'e's ill-tempered, inconsiderate, a right prig when he wants, stubborn, proud, imperious, in his cups half the time, and blue as megrim the other. 'e's—" Pip stopped midrant as a sudden realization came crashing down on him.

"Bloody 'ell. I'm in love."

Pip stood frozen in dismay until the horse grew impatient with him and gave him a good hard nudge with its head to remind Pip what he should be doing. Pip went back to brushing, but his mind was miles away.

It all made sense now. Why else would he put up with all Ash's nonsense? Why else would he keep coming back for more when there were plenty of willing young ladies who'd pamper him and flatter him? That bit about Ash being convenient was bloody rubbish. Ash was the most *inconvenient* lover Pip had ever had. And the worst of it was, he couldn't even blame Ash for his broken heart, because Ash hadn't asked for Pip's love in the first place.

Pip buried his face in the horse's shoulder and continued to brush it absently. The beast allowed him to seek comfort there and even nuzzled him a few times as Pip simply breathed against its neck.

As the shock began to fade and the reality of his predicament sank in, Pip felt a sudden and intense desire to run. He desperately wanted to leave the cottage, to go home to Maud and Master Carey and forget about this cold, lonely place forever. But he didn't move. His blasted traitorous heart wouldn't let him. It rebelled at the very thought of leaving Ash to waste away with only the Applethwaites for company—even if it was the stubborn bastard's own fault if he did—so instead of running, Pip lifted his head, stiffened his spine, and resolved not to let a little thing like love get the best of him. He was stronger than that. He certainly had more pride than that. And when he thought he could manage it, Pip closed the animals in and returned to the kitchen, his supper, and another night alone in his bed.

During the days that followed, Pip completed the mounting block in the yard as he'd promised. He went to the village when sent, and he wrote to Maud regularly about the horse and the weather and whatever village gossip he managed to pick up. The few times Ash did ring for him, Pip stayed with the man in the library and made no attempts to repeat their last encounter. He read to Ash and sat with him. Once they sucked each other's cocks before Ash sent Pip off to his own bed again, but the physical connection gave Pip no joy or comfort.

His life stretched out bleak and formless, like the mists and seemingly endless November rains that year, and Pip didn't know when he'd have the strength to turn from it, the strength to walk away from Ash.

Perhaps in the spring.

AT THE end of the last week of November, Pip was finishing up in the barn for the day and looking forward to thawing out by the fire, when the thunder of hooves reached his ears. Concerned for no reason he could name, Pip set down his rake and went to investigate.

The carts had already come and gone to deliver the coal and feed for the animals. The post had come the day before, and it was much too late in the afternoon for that at any rate. The sun was almost gone.

As Pip stepped out of the barn, a horse and gig crested the hill closest to the cottage. They were moving fast, so Pip ran to the gate, opened it, then hurried over to grab hold of the horse's lead as the carriage drew to a stop in the yard.

A man, probably only a few years younger than Pip, jumped out of the carriage as soon as Pip had the horse. He was wide-eyed and out of breath, and he rushed over to Pip.

"I'm John Ingram from the Dog and Duck in the village. Is yer master at 'ome?"

Pip opened his mouth to answer, but Mrs. Applethwaite came bustling out then, and the young man turned to repeat his greeting to her instead.

"Perhaps," the housekeeper replied cautiously. "What is your business?"

"Please, ma'am. Doctor Fields sent me. A couple o' travelers came to the inn not an hour ago, and one of 'em were badly injured on the road. The carriage got stuck, and the man caught 'is hand in the wheel when they tried to push it free."

Mrs. Applethwaite's own hand flew to her breast, and she gasped. "My word. How awful. But I don't understand. Why would the doctor send for our master?"

"Mr. Leyes, the barber, is out of town, ma'am. Doctor says 'e needs a surgeon."

Mrs. Applethwaite frowned and wrung her hands, obviously unsure of what to do, but then the front door of the cottage opened and Ash stepped out, saving her the trouble of making a decision.

"What is going on here?" Ash demanded with all the haughtiness and command Pip knew he was capable of.

The young man, John, started and seemed to shrink in on himself. He hurried over to repeat his plea to Ash after doffing the cap he'd earlier forgotten in his haste.

Ash stood silently while he heard the man out, his expression betraying nothing, and he continued to stare at the young man for some time after he finished his message. To anyone who didn't know him, Ash would have appeared completely unmoved. But Pip could see the tightness in Ash's lips and the white of his knuckles on the handle of his walking stick.

Pip shifted restlessly from foot to foot, anxious to go to the man, to talk to him, to know what he was feeling and offer to help if he could. But he couldn't do any of those things, so he stayed where he was and patted and soothed the horse instead, silently cursing Ash, the housekeeper, and the world in which he lived.

Ash glanced in Pip's direction only once before he turned back to John and said, "I left that profession behind when I sold my commission, but... if there truly is no one else, then I cannot in good conscience refuse."

"Oh, thank you, sir. Thank you. I'm to take ye directly, when ye'r ready," John said, hurrying over to the gig in his eagerness to be gone, instead of waiting for Ash to lead as was proper.

Mrs. Applethwaite frowned at the man, but Ash didn't seem to notice or care. He turned to Pip and said, "I need my instruments and the box of medicines from my rooms."

Pip left the horse with John and ran past Ash into the house. He took the stairs two at a time. He heard Mrs. Applethwaite bustle in behind him, probably fetching the master's coat, hat, and gloves, but he didn't stop to look. Pip purposefully turned away from the bed as he stumbled into the room. He simply grabbed the leather tool kit and box of glass vials from the trunk in the corner and hurried back with them.

Ash was shrugging on his coat when Pip returned. Pip hovered nervously behind him as the man limped his way to the gig. John made a hesitant attempt to help Ash into the seat, but one warning glare from those ice-colored eyes froze him in his place. When Ash had finally settled his stubborn arse into the seat, he turned to Pip, reaching for his tools. Pip held Ash's gaze, trying to convey both his concern and his support with a single look as he handed it over, making sure their fingers touched briefly in the exchange, but Ash's expression betrayed nothing as he tucked the items in his lap and turned to face forward.

When Mrs. Applethwaite hurried inside, saying she should fetch a blanket for the master, Pip leaned close and whispered, "I'm comin' with ye."

Ash looked up from tugging on his gloves then, and something flickered in his eyes before he simply nodded and turned his attention to John, "I'm ready."

The seat had only enough room for two so Pip hurried around to the boot and hopped on as John flicked the reins and the horse took off.

The ride was a little harrowing for Pip. John pushed the horse faster and faster down the narrow and rutted road from the cottage, and Pip clung white-knuckled to the back as the gig bounced and tipped precariously on the turns. When at last they reached the inn, he had to pry his hands loose from the frame, the grain of the wood etched deeply into his palms.

Ash handed Pip the box of medications and went straight into the inn as soon as the gig came to a stop, without waiting for anyone to help him down, and Pip followed as soon as he was sure his legs would carry him.

A tall man with a thick salt-and-pepper beard Pip recognized as one of Ash's first callers at the cottage rose from his place by the large stone fireplace and came to greet them. He wore a finely tailored dark blue wool jacket, tan trousers, and a gray waistcoat, and his smile was relieved as he held out his hand. The background conversation of the other guests in the common room fell silent all around them.

"Major McNulty, thank you for coming so quickly."

"Doctor Fields." Ash nodded cordially as he shook the man's hand. "Where is the patient?"

"This way." The doctor led the way through a door on their left. Pip could feel everyone's eyes on them as they went, but this time he was fairly certain none of them even noticed he was there.

The room they were taken to was small and dark, perhaps a private dining room of some kind for more particular guests. It contained a large wooden table on which a man in his shirtsleeves lay, holding his bandaged arm and moaning while a thin woman in a green travelling cape and bonnet stood at his head, soothing his brow and weeping silently.

"Mrs. Brown? Mr. Brown? This is Major McNulty. He's come to take a look at you," Doctor Fields said.

The man on the table opened feverish blue eyes and said through pale, trembling lips, "Major."

"Has he been given anything to dull the pain?" Ash asked.

"Yes. I gave him some laudanum an hour ago. He could use another dose, but I wanted to wait until you arrived before I decided on the amount."

Ash nodded and limped nearer to the table. He set his tools by the man's feet and reached for the bandaged hand. "I will need to remove these to have a look at you. I'll try to be as gentle as possible," he said to Mr. Brown.

Pip's stomach twisted with each layer of bloodied cloth that was removed. He had no idea why he was so squeamish. He'd seen his fair share of illness and injury over the course of his life—in the stews, where most couldn't afford a doctor or even a barber surgeon to help them. Pip blamed it on his traitorous emotions. He felt everything more keenly since he'd met Ash, and he cursed the man under his breath yet again for turning him into a bloody girl.

Mr. Brown moaned loudly through clenched teeth as the bloody ruin of his hand was exposed, and halfway through the process, Ash asked Pip to escort Mrs. Brown from the room. When Pip returned after handing the woman over to the innkeeper's wife, the bandage was gone, and in the light of the lamp Ash was closely examining what looked like something the butcher would turn into sausage. Pip's stomach revolted and he had to look away, swallowing back the sourness in his throat. He watched Doctor Fields at the sideboard instead, pouring liquid from a small vial into a cordial glass.

When Ash sighed behind him, Pip turned in time to see him carefully set Mr. Brown's hand back down at his side. "I'm sorry, Mr. Brown. But I agree with the doctor's assessment. We cannot save it. The hand will have to come off before it begins to putrefy and poison your blood."

Mr. Brown closed his eyes and stifled a sob as Pip's stomach did another flip.

"Phillip, tell them we need more lamps, hot water, a bottle of spirits, plenty of clean linen for bandages, and blankets," Ash ordered as he helped lift Mr. Brown's head so he might drink from the glass Dr. Fields held to his lips.

Glad to be given something to do, Pip hurried from the room again and hunted down the innkeeper. When he returned with a bottle of gin in one hand and another lamp in the other, Ash's instruments were spread out on a sideboard against the wall—the wicked-looking fine-toothed saw prominent among the various blades, hammers, and pliers. Pip swallowed more bile and set the lamp on the sideboard as Ash directed, before handing over the gin bottle.

"Here. Drink," Ash said, holding out the bottle to Mr. Brown. "I will be as quick as I can."

Pip could see nearly all the whites of Mr. Brown's eyes as he drank liberally from the bottle. The innkeeper came bustling in a moment later with a bowl, a steaming kettle, a pile of folded white linen, and two thick wool blankets.

"Thank you, Mr. Tulley. We're going to need you to stay as well," Doctor Fields said as he took the linens from the man.

The innkeeper placed the bowl and kettle on the sideboard for Ash, and then Pip helped Mr. Tulley tuck the warm blankets around Mr. Brown as the doctor tore strips of linen for bandages. When all seemed ready, Ash went to the sideboard and washed his hands in the hot water before he turned to them and said, "The three of you will have to hold him down while I work. He will fight, but he must be held as still as you can manage."

Pip swallowed and nodded along with the other two men, and they each took up a position. Pip was on Mr. Brown's left side, so he would concentrate on keeping the damaged limb in place while the other two tried to hold the rest of his body. The innkeeper draped himself across Mr. Brown's legs and Doctor Fields placed a piece of leather strap between his teeth before bracing his arms across the patient's chest and other arm. Mr. Brown's breast heaved with each frightened breath he took, and Pip couldn't look at his face. Instead he put his entire weight on the arm and shoulder beneath his hands and fixed his eyes on Ash.

123

Ash met his gaze for the first time then. He looked drawn and pale, but the set of his jaw was determined. "Are we ready?" Ash asked, his saw poised above the poor man's wrist.

What happened next, Pip chose not to remember in any detail. He stubbornly refused to look anywhere but at Ash's face while Ash worked. He quickly, deftly severed Mr. Brown's hand, cut away the damaged flesh, then closed the wound. Mr. Brown screamed and cried at first, but toward the end, he thankfully collapsed into unconsciousness. Blood spattered Pip's hands and clothes, but he pretended not to notice it, nor did he look at the red liberally coating Ash's hands, forearms, and the front of the apron the innkeeper had provided.

When it was finally over and the innkeeper and his staff were left to do the cleaning up, Pip followed Ash and the doctor out of the room, enormously grateful to be free of the closeness of it.

"Thank you, Major," Doctor Fields said as they moved in front of the fire. "I've had to learn some skill at this sort of thing since coming to Keswick with her ladyship—the village being so far removed from a town of any size—but it is definitely not what I am trained for. I would never have been able to do it as quickly and skillfully as yourself."

Ash looked positively ghostly to Pip, but he dredged up a polite smile for the doctor. "Thank you, sir. That is the highest of praise coming from a man such as yourself."

Pip swallowed a snort, turning his face away before either Ash or the doctor could see him roll his eyes. He was glad he didn't have to listen to Ash play the games of polite society often. It didn't suit the man at all. Though the kind of society Pip had to offer didn't seem to suit Ash of late either, so perhaps Pip was wrong in assuming he knew the man as well as he believed.

"You have done more than your fair share, sir. I will see to Mr. Brown's care from here, and you should get some rest," the doctor said, interrupting Pip's thoughts before they could become too sour.

Ash nodded tiredly. "Thank you, sir. I believe I am a little weary."

"John fetched you in my carriage. I can send someone to find him to drive you home again."

The doctor lifted his hand to one of the serving maids, but Pip cautiously interrupted him. "Beggin' yer pardon, sir. But, if we can

124

borrow yer gig, I can drive the master 'ome and bring yer horse and carriage back in the morning."

Doctor Fields turned and gave Pip a look, as if he'd forgotten he was there. "Oh…. Yes, certainly. If that is your wish?" He directed the question back at Ash, who had started swaying on his feet.

Pip ground his teeth to keep from snapping at the man and waited for Ash to reply.

"What? Oh, yes. That would be fine," Ash answered absently, and Pip had had enough of dithering about.

"Right, then, sir, I'll fetch the carriage."

Pip hurried out of the room and roused one of the inn's stable hands to help him get the horse in the rig. Ash was tired enough he didn't object when Pip bundled him into the seat, practically carrying him most of the way, and set off with only a short nod and a wave of thanks to the doctor.

"Are ye all right, Ash?" Pip asked when they were free from prying ears.

"No. I swore I was done with that business after I left the Cape." His voice was quiet and shaking with emotion and exhaustion.

Pip longed to pull the gig over and wrap his arms around him, to give what comfort he could, but they were still in the village.

"Is there naught I can do to 'elp?"

"No."

The word was said with a finality Pip didn't doubt. He snapped his mouth shut on any other offers and turned his attention to the road ahead, and a heavy silence fell between them.

It started to snow just as Pip reached the edge of the village, but despite the cold, he kept the horse to a slow trot. Ash was wrapped tightly in his greatcoat and blankets, tucked up warm against Pip's side. He'd begun snoring lightly, and Pip refused to risk jarring the man by quickening their pace.

The lamp hanging from the front of the carriage swung back and forth as they bumped over the uneven road, illuminating the crystal white snowflakes swirling lazily around them. The horse appeared to know what it was doing, so Pip settled a little lower in the seat and pulled Ash closer, wrapping an arm around Ash's shoulder now that he was sure the man was asleep.

A fresh wave of melancholy descended over Pip as they rode. The night was so peaceful and beautiful, and Pip wished they could have had more moments like this. But he had a sinking feeling that would never be.

Tonight he'd seen a hint of the man Ash was before his injury, and Pip was a little in awe of him. Watching Ash work on Mr. Brown, doing a procedure that would surely save his life while ignoring his own pain, emotional distress, and fatigue had been... beyond words. It forced Pip to realize once and for all how great the distance was between them. And not simply because of an accident of birth but because of the kind of man Ash was.

Pip could read and write and do his figures. He had some learning in the classics and other areas besides. His current position was respectable, if not particularly lofty, a far cry from his birth at any rate. But no matter what Maud and Mr. Carey thought him capable of, Pip was only a laborer, common as dirt. That was all the world saw when it looked at him, and that was all Ash saw, judging by the way he treated Pip at the end of each night, *after* he'd obtained what he wanted out of Pip. Ash might think him beautiful dirt, but dirt all the same and just as easily discarded.

Pip needed to stop ignoring the facts and acknowledge that Ash would never feel for him anything near what Pip wanted him to. And after weeks of sleepless nights, Pip also had to admit to himself that he wasn't happy with less.

A cold lump formed in the middle of Pip's chest as Ash shifted and cuddled closer, knocking his hat askew. Pip wanted to weep. Ash needed someone to take care of him, to distract him from his troubles, but Pip wasn't enough. Ash needed someone who could visit openly with him, someone of equal station and equal consequence. No one would ever believe Pip worthy of that. Any connection between them would always draw unwanted curiosity no matter where they went, even if Ash was willing to take that risk.

What Ash had done tonight would soon be all over the village. Callers would begin to come again, braving his queer and irascible ways for a chance to know him, whether he wanted them to or not. *Someone* would befriend him eventually, and the only thing Ash would need Pip for would be a good rogering every now and again. And Ash could travel to a

126

larger town to find that when he needed it, or someone he knew from London or his travels might oblige him if Pip were out of the way. He didn't really need Pip at all.

They arrived at the cottage before Pip could collapse beneath the weight of his misery and self-pity. Pip helped a mostly unconscious Ash up to his rooms, followed closely by a deeply concerned and curious Mrs. Applethwaite. When Ash was seated on his mattress, Pip went directly back out to find a place for the doctor's horse and carriage for the night, leaving Mrs. Applethwaite to tuck the master in this time, because Pip didn't have the heart for it.

He settled the horse in an open space far enough from their own horse's stall that they wouldn't trouble one another. And then he dragged his weary body back to the kitchen. Mrs. Applethwaite wanted to hear all about their adventure but took pity on him when she saw he was asleep on his feet and sent him to bed. Pip barely took the time to shed his coat and heavy trousers before crawling beneath the blankets.

He woke in the middle of the night to a loud clatter and the sound of glass breaking. Fairly certain of what he would find, he hurried from his room and through the door to the house, not pausing even long enough to light a candle. Light flickered through the open library door, and Pip rushed to it. He found Ash collapsed in his usual chair in front of a cold and empty hearth, in nothing but his trousers, boots, and shirtsleeves. The small table by his chair was overturned, and Ash's usual glass was in pieces on the floor, glittering wetly in the light of the single candle on the sideboard.

Pip frowned and sighed irritably, loud enough for Ash to hear his displeasure, if the man had still been conscious. At least the fool had set his candle somewhere safe before downing half the contents of the crystal decanter.

Pip was only in his stockings so he stepped carefully around the shards of glass. Ash's skin was icy when Pip reached out to touch his face and some of Pip's irritation ebbed in favor of concern.

"Ash?" The man's eyelids didn't even twitch. "Ash!" he hissed again, louder this time. That got a frown and a grumble from Ash, and Pip's tension eased. He grabbed Ash's arm, draped it over his shoulder, and dragged him to his feet.

As before, Pip was sweating and out of breath by the time he got Ash back in his bed. He stood looking down at the pale figure of his master and sometime lover and couldn't seem to bring himself to leave. His earlier thoughts and conclusions swam to the surface, and a crushing sadness followed quickly behind. Desperately in need of some comfort, no matter how short-lived, Pip climbed into bed behind Ash and wrapped his arms around the man's chilled body.

A minute or two, that's what Pip promised himself. He'd only stay a minute or two, and then he'd leave before Ash sobered enough to kick him out. But it had been a very long day, and Pip fell asleep before he knew it.

He couldn't have been asleep long. The sky was still dark when Ash's moaning woke him for the second time that night.

"Shhhh, Ash, wake up. It's only a nightmare," Pip soothed as Ash continued to thrash next to him. Pip reached out to shake the man, but his wrist was caught in an iron grip.

"Ash?" Pip gasped as the fingers imprisoning his wrist tightened painfully.

"Colin," Ash mumbled drunkenly just before he lunged, forcing Pip onto his stomach and pinning both of Pip's wrists to the mattress.

Panic surged in him, but Pip fought it down. "Ash, let go. Let go of me," he hissed, struggling to keep his tone calm as his heart beat a frantic rhythm in his breast.

Instead of easing off, Ash put his full weight on Pip's back and dragged Pip's wrists together above his head. "Why, Colin?" Ash's voice was mournful and hollow. "Why must it always be like this?"

Despite his resolve to stay calm, Pip started to struggle. He couldn't help it. His blood was pounding in his ears, and he was beginning to feel feverish and chilled at the same time. He had to get free before he lost what sense was left to him.

"Please," Ash whispered before he squeezed Pip's wrists together in one hand and began clawing at Pip's trousers with the other. The sound of tearing cloth split the air.

"No!"

Fear claimed him as it had before, and Pip bucked Ash off him. They grappled a bit, but Pip had the advantage of sobriety and muscle. He felt his elbow connect painfully with something, and Ash grunted. Pip sprang from the bed before Ash could recover, and he was through the door only

128

a moment later. He kept enough of his wits this time that he didn't go running out into the snow, but only just. He threw himself through the door to the kitchen and down the hall, banging his shoulder and smashing his toe in the darkness.

A moment after he slammed his door closed and bolted it, he heard Mrs. Applethwaite's frightened voice from the hall. "Pip? Pip is that you? What's happening?"

Pip's chest heaved as he struggled to breathe normally. "Nothing, Missus." He dragged in a ragged breath and tried again. "Master couldn't sleep. Needed me 'elp getting back to bed is all."

"I thought I heard a shout."

"Nightmare, Missus. The master were a bit shook up from this evenin'. Memories of the wars and all."

She was silent for a time, and Pip thought perhaps she'd gone until she said, "All right, then. If you think he won't need me, then I'll go back to bed and check on him in the morning."

Pip blew out a breath and buried his face in his shaking hands for a moment before he cleared his throat. "I don't think he'll need any more 'elp tonight, Missus."

Her footsteps receded along with the sliver of candlelight from beneath his door, and Pip stumbled the last few steps to his bed. He didn't sleep for the rest of the night. He sat huddled beneath his blankets in the center of his mattress, shaking and tormented by his memories until the gray light of predawn began to chase away the shadows in his room.

Chapter Seventeen

EVENTUALLY, HE dragged himself out of bed and pulled on his clothes before making his way to the kitchen. Despite the early hour, Mrs. Applethwaite was already bustling in front of the fire when Pip entered the room.

"You look awful," she said by way of a greeting.

Pip simply nodded wearily and sat down at the rough wooden table.

"You aren't ill again, are you?"

"No, Missus. Only tired. I 'ad trouble sleepin'."

The housekeeper clattered about and a steaming mug appeared before him.

"Drink this."

Pip cupped his hands around the mug, warming them, and took a cautious sip. Tea and milk, sweetened with a generous amount of honey. Pip glanced at the woman in surprise, but she'd already gone back to fussing over the bread she had rising near the fire.

Why was she being so kind to him?

Pip sipped his tea and watched her warily. He was still a bit shaken from the night before, so he was doubly grateful for her tiny bit of mothering, but it wasn't like her at all. It made him nervous.

A bell rang from the far end of the cottage, making Pip jump where he sat. His stomach twisted as he looked at her husband's vacant chair, but Mrs. Applethwaite was already removing her apron. She shook her head when Pip made to rise.

"I'll see to him, Pip. I think you've done enough for the master. I saw the broken glass in the library... and the nearly empty decanter. Mr. Applethwaite and I will take care of things from here. I assume you'll need to take the doctor's carriage back this morning?"

"Yes, ma'am."

"Then go and see to it, and leave the master to us."

Pip watched her go with a profound feeling of relief. He knew Ash had been drunk and hadn't known what he was doing. But Pip wasn't ready to face him yet. His emotions were so jumbled he didn't know how to even begin to explain them to himself, let alone to Ash.

The only feeling clear in his head that morning was a longing to go home. The tiny bit of mothering the housekeeper had given him made him almost desperate for Maud. Maud would know what to do, if only he could speak to her now. A letter just wasn't the same, and he couldn't be completely honest about Ash in pen and ink at any rate.

Pip drained the rest of his mug and left for the barn before Mrs. Applethwaite could change her mind. After seeing to Molly, he rigged the horse to the gig and drove them to village as the sun peeked over the fells and painted the snow-covered hills with orange fire. The countryside was breathtaking, and the beauty of it soothed him for a time.

Only the stable hands were about when Pip delivered the gig to the inn. The hour was still early, and the air outside bitter, so he hadn't truly expected to see anyone else. Once the horse was handed off, Pip was at a loss as to what to do next. He didn't want to return to the cottage, but Mrs. Applethwaite had given him no other errands to run. He dithered outside the inn until a sudden idea struck him, and he smiled. Both Ash and Mrs. Applethwaite would want to know how Mr. Brown fared, and Pip was curious as well. He could wait in the common room until the doctor rose and ask the man himself. Not only would Mrs. Applethwaite excuse his absence, but she'd probably thank him for his thoughtfulness.

Pip doffed his cap and entered the inn through a set of doors by the stables. He snuck into the common room and sat on a bench near the fire, feeling self-conscious in his rough clothes. A quick look around showed him the doctor wasn't there, but a few other early risers were breaking their fast. Most of them ignored Pip, but he felt furtive glances from a couple of young ladies in one corner and a disapproving glare from their matronly traveling companion. Pip kept his head down and his back to them, not once glancing openly in their direction, but that apparently wasn't enough for the matron. Out of the corner of his eye, Pip saw the woman wave the innkeeper over to her before whispering and nodding in Pip's direction.

Pip let out an aggrieved sigh as he saw the man turn and bustle over to him. "Oi, what ye doin' 'ere, lad?"

"I'm Major McNulty's man, sir. Just returnin' the doctor's gig. Me master told me to ask after Mr. Brown, so I were only waitin' for the doctor."

The innkeeper's forbidding scowl eased, and he nodded sadly. "Oh, right. I remember now. Poor man. It were a bit o' luck, then, yer master bein' so close."

Pip nodded and smiled politely as the innkeeper cast a worried glance back at the woman who'd sent him. "The doctor ain't left 'is rooms yet. He were up into the wee hours with Mr. Brown. But ye can tell yer master that 'e seems to be on the mend now, and 'e were sleeping peacefully the last time I saw 'im."

"My master wanted to hear it from the doctor 'imself, but—" Pip glanced at the pinch-lipped matron and shrugged. "I s'pose that's enough for 'im. Thank ye, sir."

Pip nodded to the man and donned his cap as he walked out of the room and reluctantly stepped back out into the cold. There was no help for it. He'd have to go back sometime.

Pip pulled his collar up, tucked his hands under his arms, and set off for the cottage. If the weather had been only a touch warmer, he might've taken his time on the walk back, but the air was too cold for that. He reached Mr. Cooper's shop in no time and was about to turn toward the road back to the cottage when Agnes stepped out onto the stoop. Pip stopped in his tracks as he felt a genuinely happy smile spread across his face for the first time in weeks.

Agnes wasn't Maud, but Pip was suddenly desperate for her company, the familiarity and lack of complication she represented.

"Agnes!"

She turned from tucking a wrapped bundle into her basket, but when she spied who it was, the welcoming smile fell from her lips. "Pip," she replied with a sniff as he hurried over to her.

"Agnes, dove. Don't be cross wit me." Pip's pout was not feigned.

"What do ye want, then?"

"You, my sweet."

Her lips twisted and she turned to leave, but Pip threw out a hand to stop her. He was still a good five feet from her as propriety dictated, so she could have simply walked around him if she'd wanted to, but she stopped and cocked her head impatiently at him.

Pip dropped his usual mask and let all of his weariness, confusion, and sadness show in his countenance as he said, "I'm sorry I 'aven't come to see ye. I miss ye, Agnes. I need to talk to ye. Please?"

She pursed her lips and studied his face. After a while, Pip saw her displeasure melt, replaced by a mixture of exasperation and concern. "Mary's waitin' for me down the lane, but I'll try t' sneak away tonight after everyone goes t' bed."

Pip blew out the breath he'd been holding, and his smile returned. "Thank ye, Agnes." Now he had something to look forward to, and it helped make the long walk back to the last place he wanted to go bearable.

Ash's night must have been as restless as Pip's, because the man spent the entire day in his bedchamber. Mrs. Applethwaite and her husband were kept busy tending to him, and of course that made both of them cross and out of sorts. Pip spent as much of the day as he could in the barn. He was practically frozen through by the time he came in for supper, but that was better that than being pecked at all day long. Supper was a quiet affair, and Pip excused himself early.

He lay in bed for a long time, trying to read but not able to get through more than a few pages as the hours ticked past. And when the house was completely silent, he tucked his blankets under his arm and crept from his room to the kitchen. He stole a heel of bread and some jam, along with a few hot coals from the banked kitchen fire. He was allowed to have a tiny brazier in the barn, but Mrs. Applethwaite had cautioned him not to use it unless the weather turned cold enough the animals were at risk. Tonight he intended to use it, and if the old crow found out... well, he wasn't sure he gave a damn anymore what she'd do.

He built a nest in a pile of straw with the blankets, as near the brazier as he could safely manage. Molly and the horse shifted in their stalls every now and again, unused to having company so late, but otherwise the night was quiet while he waited. He must have dozed off at some point because a scratching at the back of the barn woke him some time later.

"Ye better be willing to show yer gratitude," Agnes grumbled as Pip helped her through the opening and then closed and bolted the shutters behind her.

"Come on. Let's get ye warmed up, dove." Pip led her to the nest he'd made, draped a blanket over her shoulders, and sat down beside her.

As soon as she stopped shivering, Agnes tugged the mittens from her hands and reached for the front of Pip's trousers. Pip should have expected it, but the move somehow caught him by surprise and he jumped, grabbing her wrists and holding them away from him. "Wait, Agnes. I truly did want to talk to ye."

"What for?" she asked impatiently.

Pip supposed she had a right to be confused. He'd asked her to come only thinking of how soothing her presence would be, but he should have remembered *talking* was rarely what they started with when they had a bit of privacy. Unfortunately, he didn't think he'd be able to give her what she wanted, now that he had her there, and a wave of guilt crashed over him.

"I wanted to apologize for any 'urt I might've caused ye, Agnes," he began, only then realizing the full truth of those words. "I haven't given ye half of what ye deserve, and if I caused ye any pain in me carelessness, I hope ye can forgive me."

When Pip mustered the courage to meet her gaze, Agnes was looking at him as if he'd gone daft. "What are you goin' on about?"

A bit flustered now, Pip tried again. "Ye'r a fine girl, Agnes. And I'm sorry if I led ye t' believe there were more between us than there is, if I were careless with yer feelings. 'Tis all me own fault. I know it now. And ye have every right to be angry with me."

Agnes pulled back and turned her face away as her shoulders began to shake. But when Pip set a comforting hand on her arm, she let out a loud snort, and Pip realized she wasn't crying. She was laughing. "Ye'r barmy, you are," she sniggered, and Pip pulled his hand away and frowned at her.

"It ain't that funny," he grumbled, all hurt pride.

She snorted again and made a show of getting a hold of herself. "Sorry. Pip, ye know I'm fond of ye. Sure'n ye'r the prettiest man I ever laid eyes on, but I'm not a bloody idiot. No girl in 'er right mind would set 'er cap on ye."

Pip crossed his arms over his chest and pouted. This wasn't going at all as he had hoped. If anything, he felt worse now than he had before.

Agnes must have noticed his pique, because she stopped grinning at him and tried to look contrite. "I'm me father's eldest daughter. Someday soon, when Roger Olmsley's got enough money saved up, he'll ask for me hand, and I'll move from me father's farm to Roger's, an that's 'ow it is. Ye ain't the kind o' man a girl marries, Pip, and ye know it."

She was right, but it still stung—especially now because it came all too close to the thoughts he'd been having about Ash. Not only was Pip not the kind a girl would take seriously, but he wasn't the kind Ash would ever take seriously either. That fact had never really mattered to him before. He'd happily taken full advantage of it in the past. But it did now, and it hurt to have Agnes say the words out loud.

A warm hand cupped his cheek, and Agnes said, "I am sorry, Pip. It weren't Christian o' me to laugh at ye."

Pip could only nod. His thoughts had turned back down the road he'd been trying to avoid, and it looked like there'd be no redirecting them now.

Agnes sighed loudly next to him and let the blanket fall from her shoulders as she rose. "I'm thinkin' yer troubles 'ave less to do wit me than somethin' else. But either way, I don' think ye'r gonna be payin' me back for me long, cold walk tonight."

Pip did a quick inventory of his body, but he felt not a single spark of passion, not a tingle anywhere. He began to fear Ash had ruined him in that respect, but perhaps all he needed was time, time to find his swagger again.

"Can I walk ye 'ome?" Pip asked as he too rose to his feet.

"Aye." Agnes picked up her mittens from the straw and put them back on after straightening her shawl and brushing off her skirts.

Pip covered the brazier and set it safely away from anything flammable before offering his arm to Agnes and leading her out the front doors. He didn't feel right making her climb out the back again. As he led her across the yard, Pip thought he saw something flash in an upstairs window, but he looked again and found nothing.

Only a sliver of moon hung in the sky, but the reflection on the snow provided plenty of light to see by. When they reached the edge of the yard in front of her father's farmhouse, Agnes stood up on her toes and kissed Pip on the cheek. The gesture had a sense of finality, but Pip didn't comment on it, he simply watched in silence as Agnes hurried to the house and her sisters helped her through a window at the side.

Pip ran the short distance back to the cottage to keep warm, collected his blankets from the barn, and crept back through the kitchen to his bedchamber. By that time, the storm inside him—memories trying to break free and feelings he no longer wanted—had subsided, replaced by a shield of numbness. And when Mrs. Applethwaite called for him the following morning, Pip rolled out of bed and prepared for work as always.

But that day, as he entered the kitchen to break his fast, the housekeeper blocked his path.

"The master has sent for you."

"I didn't hear the bell," Pip said as a sudden jolt of nerves threatened to shatter his illusion of detachment.

"That's because he didn't ring," she replied irritably. "Not that it matters, but he was awake and dressed when I went to stir up his fire and bring him his tray. Now he's waiting in the library, so get along with you."

Pip swallowed at the stone that now seemed lodged in his throat and went to the library as he was bid. Instead of sitting in his usual place, Ash stood in front of the mantel staring at the coals.

"Close the door," Ash ordered without looking at him. The man looked as haggard as Pip felt. His cheeks were hollow, the pale gray light from the windows making his skin look ashen and casting ghastly shadows over his face.

Pip's heart ached just looking at him, but Ash didn't give him time to fret. He began to speak as soon as the latch clicked into place. "I saw you last night with that girl. I assume she's the same one as you were with before." Pip opened his mouth to make excuses, but Ash didn't give him the chance. One of his elegant, long-fingered hands slashed through the air. "I don't wish to hear another word. I brought you here to tell you you're dismissed. Mrs. Applethwaite will give you any wages you are owed, and you may take any gifts you have received, but I want you gone within the hour."

The numbness lifted quickly, but Pip feared if he gave in to even one of the emotions suddenly raging inside him, all of them would come rushing out, damning both of them in the process.

Ash still wouldn't look at Pip, and his next words cut Pip even more deeply because of it. "If you're thinking of blackmailing me or telling *anyone* about what happened between us, remember it is your word against mine. You would be up before the magistrate and facing the gallows long before I ever did."

Pip took a step back, as if he'd been slapped. He knew Ash didn't think highly of him, but he'd assumed the man had more regard for him than this. Silence hung heavily between them until Pip managed to force a single "Yes, sir" from his throat. He spun around and left before he broke down.

As he exited the library, Ash's bell began ringing for Mrs. Applethwaite. She passed Pip on his way to his room, but he didn't look at her. He clenched his jaw against the tears that threatened to unman him and rushed on without stopping. He dragged his bag, a gift from Maud, out from under the bed and began throwing his few possessions inside with a ferocity that betrayed his anger. When he came to the house slippers, the beautiful waistcoat, and other articles Ash had given him, Pip nearly broke down, but he quickly shoved them into the bag and moved on.

Once his dresser was empty and the small pile of coins he'd managed to save were safely in his pocket, Pip cast about the room one more time to make sure he hadn't forgotten anything, and his gaze fell on the small stack of books resting on the windowsill by his bed. The bag dropped from his numb hand. He went to the books and traced his fingers over the spines until he touched one at the bottom of the stack—*Posthumous Poems of Percy Bysshe Shelley*. Pip opened it and leafed through the pages until he found the one he was looking for.

"Love's Philosophy." He didn't have to read the words. He'd memorized the poem weeks ago.

Without stopping to think, Pip rifled through his bag until he found the stack of letters from Maud. He tore the bottom off one and scribbled a few words on it in pencil before tucking the slip of paper into the book and putting it back on the bottom of the stack.

His wages waited for him on the kitchen table, but the room was otherwise empty. He would receive no parting remarks from the Applethwaites, not that he'd really expected any. He didn't stop or turn his head as he left the yard. Nor did he take any time to say good-bye to the horse. He didn't dare. One word of farewell, even to a bloody horse, and he'd be weeping like a babe for sure. He simply closed the gate behind him, threw his bag over his shoulder, and took off down the road toward the village. This early in the morning he hoped he'd be able to catch the post home to Penrith and not have to spend a minute longer in Keswick than he had to.

Chapter *Eighteen*

THE MOMENT Maud opened the door, she took one look at him, dragged him into her kitchen, and pushed him into a chair. Before Pip could utter a single word, he was handed a steaming bowl of stew, a plate of buttered bread, and a mug of tea. Pip decided he must have looked damned awful, because the five other times he'd come home again after being sacked, he'd received a dressing down and had hours of making excuses and cajoling to do before Maud even thought about mothering him.

As it turned out, he didn't have to explain himself that night either, because he nodded off as soon as his dishes were empty, and Stubbs was the one to drag him to his bed. Maud's husband was taciturn at the best of times, and thankfully, the man merely grunted a few times and walked out as soon as he'd dumped Pip onto his bed without requiring any conversation.

Pip slept the sleep of the utterly exhausted. He didn't remember dreaming anything at all, and his limbs were so stiff upon waking that he must not have moved an inch all night. The next day, the house was alive with noise as it always was, but Pip slept through it until close to noon, judging by the sun outside his window.

A sense of peace settled over him when he finally opened his eyes. His room was exactly the same as he'd left it. The tables and dresser were still littered with the bits of string, rocks, baubles, and paper flowers the children had given him. The worn and patched blue coverlet beneath his hands was as familiar and comforting as always. He closed his eyes and drew it up to his chin again, hoping the world would forget him for a few more hours.

But it was not to be.

The moment he got settled again, Maud tapped once on the door and then came in. Pip pretended to be asleep, but he watched her through slitted eyes while she set a steaming ewer on his dresser and then stood by the bed, staring down at him. "Ye've been abed since nine last night. Time to get up, ye lazy lout."

When Pip opened his eyes the rest of the way, her hands were propped on her hips, and she was trying to look stern. But Pip could see the worry underneath. Maud had never been very good at hiding her feelings, and after months of dealing with Ash, she was a most welcome change.

In a sudden rush of gratitude for her presence alone, Pip reached out and took one of her hands in his. "I've missed ye, Maud."

Her frown deepened as her concern overshadowed any other feeling. In an attempt to soothe her, Pip did what he should have from the start. He plastered his cocksure grin on his face, kissed the hand he held, and winked at her. "Who else would bring me a bit of toast and sausage in bed whilst I recover from me long journey 'ome?"

The performance lacked his usual rakish charm, and Pip could tell Maud wasn't falling for it, but she played along just the same. "Get off with ye. If ye want to eat, ye'll come to me kitchens like everyone else. An' ye won't get no supper lyin' about in bed all day neither. There's plenty t' keep ye busy, so get yerself dressed."

Pip's grin faded quickly after she left, but he dragged himself out of bed and washed and shaved in the blessedly warm water she'd brought him. The meal she fed him when he finally appeared in her kitchen bespoke her concern for him. His plate was piled high with eggs, sausages, and toast with jam, and Pip tucked in with relish.

She waited until he was done before shooing the rest of the maids out of the kitchen and sitting down next to him.

"Are ye goin' t' tell me what 'appened now?"

Pip swallowed and he suddenly regretted stuffing himself with quite so much sausage. "I were sacked, again," he answered simply.

Her lips twisted and she rolled her eyes. "I know that. What I don't know is why, and whether or not the girl's parents'll be seeking reparations, or if we should expect an angry 'usband bangin' on our door someday soon. Ye didn't even last 'til Christmas, this time."

139

Pip's lip turned up at her exasperated tone, and he chuckled tiredly as he shook his head. "No fathers, husbands, or brothers. Ye don' need to worry about that."

She studied him for a bit before she reached over and took his hands in hers. "What's wrong, lamb. I haven't seen you like this, since—"

Pip stood up, cutting her off before she could finish that sentence. "I'll be all right. I can't talk about it now. I need time and I hope I can 'ave it 'ere. I don't plan to leave again, Maud. I'm 'ere t' stay, if ye'll 'ave me."

Maud rose and wrapped her arms around him, squeezing him tight with all the softness and warmth he'd come to count on since he was a child. "Of course, my beautiful boy. Ye're famly, always. Master Carey'll want t' speak to ye. But I think that can wait until ye've 'ad a little time. Go down to the stables. There's someone there who's been missin' ye somethin' awful. 'e'll be sure to lift yer spirits if anyone can."

Pip's smile this time was genuine as he squeezed her ample form back and then headed for the door. He'd just reached for the knob when Maud called after him, "Did ye love the girl? Is that what it is?"

Pip closed his eyes for a moment before he replied, "Weren't a girl."

Maud harrumphed. "Woman, then."

"Nor that neither," Pip said, a tiny bit of his good humor rising with baiting Maud.

"Ye weren't alone so long ye started on sheep, were ye?"

Pip snorted. "No."

He stepped through the door and closed it behind him before she could ask him anything else. He took the path down the hill to the stables at a run, the quicker to get out of the bitter wind. For a while, Pip hovered over the brazier set up just inside the building, thawing his hands, before he went in search of Peter.

The boy was in one of the stalls at the far end of the stables, brushing Clover, the pretty little pony Master Carey had bought for the children to ride. At seven years of age, Peter's little blond head barely reached the pony's shoulder, but he handled the brush and Clover with practiced ease.

Pip hovered outside the stall and simply listened to Peter croon nonsense to the creature until he felt its soothing effects himself. Eventually Peter finished his work, threw a blanket over Clover's back, and stepped out of the stall. When he finally spotted Pip waiting for him, he dropped the brush and any pretentions of decorum and launched himself into Pip's arms.

"You're back!"

Pip grinned and spun Peter around in a circle. "Aye, lad. Ye're a sight for sore eyes."

"Are you staying for Christmas?"

"I 'ope so. I 'ave no plans to be anywhere else, at any rate."

He set Peter down, and the boy stared at him, his face scrunching up into an adorable frown. "You look awful."

Pip put a hand to his chest and pretended to be deeply wounded. "What a thing t' say. An' me only just come 'ome."

Peter stuck out his tongue. "You know what I meant. You haven't been ill, have you? You look ill."

"Only a little fever, months ago. Nothing to worry ye."

"Then why do you look like that?"

Heaven preserve him from tenacious and inquisitive children. What happened to his air of rakish charm, infamous throughout the countryside, if even a child could see through it?

"I'm only a bit tired, is all. I'll be good as new in a couple o' days, ye'll see."

The look Peter gave him then was a near perfect imitation of the one Master Carey usually reserved for him—eyebrow raised in haughty disbelief while his mouth quirked to the side in both amusement and resignation. Pip knew Master Carey was fond of Peter. And Peter had certainly begun to sound like the gentleman. But Pip hadn't realized they'd spent enough time together for Peter to start looking like the man as well.

Peter used to mimic Pip. But Pip supposed it was better that the boy had chosen to begin aping the master instead. He'd get further in life that way. That was sure.

"Come along," Pip said, suddenly anxious to take his thoughts down a different path. He reached out and tousled Peter's hair before putting a hand between the boy's shoulders and giving him a shove toward the stalls. "Let's reintroduce me to all our lads and lasses 'ere. An' then I can supervise while ye muck a stall or two."

Peter stuck his tongue out again, but he giggled as he ran to the next stall down from Clover's. Pip didn't know where Turner, the stable master, was, but it appeared as if Peter had things well in hand. That thought made him a little sad as it occurred to him that he wasn't really needed here either. But he pushed it away and set to work before he became any more maudlin than he already was.

Less than an hour later, the sound of a horse approaching shattered the small contentment Pip had managed to achieve, working up a sweat in familiar surroundings. He assumed it was Master Carey returning from his ride, and he hadn't taken any time to prepare himself for the inevitable interview that would follow. Pip set down his shovel, wiped his hands on his trousers, and stepped out of the stall. But it wasn't Asmodeus's reins that Peter reached for but Gabriel's.

Master Carruthers dismounted, smiling down at Peter, and patted the boy's shoulder as he stepped away from Gabriel. "He's had a good run today, Peter, so walk him about a bit and take care when you rub him down. Make sure he's dry before you put him away and add a little extra treat to his feed."

"Yes, sir."

Peter turned Gabriel around and led him out the way they'd come in, talking gibberish to the creature as he went.

"Sir?" Pip called from the shadows, and Mr. Carruthers turned and smiled in welcome.

"Pip? I hadn't heard you were back."

In the past, Pip had always found Mr. Carruthers to be a bit on the reserved side, perhaps even a little standoffish. He was a master of the house, and Pip followed his orders, but they hadn't had much interaction beyond that. Mr. Carruthers was a farmer to the heart of him and spent most of his time either out with his livestock or in private with Mr. Carey. Pip didn't have the love for the man that he did for Mr. Carey, but Mr. Carey loved Mr. Carruthers, so that was enough for Pip to feel at least a little warmth toward him.

"I only got back last night, sir."

"How long do you plan to stay this time?"

Pip supposed he should have been grateful it was Mr. Carruthers he saw first. Mr. Carey knew Pip too well, so an interview with him would turn out to be a great deal more... *personal* than one with Mr. Carruthers. With any luck, Carruthers would convey the information to Mr. Carey and Pip could avoid that conversation altogether.

"I'm thinkin' I'll be stayin' on permanent this time, sir... if that's all right with ye and Master Carey, that is."

Pip's answer seemed to surprise the man, and Carruthers took a few steps closer, studying Pip.

"Are you unwell, Pip?"

Why does everyone insist on asking me that?

Pip opened his mouth, but only a pathetic croaking sound emerged. And much to his eternal mortification Pip felt tears spring to his eyes as his throat closed. Pip blinked rapidly and opened his eyes wide to dispel any hint of moisture, but it was too late. Carruthers had seen it. The man came closer still and put a hand on Pip's shoulder, his eyes filled with concern.

Pip had never really noticed how unique a shade Mr. Carruthers's eyes were, more reminiscent of amber than the light brown Pip had always thought them. They weren't as beautiful as Ash's, but they were certainly striking.

And when had he started noticing the color of other men's eyes?

Oh God.

Pip buried his face in his hands to cover the fire in his cheeks as the rest of his body turned ice cold.

"Come on," Carruthers said gently.

Using the hand on Pip's shoulder, he steered Pip to Turner's small office at the back of the stables. The room was vacant, but the stove was blessedly warm, and Carruthers pushed Pip into the chair in front of it before settling himself on a stack of crates opposite. Pip could only glance at the man from the corner of his eye because he was too ashamed to meet his gaze.

What was the matter with him? Did he have no pride left?

"I'm sorry, sir. I don't know what came over me."

Carruthers removed his hat, set down his riding crop, and ran gloved fingers through his rather unruly blond-tipped curls, looking as uncomfortable as Pip felt.

"There's no need to apologize, Pip. I realize we have never been close, but William loves you… and Maud and Stubbs. I would love you for their sake alone, even if I didn't know you to be a good man in your own right. You're obviously troubled. If there is anything I might do to help, I hope you would feel you could come to me with it."

Pip shifted in his seat and looked down at his boots. If he kept looking at Carruthers's earnest face, even askance, he might break down again, and he wasn't sure his pride would survive another blow. He didn't even know where the outburst of emotion had come from.

"Thank you, sir," he answered quietly.

Pip took a few deep breaths, and when he thought he could manage it without making a fool of himself again, he met the man's gaze. He'd also never noticed before how handsome a man Mr. Carruthers was. He wasn't that much older than Pip, and Pip could easily see now why Master Carey had been taken with him from the moment he set eyes on the man.

Pip dropped his face into his hands, shaking his head. "I don't know what's the matter with me."

That was a lie. He knew exactly what was the matter with him. He just didn't know how to cure himself of it.

"I can't speak to that, since I know nothing of the events leading to your return. But, given your past exploits, I can only hazard to guess it has something to do with an affair of the heart?" Carruthers said with a trace of gentle humor in his voice.

Pip smiled at that. It would be the obvious assumption to make, and he appreciated the man's word choice. "I fear that's the problem, sir. Me past exploits had nothing to do with me 'eart."

"But what happened this time does?" Carruthers asked, showing a surprising amount of insight.

"Aye."

Pip wasn't sure how much he should impose on the fragile intimacy they had begun. Carruthers was his master, along with Mr. Carey. But it suddenly occurred to him that of all the people he knew, Mr. Carruthers might be one of only a very few who might understand what he was going through. After all, Master Carey had to hunt the man down and practically force him to accept Carey as part of his life. Mr. Carruthers might well understand Pip's fears and his hurt.

"Sir? Did ye know it when ye fell in love with Master Carey?"

Carruthers had been leaning toward him before this, but he suddenly sat back with a look of surprise.

"I'm sorry, sir," Pip quickly added, "I shouldn't 'ave asked that. It isn't any of me affair."

"No, no, Pip. I offered to help. You simply caught me by surprise." Carruthers pursed his lips a moment, considering. "I suppose my answer would have to be no. I didn't know it straight away. I think too much had come before, and I wasn't willing to trust in anyone but myself. William had to do a great deal of convincing before I could believe in him. But he's an expert at that, as you well know," he finished with a chuckle and a wry grin, and Pip couldn't help but mirror it.

"'E is that, sir."

"Is that what this is about? Are you wondering if you're in love?"

Pip's smile fell away, and he shook his head. "No, sir. I know I'm in love. It wouldn't 'urt this much if I weren't. The problem is, 'e don't love me back."

Carruthers's eyes went wide as he said, "He?"

"Aye, sir." Pip's lips tried to twist into another wry smile. He hoped it looked better than it felt.

"I see." Carruthers blew out a long breath before he continued soberly, "This isn't a safe or easy road to follow, Pip. You know that, don't you?"

Pip barked out a bitter laugh. "Ye don't 'ave to tell me, sir. But don't worry. It don't look like I'll be followin' it, at any rate. 'e sent me packin'.""

"You're certain he does not care for you as you do him? That there wasn't some other reason he sent you away?"

Don't leave me.

"There were a time or two I thought... maybe. But I were wrong. It were only me wishin' for somethin' that 'e couldn't give. I can't blame 'im for that, now can I?"

"Of course you can." Carruthers snorted, and Pip laughed, feeling a little better despite himself.

Pip was beginning to think he'd missed out on something by not getting to know Carruthers better before this. They were certainly closer in station than Pip was to Mr. Carey.

"Thank you, sir… for listening to me, for being so kind."

Carruthers shook his head. "I only wish I could do more, Pip. I know what heartache is, and I wouldn't wish it on anyone. I don't know the particulars of your situation, and I would not give you false hope. But did you ever tell the man how you felt? Does he know you love him?"

Pip shook his head miserably.

Carruthers sighed and leaned forward again with a grave expression on his face. "I should be advising you to forget him. It would be the safer course. But I remember a time when I thought all was lost between William and I. I remember that pain, even though I thought it was the only way. If he hadn't come to me, if he hadn't taken that risk and opened his heart to me utterly and completely, I know I would have spent the rest of my days in regret. And I never would have known the joy I have now, with him and all of you filling that drafty old house I was trying so desperately to save."

A tiny spark of hope stirred deep inside Pip at his words. Pip was so immersed in thought, he didn't realize Carruthers was still waiting for some kind of response until someone knocked on the door.

"Stephen?"

"I'm here, William."

Master Carey opened the door and looked back and forth between the two of them, frowning. "Is something wrong?"

Carruthers stood up and went to him. "No. Pip had something on his mind, so we sat down to have a little chat."

A look passed between the two of them, and then Mr. Carey shrugged. "Peter said you'd come in, but Maud said neither one of you were up at the house. Can Turner have his office back now?"

"Yes, I think so," Carruthers answered for both of them. He grabbed his hat and his riding crop, but he paused in the doorway. "Be honest, Pip. If you get the chance of it, always be honest."

Mr. Carey watched his lover leave with bemusement before he turned back to Pip. "Welcome home, Imp. We'll talk later," he said. He turned to leave, and Turner came into the office before Pip could do more than nod.

Turner shook Pip's hand briskly and began peppering him with questions about his latest adventure straight away. Pip let them roll over him like a warm summer breeze, familiar and comforting, a balm for the torn and ragged edges of his heart. He answered as best he could, telling the man about Keswick, the beautiful gelding, and Greer cottage but leaving out anything that would bring on another episode of blubbering. Pip couldn't shame himself twice in one day. And while Turner probably knew about their masters' relationship, the man was one of the many on the farm who preferred to pretend otherwise. Pip would never feel comfortable sharing anything about Ash with him.

By the time Pip came in for supper that evening, he could tell that word had spread. He hadn't expected any less. Mr. Carruthers would certainly have told Mr. Carey all about their conversation. And, of course, Mr. Carey would have then told Maud. That was how things went with a family.

She was waiting for him in her kitchen. Without a word, she wrapped him in her arms and hugged him tight, murmuring words of comfort against his cheek. Pip felt his lips tremble a little at that, but he hid it well and his eyes were dry when she sat him down at the table with a mug of tea until supper was ready.

As always, after the masters had their dinner in the dining room, all the servants came to the kitchen to eat their own meal—Maud and Stubbs, the three downstairs maids Maud had rescued from a life of ruin on the streets of London, Peter and Joanna and the younger children, plus a new boy Pip had never seen before, introduced to him as Adam, orphan and new apprentice shepherd. Maud had picked him up from somewhere or other, like the rest of their motley little family.

The noise in the room was almost deafening after his months in Keswick, but Pip reveled in it. The downstairs maids—Pip could never remember their names because Maud had always made him keep his distance—were giving him calf eyes and giggling among themselves, making Pip preen even in his depressed state. But when he glanced guiltily over at Maud, she seemed completely unconcerned.

That rankled a bit.

He falls for one bloke and all of the sudden he's harmless, no longer a threat to their already somewhat tarnished virtue?

Admittedly, Maud never had anything to fear at any rate. The girls were much too young when they'd come to the farm, and Pip had never been able to look at them any other way. But it still stung his pride… especially since Pip knew she was right. As he was now, no woman—or other man for that matter—was in any kind of danger from him.

That night in his room, Pip thought long and hard over Mr. Carruthers's advice. Ash had hurt him more than once with the coldness that seemed to come over him at the end of their nights together, but Pip had never called the man out on the subject. Perhaps he should have been brave enough to come out and say what he felt, once he'd figured it out. He'd left that slip of paper in the book of poetry, but the gesture seemed cowardly and childish now. He wasn't certain what he'd hoped to accomplish by it other than to hope Ash would feel a twinge of *some* feeling when he eventually discovered it.

Pip thought about writing Ash a letter now. But how would he say what he needed to without endangering both of them? And even if he did manage it, could he risk raising his hopes only to have them dashed when Ash didn't respond, or worse, responded with only coldness and regrets? He should at least set the man straight about what happened with Agnes that night, shouldn't he?

Pip groaned aloud to his empty room and drew his blankets over his head, snuggling down into the warmth and darkness. He was tired, tired of hurting, tired of wanting, tired of thinking and agonizing over matters he had no answers for. And he blamed Ash entirely. Ash had done this to him and then left him to manage the wreckage on his own.

Bloody bastard.

Chapter *Nineteen*

BY THE end of his second week home, little had changed. He hadn't been able to bring himself to write the letter to Ash as yet. Instead, he concentrated on settling back in on the farm. He packed away the gifts Ash had given him at the bottom of a chest in his room. He put on a brave face for Maud and for his masters. He did whatever needed to be done around the farm while Maud and everyone else got used to the idea that he intended to stay this time.

Playing with the children and eating his meals amid the family Maud had created helped. But beneath it all, his heart was still broken, and his confidence remained damaged. He rarely flirted at all anymore. Maud accepted his newfound solemnity reluctantly, but she watched him and fussed over him constantly… and Pip loved her all the more for it, even if it rankled a bit.

The nights grew even colder as Christmas approached, and Pip took to filling them with trips to one or more of the overabundance of pubs in Penrith, rather than sitting under Maud's watchful eye by the kitchen fire. He would walk or ride into town and drink with Turner or Myers, Mr. Carruthers's master shepherd… or with any of the other men who haunted the pubs at night and would welcome his company at their table. The ale flowed freely and the rooms were noisy and warm, full of life and distractions that kept him from dwelling on his sorrows.

One of those nights Pip returned to a house gone dark and quiet, warm to his bones on good ale, despite the frigid walk. He crept through the kitchen to his room, careful to keep quiet so he wouldn't wake anyone.

But before he could open the door and disappear inside his bedchamber, Stubbs appeared at the end of the hall, carrying a single candle.

"Oi, lad, we've been waitin' for ye. Ye have a visitor."

Pip swung around a little unsteadily and frowned at him. The ale was making his mind a bit slow, but he was sure he couldn't have heard the man right.

"A visitor?"

"Aye. 'e come just after dark. Major Astley McNulty," Stubbs ground out the name carefully, as if it didn't sit well in his mouth. "'E were ghastly pale, and the masters decided to put 'im in a guestroom upstairs afore he fell over dead."

Pip barely heard anything after Stubbs said the name. Ash was here, now. The pleasant and sleepy haze he'd been laboring under disappeared with the pounding of his heart.

"Where?" It was the only word he could manage.

"Upstairs," Stubbs replied unhelpfully, and Pip growled. Stubbs's craggy face quivered a bit in the candlelight before the corner of his mouth lifted a tiny fraction. He was enjoying Pip's agitation. "Last room on the right."

It wasn't the largest of the four guest rooms, but it would be the easiest to keep warm and, perhaps not incidentally, the farthest from the masters' bedchamber. Pip nodded, but he remained rooted to the spot, unable to think of what to do next.

Eventually Stubbs grunted, closed the distance between them, handed over his candle, and stumped back the way he'd come without another word. The sound of a door closing finally shook Pip out of his stupor, and he rushed to the stairs and took them as quickly and quietly as he could. He was down the hall and through the bedchamber door before any second thoughts could stop him.

Once inside, his candle cast wavering shadows across the room and at first, he thought it a trick of the light when the midnight velvet bed curtains moved, but then a tired voice confirmed he was not imagining it.

"Phillip?"

Ash was the only one who ever called him that, and hearing his name in that beloved voice sent a stab of joy and pain through his chest.

"I'm here."

Ash pushed the thick bed curtains aside and swung his legs to the floor. He was still in his trousers and boots, and the room felt inexcusably cold. Pip stepped away from the door and hurried to the grate. He set his candle on the mantel and stirred up the coals before pouring another shovelful on, embarrassed and angry that Ash hadn't been properly seen to. "Did no one come t' take care of ye?"

"I was well taken care of. Your masters Carey and Carruthers were very generous with their hospitality. The housekeeper, Maud, offered any service I required, but I told her I could manage on my own. I simply hadn't expected to sleep as long as I did. I must have been more tired than I thought."

Stubborn bastard.

Silence fell as the coals began to warm the room, and Pip drank in the sight of his former master. Ash still looked pale and careworn. He also appeared thinner than when Pip had left him, and the tightness around his eyes and mouth betrayed his suffering. Pip wanted to go to him, to wrap his arms around him and soothe away his hurts, kiss him until Ash forgot his pain. But he stayed where he was, hurt and fear of rejection keeping him frozen to the spot.

"Why 'ave ye come?" he asked, hope creeping in despite all that.

Ash made to rise but seemed to think better of it. He dropped his hands to the mattress by his thighs and sighed. "I had much to say to you, and none of it could be put in a letter."

Pip swallowed and took a steadying breath, fighting the urge to run to the man again. Crossing his arms over his chest, he feigned an air of patience and unconcern he did not feel.

Into the silence that fell between them, Ash chuckled ruefully. "I suppose that is only partly the truth. But I think it is where I should start, even if I may wish some of it had remained unsaid by the time I am finished."

He spoke so quietly that Pip began to think he was speaking more to himself than for Pip's benefit. "I don't understand."

"I know, and for that I must apologize along with all the other injustices I must redress." Ash blew out a long breath before continuing. "I have done you great wrong, Phillip. I have thought ill of you when I was given no cause. I have made assumptions I should not. And I have not once taken the pains to understand you, as I should."

Pip growled. "Speak plainly, man. Ye know I'm only a simple—"

"But you aren't," Ash interrupted earnestly, straightening his spine and leaning toward Pip, as if to compel him to understand. "I knew you weren't. I *knew* there was so much more to you, and yet I still...." He slumped back and dropped his head into his hands. "From the very first, I believed you were only toying with me, Phillip. I thought you might prove the ruin of me, once and for all. But I didn't care. A quick end was almost preferable to the slow one I had planned for myself, as long as I had a few bright moments with you before it happened."

When Ash gazed up at him again, Pip's stomach twisted at the resignation in the man's eyes. Ash must have seen when his words finally sunk in, because he nodded and smiled sadly. "Yes. When I purchased the cottage, I fully intended to die there. Oh, nothing so dramatic as a pistol or a length of rope, but I believed I'd waste away quietly with my books and my drink, no trouble to anyone. But then I met you. The first time I saw you, I looked at your face, and I thought I had never seen a more beautiful man."

Pip snorted loudly and began to pace in front of the grate, unable to keep still any longer. "Ye weren't lookin' at me face that first time," he said tartly, eager to dispel the heaviness in the room before it crushed him.

Ash barked out a surprised laugh, and some color actually returned to his cheeks. "No. I suppose I wasn't." He shook his head and turned his face away. "At any rate, I saw you and the tiniest of flames sparked to life where I thought all was dead and gone. I decided then I needed more of you, even when I believed nothing could happen between us. And when the miracle happened and you did let me have you, I couldn't allow myself to believe you could want me for myself alone. I was a wreck, a ruin. What on earth could you possible see in me if not my money or some other means of advancement?"

Pip clenched his jaw and wrapped his arms tighter around himself. Again, he'd known by the way the man treated him that Ash thought little of him, but he hadn't realized it was as bad as this. He felt like even more of a fool now than he did before he'd left, but he couldn't help but ask, "If that's what ye thought, then why are ye 'ere now?"

"Because I found this," Ash answered, drawing a book from under the pillows and opening it to the page marked by a torn bit of paper.

Even in the dim light of the candle, Pip knew the volume, and as Ash began to recite the lines, Pip had to fight the lump in his throat and the sudden sting of tears in his eyes.

> The fountains mingle with the river
> And the rivers with the ocean,
> The winds of heaven mix for ever
> With a sweet emotion;
> Nothing in the world is single;
> All things by a law divine
> In one spirit meet and mingle—
> Why not I with thine?
>
> See the mountains kiss high heaven
> And the waves clasp one another;
> No sister-flower would be forgiven
> If it disdained its brother;
> And the sunlight clasps the earth
> And the moonbeams kiss the sea:
> What is all this sweet work worth
> If thou kiss not me?

By the time he finished speaking, Ash was standing only inches from Pip. He did not reach out or move any closer, but Pip could feel him on every inch of his body, as if they were already wrapped around one another.

"I will not lie to you, Phillip. I would have sent for you eventually, even if I hadn't found it. After only a fortnight without you, knowing I might never see you again, I was almost ready to damn what little pride I had left and risk ruin and public disgrace to have you, even if only for a little while longer… to beg you to return, whatever your motives were.

But when I found this," he continued, holding out the torn slip of paper, "I realized how wrong I had been. I have no excuse for it. Simply because I'd been played for a fool before did not give me the right to paint you with the same brush. I sent for a carriage at once. I had to know...."

Pip took the slip of paper from Ash's shaking hand and smoothed it out with his fingertips.

"All is ash."

The words he'd scribbled in pencil, what felt like a lifetime ago, were blurred and smeared but still legible.

"How did ye find it?" he asked, because it was the only thing he could say.

"I went in search of the book not long after you left. I couldn't bring myself to read it at first, knowing how well you loved it, but I kept it with me during those first terrible days. Every minute of every hour, I thought of you."

Pip let the slip of paper fall to the floor. Then he closed his eyes and buried his face against Ash's neck. "All I ever wanted was more time with ye. No blackmail, no presents, just you," Pip whispered against his skin.

Ash's breath sobbed from his chest a moment before he wrapped his arms around Pip and drew their bodies together. They stood like that, sharing one another's warmth, until Pip felt Ash's legs tremble. He drew back and took Ash's hand and led him to the bed.

Without a word, Pip pushed him down onto the mattress and crouched to tug off his boot. When Ash began to object, Pip shoved at the man's shoulders until Ash was flat on his back. Then Pip unfastened Ash's trousers and yanked them off before setting to work on Ash's false leg. The thigh beneath the lacings looked swollen and painful, the end rubbed raw, and Pip had to stifle a whimper of sympathy as he eased the contraption off and set it aside.

Pip then littered the floor with his boots and outer clothing before he climbed onto the mattress and shoved the two of them beneath the blankets. Pip reached for Ash then, drawing him near with a hand behind his neck. Their kiss was gentle. As desperately as Pip needed Ash's touch, reassurance that he was solid and real, he knew he had to hold back. Ash still needed more time to recover from his journey.

"Phillip, I have missed you so. But I don't know if I am able to—"

Pip shut him up with a long, intoxicating kiss. He sucked and nibbled on Ash's firm lips and tongue. He teased and tormented until he was certain Ash had never been kissed so thoroughly in his entire life. And then, when Ash was panting and quivering in his arms, Pip whispered, kissing lightly over Ash's cheeks and his eyes, "I know. You've come a long way. And you need to rest. Sleep. I'll be here when you wake."

Fatigue and Pip's ministrations were obviously dragging him down, but Ash retained enough of his senses to frown and shake his head. "What if someone comes? You can't be caught here."

Pip smiled and kissed him again, until Ash's mouth was chasing his, begging for more. "Don't worry," Pip whispered hotly against his lips. "We're safe." Ash looked as if he wanted to argue, but Pip said, "Trust me," and Ash surrendered to exhaustion, relaxed back into the pillows, and closed his eyes.

Pip watched him sleep for a time, while echoes of all that remained unresolved between them floated about in his head. But, eventually, the warmth and comfort of Ash's body next to his and the quiet rhythm of Ash's breaths drew him into slumber's waiting arms as well.

Pip was not a religious man, not by a long stretch, but a prayer was on his lips as darkness swept him under.

Please, Lord, this is all I want. It isn't so much to ask, is it?

Chapter Twenty

ASH'S ANXIOUS voice woke him the following morning. "Phillip, you fell asleep. It's morning. You must go before anyone sees you."

They were nestled together in a warm cocoon of blankets. The bed curtains were drawn so only a tiny shaft of light pierced the gap on either side of them, making it feel as though they were suspended in some ethereal twilight where no one could encroach. Ash's body remained splayed across Pip's chest—where it had migrated sometime in the night—and he didn't appear in any great hurry to move, despite the urgency of his tone.

As soon as he was fully awake, Pip felt a familiar ache in his loins. He stretched and wrapped his arms and legs around Ash, gaining some much-needed friction against his cock as it nestled into Ash's hip before he grinned up at the man.

"Phillip." Ash's voice was strained, and Pip could feel an answering hardness against his belly.

It took some thorough convincing, but eventually Ash forgot his fears and succumbed to Pip's ministrations. Pip began with Ash's mouth, kissing and nibbling away any protests before they could form. And he didn't release those lips until he was sure Ash was incapable of speech, owing to the fact that Pip's his hands were doing so many naughty things everywhere else.

As Ash gasped and panted in his ear, Pip wrapped his fist around both of their cocks and stroked them together while the fingers of his other hand toyed with Ash's back entrance, and he sucked marks onto the man's neck. Ash shuddered in his arms, thrusting into Pip's grasp and clutching at Pip's body hard enough to leave bruises. Pip was drowning in Ash, the feel of his skin, the smell of him, the sounds he made. Ash's sweat mingled with Pip's and his breath ghosted through Pip's curls as they both strained against one another, desperate for release but at the same time never wanting it to end.

Ash spilled first, the proof of that hot and wet between them. With Ash's muffled cries caressing his ears, Pip succumbed soon after, mingling their seed. He bit down on Ash's shoulder as the final throes washed over him and then he collapsed back onto the mattress, happy and replete.

By the time Pip regained his breath and was able to open his eyes again, Ash's usual solemnity was back, and he was studying Pip with a grave expression, concern deeply knitting his brow. All Pip could do was grin happily in response. His world was finally set to rights again.

Ash opened his mouth to speak, but a sound from the hall had the man paling before Pip's eyes. A moment later, a knock came at the door. When Ash appeared incapable of answering, Pip called out, "Come," and Maud came bustling into the room. He knew it was Maud because none of the other servants, except for Stubbs, were allowed upstairs when any of the rooms were occupied. As she bustled about, he heard a small thud as if she set something down, the clank of iron when she stirred the coals in the grate and added more, and then the huff of the bellows.

Ash lay frozen in Pip's arms, a look of horror on his face, and Pip tried to draw him nearer to soothe him, but the man would have none of it. His arms remained rigid between them, and he looked at Pip as if he'd lost his senses. The sound of Maud dusting her hands drew their attention back to her, and a moment later she cleared her throat.

"Beggin' yer pardon, *sirs*, but the masters wondered if ye were well enough to join 'em at breakfast." The extra inflection on sirs was not lost on Pip. She was teasing him for lying abed when he should have been out working hours since. But he wasn't overly concerned. He knew even without seeing her face that he would be forgiven. He could hear the smile in her voice. She was happy for him.

Unfortunately, Ash did not know her so well, and he looked positively ill. He was gaping like a fish, his pale eyes wide with panic, and Pip sniggered despite himself.

"Thank you, Maud. Tell the masters we would be delighted," Pip answered in his best imitation of Ash.

Maud chuckled and swept out of the room. When Ash continued to stare incredulously at him, Pip swooped in to steal another kiss from his parted lips, but a hand clamped across his mouth stopped him.

"What just happened here?" Ash demanded.

Pip shrugged and teased his tongue over Ash's palm until the man released him. "I told ye to trust me."

"I trusted you to leave before we were discovered, not this. And now you laugh as if this were all a joke. You do realize what could happen to us?"

Pip's grin faded and he smoothed the backs of his fingers over Ash's cheek to soothe him. "Ye don't need to fear any o' that from Maud. Ye 'ave me word. We're safe 'ere."

Outrage was slowly replaced by confusion on Ash's face as the man relaxed his cheek into Pip's palm. "You're certain of that? Enough to risk your life on it?"

"Aye. While ye'r 'ere, ye don't need to kick me outta yer bed, unless that's what ye really want." Pip said the words teasingly, but a hint of the real hurt behind them must have come through, because Ash's expression softened, and he reached to cup Pip's face as well.

"I only ever sent you away to protect you, Phillip. If we were caught, my brother would have ensured my safety. I might have been sent away in disgrace, but you... you would have more than likely faced the gallows. I couldn't have allowed that to happen, no matter how much I wanted you. Do you think I *wanted* to sleep alone?"

Pip closed his eyes against a surge of emotion. "I didn't know," he whispered. "I thought...." His words trailed off, choked by the stone lodged in his throat.

A moment later, he felt Ash press their foreheads together, and the man sighed and whispered, "It isn't easy for me to share my feelings, Phillip. I have only ever tried twice before in my life, and both times I came to regret opening my heart. I assumed the worst of you because that was what experience had taught me. I don't know if I truly believed those things or if I only chose to believe them because it made it easier to keep distance between us. The last time nearly killed me, and despite my resolve to end what life I had left at the cottage, I was afraid… for both of us. I still am."

Pip was tired of secrets and half-truths. Carruthers was right. They needed to speak plainly. If they could not be honest and open with one another, even in the privacy of their own bed, they would have no chance of surviving the challenges they would face. Of course, that meant that Pip would have to be honest as well, but he thought perhaps he could manage it… soon.

He drew in a shaky breath and then another before asking baldly, "What happened to you, Ash?"

"You want my tale of woe, Phillip? Are you certain?" Ash chuckled as he said it, but the sound had a bitter edge.

"Aye."

Ash tilted his head and pressed a kiss to Pip's lips. "I will tell you, if you really want to know, but not now. Your masters are awaiting us, and as I am a guest in their home. I would not be late. Provided we aren't dragged in front of the magistrate, we can talk after breakfast."

Pip tried to ignore Ash's air of command in favor of the practicality of his words. Ash was used to giving orders and having them obeyed. It might be a long time before Pip broke him of that habit when they were alone together, but he thought the effort would be worth it in the end. And the road there could be a lark, if Pip chose to make it so.

When Ash drew away from him and sat up, pushing the curtains aside with determination, Pip remained as he was, his shirt pushed up revealing all from his belly to his feet. His spent cock lay against his thigh, now showing signs of renewed life, and he raised an eyebrow at Ash as his grin turned wicked. Unfortunately Ash's own shirt fell as he sat up, shielding his gorgeous arse from Pip's gaze. But the look the man gave him when he realized Pip hadn't moved was worth the disappointment. Ash's eyes, at first impatient and scolding, lit from within as they roved over Pip's body. Whatever words of censure were poised on the man's tongue got lost in the rumbling groan that issued from the back of his throat.

"You will be the death of me yet. Please get dressed, Phillip, before I forget good manners entirely," Ash pleaded as he deliberately turned his head away again and reached for his false leg.

Better pleased with Ash's words this time, Pip grinned to himself and clambered to his feet. He picked up the clothes he'd strewn across the floor and dressed quickly. He needed a wash, but that would have to wait until he could change.

When he was mostly clothed, Pip moved to Ash's side. "I need to go back to me rooms afore I go to breakfast. Do ye need aught afore I go? A hand with yer washin' per'aps?"

Ash's initial polite refusal died on his tongue as Pip waggled his eyebrows suggestively, and the man threw a pillow at him. "Be off with you," he said, chuckling.

Pip dodged the projectile effortlessly and swooped in for another kiss before beating a hasty retreat. He took the stairs two at a time and hurried to his room before anyone else could see him in dishabille, grinning like a fool. He could hear Maud in the kitchen as he stepped into his room, and he sighed happily when he spotted the steaming kettle wrapped in cloth waiting for him on his dresser. The woman was a saint.

Pip quickly stripped down and washed while the water was still warm. Instead of putting on his best wool waistcoat, Pip dug into the chest at the foot of his bed for the silk one Ash had given him. It looked a little silly under Pip's rough wool jacket, but he wanted to wear the waistcoat and the jacket was all he had. Master Carey had enough blunt to keep his rooms warm, even in the dead of winter, but it wasn't warm enough in the house to go about in his shirtsleeves alone.

Pip shaved the stubble from his chin and ran a comb through his hair in front of the small oval looking glass mounted above his dresser. His color was high despite the twisting in his belly. He didn't think the masters would be unkind, but he didn't exactly know what they wanted either. Things were still so unsettled between him and Ash, he would rather have had more time to talk alone before they were forced to face anyone else. He only hoped Master Carey would be gentle.

As it turned out, Pip need not have been worried about Ash. Major Astley McNulty, despite being thrown off-balance by the peculiarity of their situation and unfamiliar surroundings, handled himself with all the dignity of a man of his station. He did not cower under Mr. Carey's intimidating gaze. His back was ramrod straight, his shoulders broad, and his head held high as they all sat down to breakfast.

Pip picked at his food and fidgeted uncomfortably in his seat as the gentlemen exchanged polite nonsense about Ash's journey, his health, the weather… and Pip stopped listening until silence finally descended, and he looked up to find all eyes at the table on him.

"What?"

Mr. Carey snorted into his napkin as Carruthers rolled his eyes and said, "I said, why don't we retire to the library where we might continue the conversation in comfort. If you intend to actually participate in the discussion, that is."

"Oh, right," Pip replied stupidly. He could feel his cheeks heat even as Ash's lips quirked the tiniest bit at one corner.

"Would you show the major the way?" Carruthers requested, with exaggerated patience.

Pip stood up quickly, grateful to have something to do other than sit and listen to nothings, and Ash followed him after murmuring his compliments for the meal.

Ash's limping gait was stiff when he entered the library, and Pip felt a stab of concern. "Are ye all right?"

Ash glanced toward the door, but when the masters didn't immediately follow, he replied quietly, "I'm simply trying to understand what is happening here. You told me what Mr. Carey has done for you. And for that I am willing to excuse much from the man. But I have no idea what I am to expect from this interview, for that is what it appears to be. I am assuming we are not simply engaging in a social call. What do they know, Phillip? Who are these men to you, really?"

Pip tried to smile reassuringly. He would have gone to Ash and offered more, but he could hear the two masters approaching, and there wasn't time, without embarrassing Ash and shaking their already fragile connection. Instead of doing or saying the things he truly wished to, Pip settled for a few words that would convey a world of meaning.

He hoped.

"Better to ask what they are to each other instead."

Ash's eyebrows shot up a moment before Carey and Carruthers entered the room. The surprise was erased from his features when he turned to them, his mask of polite indifference returned, but Pip could almost see the speculation and wary understanding as it dawned.

The masters were always circumspect in company. Pip had never once seen them exchange a touch that would betray them. But if you knew what to look for, the depth of their connection and familiarity could be seen in the way they moved around one another or were seemingly able to convey worlds of meaning with only an exchange of glances or a few words.

The harsh lines around Ash's mouth eased a little, and he accepted the offer of a comfortable chair with more warmth than he had earlier at breakfast. When they were all seated by the fire, Pip and Ash on an elegantly upholstered but sturdy settee and the two masters in matching winged leather armchairs, Master Carey was the first to break the silence.

"Now that you seem to have recovered somewhat from your journey and we have seen you fed, perhaps we might learn the reason you braved the roads to pay us such an unexpected call, Major."

Pip eyed the tray of crystal decanters on the small table by the windows longingly, wishing he'd had a tipple or three before this particular conversation. But when Ash answered without a moment's pause, his voice calm and assured, Pip felt some of his own tension ease and his admiration for Ash increase.

"As I said last night, I wished to speak to Phillip. There was a... *misunderstanding*, and I reacted hastily. I should have given him the opportunity to explain himself before I terminated his employment with me. I felt, given the abrupt manner of our parting, that I would do better to discuss the matter in person rather than merely sending a letter."

Pip hid a smile and tried to keep his expression blank.

"Surely, after a fortnight had already passed, one more day to send word ahead so we might prepare for your arrival would not have made that much difference." Master Carey's words and expression betrayed nothing beyond mild curiosity, but even Pip could see the devilish twinkle in the man's eyes. Carey was enjoying himself immensely, baiting Ash.

"It is a matter of honor to me, Mr. Carey, that when I am proved to be in the wrong, I waste no time in righting it. I intended to merely speak to Phillip and then find lodgings in town. You were both most gracious to offer your hospitality, but I never dreamed of imposing on it," Ash replied swiftly and smoothly, but Pip could see a tiny bit of color in Ash's cheeks.

Carey waved a dismissive hand, clearly done toying with the man. "That is of no matter. We are most gratified to be given the pleasure of your acquaintance, and we would not dream of interfering in your private matters. I only ask for Pip's sake. He is well-loved here, and I know whatever transpired between you was the cause of great distress to him."

Now they were finally getting to the heart of the matter, without so much of that mincing about with words. Pip was warmed by Master Carey's concern for him, even though he wished again for a little more time with Ash before they had to suffer this. When Pip looked to Ash, he could see that some of the man's composure had cracked around the edges. He was looking only at Pip as he answered.

"I know that now, Mr. Carey. I will do whatever I must to make it up to him, if I can... and if he will allow it."

Pip swallowed at the tightness in his throat. He wanted to fling himself at Ash and promise to let him do whatever he wanted, but more than decorum held him still. He didn't know yet what Ash was offering nor did the current circumstances make him feel any better about what he had to offer in return.

For only the second time in the months Pip had known him, Pip was witnessing Ash in the company of his equals, and the experience was proving as disheartening as the first time with the doctor.

Silence fell on the company until Carruthers chose to speak, cutting off whatever Mr. Carey had drawn breath to say. "I believe these men have more to discuss before we badger them further, William. We should let them to it. We have business matters we should attend to, at any rate."

Carey let out a sound Pip had never heard from the man before, half groan, half whine, like a child who'd been denied his favorite toy and forced to go to lessons instead. But he stood up and followed Carruthers from the room anyway.

"We shall see both of you at dinner, I hope?" Mr. Carey said from the doorway.

"Thank you for the invitation. I accept most gratefully," Ash answered, still without taking his eyes off Pip.

"Remember what I said before, Pip," Carruthers called over Mr. Carey's shoulder. Then Mr. Carey closed the door behind them, leaving Pip and Ash to themselves.

Pip turned away from the intensity of Ash's questioning gaze, but when he did, all he saw was the richness of the room around them. It hit him all at once that he didn't belong in this room, not as a guest at any rate. This wasn't his world, and no matter how finely he might try to dress himself up and put on airs, it wouldn't change the truth of that. He'd spent years avoiding getting any nearer to this than the servants' quarters. And now....

"Phillip?" Ash's concerned voice broke him out of the downward spiral of his thoughts, and he turned back to the man. "What is going through that complicated mind of yours?"

Pip snorted. "Complicated? Not 'ardly."

Ash brushed his knuckles across Pip's cheek and smiled. "There is far more to you than meets the eye, Phillip. No matter how you try to convince the world otherwise."

Pip closed his eyes and pressed his cheek into the coolness of Ash's fingers. He took a deep breath before saying, "We need t' talk. But not 'ere."

"Where would you like us to go?"

"Back upstairs, to yer room."

Ash chuckled. "Are you sure we'll get any talking done?"

Pip grinned cheekily despite his unease. "Course we will… *after*."

Chapter *Twenty-One*

ASH HADN'T packed any oil, so despite the fact that the man insisted it wasn't necessary, Pip had to sneak into the masters' bedchambers in search of some. Pip was dressed quite scandalously in only his trousers and shirtsleeves while he raced along the upstairs halls, returning with the small glass vial clutched victoriously in his hand. He would need to return it before the masters discovered it missing, but perhaps he might be able to coax Maud into doing that for him.

She wouldn't want him to get into trouble now, would she?

Pip's stocking feet slid on the waxed wood floor as he came to a halt beside drawn curtains on one side of the bed. Ash was already beneath the thick dark blue velvet coverlet, his cravat and outer clothes discarded, his fine linen shirt open at the neck and wrists, revealing dark blond chest hair and lean, muscled forearms. Pip quickly set the vial on the night table and flung off the rest of his clothes before diving beneath the blankets and drawing Ash into his arms.

"This isn't talking," Ash chuckled against his lips.

"After," Pip promised both of them. He needed to remind himself of all the ways in which they were equal, how they fit together, that beneath the fine words and clothes, they were both made of flesh and bone with desires and hopes and vulnerabilities.

Pip threaded his fingers through Ash's soft blond hair. He'd let it grow long enough for Pip to hold on to as he plundered the man's mouth. Ash slid his palms around Pip's back, his hands playing restlessly across the muscles there as he gave back in equal measure.

Eventually, Pip pushed Ash back into the pillows and climbed into his lap, straddling the man's thighs as they tasted and teased one another's mouths. Impatient for more contact, Pip pulled away only long enough to strip Ash's shirt over his head. Then he pressed the man back again, tangling their tongues together and swallowing Ash's panting breaths while Ash's coarse chest hair teased Pip's nipples.

"I need ye, Ash. I need to feel ye around me," Pip whispered against his lips, grinding his cock into Ash's thigh.

Ash moaned and dug his fingers into Pip's buttocks, dragging his hips closer so he could grind his cock against Pip as well. Pip pulled away again long enough to grab for the oil and then dove back in for another devouring kiss. Ash clung to him as Pip pushed between his legs, nudging the backs of Ash's thighs until the man spread them wide and locked his good leg around Pip's hip. The bed creaked as Pip bent Ash nearly in half, pressing oiled fingers into his hole and invading Ash's mouth with his tongue at the same time. Ash's satisfied groan vibrated all the way to Pip's fingers, and, desperate to hear that sound again, Pip twisted and curled them as Ash's channel throbbed around him, drawing an answering pulse from Pip's loins.

Unable to wait a moment longer, Pip withdrew his fingers and slicked his cock with oil. Lining his crown up with Ash's opening, Pip pressed forward until luxuriant, silken heat gripped him tightly all the way to the root. They both groaned then, so wrapped up in one another not a hair's breadth remained between them. Ash enfolded him in his arms as Pip buried his face in the man's neck and began to thrust. Ash whispered breathless and surprisingly filthy words of encouragement in Pip's ear that only inflamed him more, driving Pip to burrow his own arms beneath Ash's back and lift his hips from the mattress, pounding down into him with ever greater force until Pip was almost struck blind with the pleasure of it.

His release took him by surprise. He barely had the presence of mind to clamp down on his lower lip, cutting off his shout, before the dam broke and all that he had rushed from him in a flood of ecstasy and fire. Ash writhed beneath him, forcing a hand between them. Thankfully, the stars faded from Pip's vision soon enough to watch Ash grip his own cock and pump furiously at it while his hips twisted and flexed, Pip's cock still embedded fully inside him.

Not long after, Ash threw his head back, his face awash in pleasure, and ropes of his seed painted his belly. Pip shuddered as Ash's channel rippled and squeezed his now sensitive cock, but the sight before him was worth any discomfort. Ash was beautiful.

And he is mine.

"Mine," Pip whispered before bending down and capturing Ash's slack lips again.

Pip tasted Ash's answering smile until his thighs began to cramp and he remembered that Ash was bent nearly in half beneath him. Pip eased off the man and fell onto his back as Ash groaned and stretched out next to him.

A few moments later, while Pip was floating contentedly on a cloud of satiation, the mattress shifted and then shortly thereafter Ash's beloved voice came to him. "It's cold. Be warned."

The mattress dipped again, and Pip barely had time to open his eyes before an icy flannel was wiped across his belly and prick. He yelped and pulled away, throwing Ash a wounded look, but the man simply chuckled. "I warned you first."

Pip grumbled a bit and quickly burrowed beneath the covers while gooseflesh rose over his skin. As he watched from the safety of his cave, Ash rolled away and tossed the flannel the short distance to the washstand. Only then did Pip notice the furniture in the room had been rearranged while they were at breakfast, and the washstand and chair had been moved to within easy reach of the bed. Maud must have seen Ash's false leg against the night table that morning and had Stubbs do it as a kindness. Clever woman, to see to it without calling undo attention. Pip would have to remember to thank her later.

Ash burrowed back under the covers next to him, and Pip rolled toward him. He pressed his body against Ash's side and draped an arm contentedly over the man's chest, feeling so much better than he had less than an hour ago. The distance and anxiety he'd felt that morning had eased and their relationship did not seem so impossible at the moment.

Of course, a release like the one he'd just had did much to improve his confidence and outlook on the world in general and he was feeling positively sunny as he propped his chin on his hand, gazed dotingly up at Ash, and said, "Now we can get back to where we left off this morning."

"And where was that?"

"Ye were going to tell me what 'appened... yer tale of woe, as ye called it."

167

Ash raised his eyebrows innocently, but the fond smile he'd been wearing as he toyed with Pip's curls dropped away. "That is a rather broad request. I fear I wouldn't even know where to start."

As the man chuckled uncomfortably, Pip narrowed his eyes and waited expectantly. But Ash didn't continue, and a spark of anger ignited in Pip's belly, his good humor quickly slipping away again.

He pushed himself up on his arms and glared down at the man. "Ye said ye thought all those bad things about me because of yer past, not because of what I am," he said hotly. "But ye won't tell me anythin'. Ye said ye knew ye were wrong now and ye want me back. But when I try to know ye better, ye push me away like ye did before, makin' me think yer fine words are all a lie. This ain't gonna work between us if ye don' even try."

Pip huffed and made a big show of throwing off the blankets. He moved toward the edge of the bed, but thankfully Ash reached out to stop him before he got too far.

"Wait. I'm sorry, Phillip. You're right. Come back. Please."

Pip frowned petulantly at the man, but when Ash settled back into the pillows with his arms outstretched toward Pip and his pale eyes contrite, Pip cautiously resumed his earlier position, perched on Ash's chest, chin propped on his arm.

When Pip was settled, Ash closed his eyes and returned his hand to the back of Pip's neck, toying with the curls at his nape, as he seemed to gather his thoughts. "You asked me once why I was mad enough to walk away from becoming a physician, only to ship myself off to war as a surgeon instead. I didn't want to answer because I didn't walk away. I ran. My brother arranged the whole thing to avoid a scandal at the hospital. I fell in love with one of the patients, you see. A young man of questionable birth and—I found out only later—questionable morals as well. I was young, and Tom was handsome and charming. Our affair only lasted a few weeks before he tried to blackmail me... or I should say, he succeeded. My brother paid him off, and I was sent away so the whispers in the hospital would eventually die down. That was my first love."

Ash's voice held nothing but self-ridicule, and even as Pip cringed inwardly about the "questionable birth," he hurt for the youth Ash must have been, risking his heart for the first time only to have it trod upon. Pip leaned forward and brushed his lips across Ash's in a gentle kiss. "I'm sorry, Ash."

Ash opened his eyes and shook his head. "It was long ago. A lifetime. Besides, it set in motion a chain of events, at least some of which I'm not sorry for. After all, I went off on my grand adventure after that. First to Belgium to rout old Boney… not single-handedly of course, but people are *always* impressed when they hear I was there." His tone had taken on a mocking edge, but Pip wasn't sure if Ash was making fun of himself or everyone else.

"Ash," Pip gently chided.

"What?"

"I don't want ye t' tell me what ye would anybody else. I want the truth, *your* truth."

"The truth?" He laughed bitterly. "It was the first time I had ever seen a battle in my life. It was chaos, and I was petrified. I was only a surgeon's assistant. I'd had training before I left but not enough. We started in tents on the field before we were ordered to fall back to Mont-Saint-Jean. It was all a blur of blood and screams and canon fire. We were overwhelmed in the makeshift hospitals. So many died that should have lived. I worked until I collapsed those first horrible days. But I learned quickly, and my mentors were impressed with my knowledge and abilities by the end, even if the whole time I was wondering why the hell I was there." He shook his head ruefully. "I was never truly cut out to be a military man. But when the battle was over, and the wounded either sent home or to their graves, I wasn't ready to go home again either. I had seen too much. I was changed. I'd like to blame my obviously damaged state of mind for what happened next, but I don't think my conscience will allow it. You see, amidst all that horror, I was idiotic enough to fall in love again, a soldier this time, my second disastrous affair of the heart, and the one that nearly ended me."

"Colin?" Pip whispered, remembering the name Ash had called him their last night together before he left.

Ash stiffened beneath him, and the fingers at his nape clenched. "How do you know that name?" he demanded suspiciously.

"Ye said it in yer sleep."

"Last night?"

"No, before, at the cottage. Ye were 'aving a nightmare an' ye kept calling 'is name."

Pip couldn't look at Ash as he said it, but his tone must have betrayed something, because Ash's fingers relaxed their grip on his neck, and the suspicion in his voice melted into concern. "Did something else happen that night, Phillip?"

Pip suddenly felt cold to his bones. He shivered and reached for the blankets, drawing them the rest of the way up to his chin. When that wasn't enough, he pressed his cheek to Ash's breast and breathed in the man's scent. That combined with the steady beat of Ash's heart soothed him.

"Please, Phillip. If I did something, I need to know. I… I have spells sometimes, spaces I don't remember, when the nightmares take me."

Or when ye'r foxed off yer arse.

Pip swallowed and forced himself to meet Ash's distraught gaze. "Don't fret. It weren't nothin' really. I stayed with ye that night because I were worried. You were fretful and yer skin so cold. I lay with ye just to warm ye up, but ye started thrashing about and callin' 'is name… and then ye climbed on top o' me and tried to hold me down. I don't remember much after that, because I panicked, like the first time ye kissed me, an' I ran away. I knew it were a nightmare, Ash. I knew ye didn't mean it, but I couldn't…." Pip shivered again, and Ash pulled him up, wrapped his arms around Pip's shoulders, and pressed a kiss to Pip's temple.

"God, I'm so sorry, Phillip."

Forcing the ugliness away, Pip cupped Ash's jaw and kissed the man hard, all thrusting tongue and punishing lips, until Ash opened to his assault, surrendering to it. Eventually whatever Pip was really fighting receded from his mind, and his kisses gentled. He soothed Ash's swollen lips with soft licks and featherlight pecks.

The man's cheeks were flushed, and his eyelids heavy when Pip finally pulled away, but his face turned grave again as he said, "I promised you from the start that I wouldn't try to force you to do anything you didn't want. I'm sorry I broke my word, but I hope you can believe I never intended to." He took a deep breath and let it out in a long sigh. "I think you deserve an explanation of what might've happened there. I… things between Colin and I were never what I would call salutary. I followed him halfway across the world, to the East Indies and then to the Cape, almost ten years. I thought I loved him, and I believed he loved me, in his own way. But Colin had a great many demons inside him. I suppose we both did. And no matter how hard I tried to make myself who he wanted me to be, it was never enough. The bed games he liked to play didn't come naturally to me. He… he liked to be forced, held down and made to—well, at any rate, it didn't matter how many times I pleaded with him, he wouldn't be satisfied unless we did things his way."

"Ye were angry that night," Pip offered.

The smile Ash gave him was both bitter and sad. "I was often angry with him… and myself. He was never faithful. We shared no tenderness, no real affection unless I threatened to leave him and never come back again. Then he would become quite solicitous for a time. But it never lasted, and still I didn't leave. Toward the end, I think I may have begun to realize I couldn't go on like that forever, but fate stepped in and took the decision from me."

Ash's hand moved beneath the blankets and began rubbing his injured thigh, as if the memory were enough to cause him physical pain. When he spoke again, his voice was emotionless, as if he was recounting something from a history book. "That January, two years ago, Colin went with the expeditionary force Sir Charles MacCarthy led against the Asante Empire, while I remained behind at the Cape. I had taken ill just before they left, and it was thought I would be of more use in the small hospital there than stumbling through the wild…. Colin never came back from Nsamankow."

Pip didn't recognize the place names, but he understood enough that he wouldn't ruin the moment by asking stupid questions. He had only one question he truly needed answered. "If ye were left be'ind, then 'ow…?" Pip swept his arm to indicate Ash's leg.

The grimace that twisted Ash's face was filled with mortification rather than the pain Pip expected. "I stayed at the Cape after the battle to fulfill my obligation, but I fully intended to sell my commission as soon as possible after. Six months before I was scheduled to leave is when it happened. A bloody supply cart. Ten years, numerous battles and skirmishes, storms at sea, and various epidemics of fever, and I'm cut down by a ruddy supply cart." He chuckled, but it held no mirth. "The wheel cracked. The cart overturned. I wasn't paying close enough attention, and my horse reared and fell on me. My leg was crushed and some of my ribs were broken. But given the conditions of the surgery, I was lucky to survive—although I didn't feel particularly lucky. By the time I returned home to England, all I saw was a path leading inexorably to my pathetic end." The faraway look in Ash's eyes receded as he focused his gaze on Pip again, and his smile turned truly happy. "Until I met you. Come back with me, Phillip. Don't ever leave me again. Even if I try to send you away, don't go."

Pip desperately wanted to say yes, anything so Ash would keep looking at him like that. But his doubts from the morning came flooding back, and the mere thought of going back to that cottage again left him cold. His throat closed, choking off the promises he would have made, and as the silence stretched between them, Ash's smile began to fade. "What is it? What's wrong?"

Pip could only shake his head. He had to clench his jaw to fight back the wave of conflicting emotions threatening to break him, and he couldn't meet Ash's gaze.

In the silence that followed, Ash's body stiffened beneath him. "Phillip, I have swallowed what little pride I have left and travelled all the way here to beg your forgiveness, to tell you how much I need you. I have done what you asked of me and shared my pathetic and humiliating tale. I am *trying*, just as you insisted. And now… what? Are you telling me it was all for naught? Was last night and this morning a fond farewell? An apology? Pity?"

"No!"

"Then what?"

"I don't know."

Ash pushed Pip away then and sat up. When he reached for his leg and made to fasten it on, Pip's indecision and paralysis eased enough for him to throw his arms around Ash's chest, preventing him from continuing. "Don't, Ash. Wait. Please?"

"What am I waiting for? You tell me to stay, but you won't tell what you're thinking. You tell me it isn't a farewell or pity, but you won't say what it is. When I beg for your promise, you won't give it. How can I understand when you won't talk to me… if you won't tell me *your* truth, as you so eloquently put it?"

Ash's words stabbed at him, all the deeper for the truth they held. Once again, Ash was proving himself the better man. All of Pip's doubts and fears, desires and wishes were suddenly overwhelming him, and he felt as if he might shake apart at the conflicting feelings inside him.

And that was when he must have taken leave of his senses, because he vaulted from the bed and began pacing the icy room in nothing but his skin, ranting like a madman and flailing his arms about without any consideration for his pride, his dignity, or his vanity. If Ash wanted the truth, Pip would give it to him in all its ugliness and utter madness.

"My truth? My truth is that I'm a bloody wreck! I 'ave been since the first day I met you, mooning about one minute like a blighted heroine in one o' them wretched novels, and then the next happier than I've been in me entire cursed life!" Pip rounded on Ash as his fury mounted. "It's all yer fault. I were doin' fine afore I met ye. I could see me road stretching straight out in front of me, smooth and peaceful, even if I didn't know quite where it were leadin'. Then *you* come along an' turn everythin' on its ear. I can't think straight 'alf the time for wantin' ye." Pip stopped and took in a deep shuddering breath. "My truth is, I love ye, ye stubborn bastard! I want to be with ye more'n anythin'. But I can't go back to that 'ouse, skulkin' about in the shadows just to spend a few precious minutes with ye afore I have to go back to me empty bed alone, not able to talk to ye or laugh with ye… or even sit and read to ye without the 'ousekeeper lookin' at me sideways! But, then, low as I am, I 'ave no right to ask any more of ye than that, do I?" Pip laughed mirthlessly. "And do ye know what the funniest part of that is? Ye don't even know the worst of it yet!"

Pip's breaths were huffing in and out of his lungs like a bellows now, and his hands were fisted at his sides so tight the knuckles cracked.

Ash's initial shock at his outburst seemed to fade and his expression turned into real concern the longer Pip went on. Toward the end Pip's tirade, Ash rose and stood beside the bed, naked as Pip, grasping the post to keep himself upright, his false leg forgotten on the floor. "Phillip, come here." His voice was soft and cajoling. He beckoned with his free arm, nothing but heart-wrenching care in his eyes, and Pip rushed to him, pressed the lengths of their bodies together, wrapped his arms around Ash, and clung to him.

"You love me?" Ash asked in a whisper against Pip's neck.

Of all the nonsense Pip had just spewed, of course the man would only listen to that part. "Aye," Pip answered grudgingly.

Ash drew in as deep a breath as Pip's viselike grip on his ribs would allow. His long exhale ruffled the curls behind Pip's ear. "What is it that you want from me?"

173

Pip made a frustrated noise at the back of his throat and gave Ash a few shakes without letting the man go. "I want *you*. I want to sleep next to ye at night and be by yer side during the day. I want to eat with ye and drink with ye and talk with ye. I want what Master Carey and Master Carruthers 'ave. That's what."

"Do you think I don't want that too? Of course I do. But you have to know how lucky those men are to have found such loyal and sympathetic servants. The rest of the world is not so forgiving, Phillip, and I couldn't bear to risk your life by pretending it is."

Pip let his head fall to Ash's shoulder, feeling suddenly exhausted from his outburst and defeated as well. "I know." Pip pulled away then and collapsed onto the edge of the bed. He propped his elbows on his knees and dropped his face into his hands as hopelessness swamped him. "It ain't only that, Ash. At least Master Carey and Master Carruthers are closer in circumstance than you an' me. We're practically from different worlds, we are. Even if we could get so lucky with a 'ousekeeper like Maud, who would ever believe I 'ad the right t' even set foot inside yer door, let alone spend me days with ye? Look at me. Coarse and common as I am, I'm not even fit t' clean yer boots. Why should ye offer me more'n ye already 'ave?"

Ash shoved Pip's shoulder hard.

"Don't talk nonsense," he snapped. "After all I've told you today, after you've seen me at my most wretched and been given ample proof of how truly damaged I am—and more than just this"—he pointed to his leg—"do you honestly think I care a whit about all that rubbish? That I wouldn't give you anything you asked if it were in my power to do so?"

"Ye might not if ye knew the whole of it."

"The whole of what?" Ash demanded, obviously feeling as frustrated as Pip was.

"Me own tale of woe, as ye put it."

Ash plunked down next to him and growled, "Then tell it to me, and let's have done so we can dispense with the pretense that my being born a gentleman—through none of my own doing, I might add—and your being born a servant are somehow to blame for why you can't come home with me." His silver eyes were ablaze, his cheeks flushed, and his jaw hard when Pip finally lifted his head to return his gaze.

Oddly enough, Pip's cock twitched in response to that flash of temper, even as he hid a smile. An angry Ash was so much better than a dejected or melancholy one. And for a moment, Pip was tempted to let all his worries go and simply attack him. He didn't truly want to ruin the fragile thing they were trying to build between them with his secrets. Ash wanted him as he was now. He didn't have to know the whole filthy tale.

But Carruthers was right. Ash did need to know. And Pip would be a coward if he didn't give Ash the same consideration the man had shown him. Pip had to make Ash understand just how wretched and low a creature he really was, or he'd always wonder if Ash would still want him if he knew. The doubt would always be there, niggling at the back of his mind, spoiling whatever they managed to have together.

"All right, then. I'll tell ye. Ye'll give me a fair 'earing, as I did for you. And in the end, if ye've changed yer mind about anythin', ye'll tell me straight. All right?"

Ash sighed in obvious irritation. "Yes, a thousand times yes. Let's put at least this much to rest, once and for all."

The tightness in Pip's chest didn't ease, but he nodded. "Right. Good. Now shut yer gob an' let me tell it."

That drew a snort out of the man, but he kept his mouth shut just the same.

"First is, I lied to ye. Stubbs ain't me real name. It's Bell, from me mum. I never knew me father, an' I don't think me mum knew 'im neither, if ye catch me meanin'. But Maud and Stubbs—and Mr. Carey—'ave been more of a famly t' me than anyone else so that's why I took it."

"*Belle* suits you better," Ash murmured with a hesitant smile.

Pip shushed him even as he preened a little over the compliment. "It weren't me ma's real name, at any rate, from what I could tell. She died when I were real young. Maud did what she could to 'elp, even though I weren't 'er boy, but she were only scrapin' by as it was. So I did what I 'ad to live. I weren't born a servant, Ash. I were born much lower than that, and I sunk lower still, stealing from carts and pickin' pockets in St. Giles. And even further when I got nipped. The new magistrate wanted to make a name for 'imself, ye see, so 'e sent me to Newgate—a whole year in that hell over a sodding pocket watch."

175

Pip fell silent and Ash asked quietly, "How old were you?"

Pretending a nonchalance he didn't feel, Pip shrugged. "Eleven, near as I can tell. Not much call for celebratin' birthdays in the rookeries."

Ash looked appalled. "God, Phillip, that must have been terrible."

Pip squirmed and turned away. "When I said Master Carey was me benefactor, I weren't completely honest. 'e were much more than that. The man saved me life. 'e got me out o' there before I went completely mad, and all because Maud asked 'im to. They sent me away to Vicar 'alford, and a kinder man ye'll never meet. I wouldn't be 'ere today if not for them." Pip's voice caught on that last, and he had to swallow hard.

The mattress shifted and Ash's hand cupped his cheek, forcing Pip to turn and face him. "I am so sorry, Phillip. I've heard the stories about Newgate. Even from the outside, it looked like hell. To sentence a mere child to that was unconscionable." He brushed his lips against Pip's. "Thank you for sharing that with me. But I don't understand why you think it would change how I feel about you."

Pip pulled away and stared at the man, trying to decide if Ash had actually heard anything he'd said or if the man had just lost his wits. He supposed he needed to speak plainer. "Because! I'm a bastard son of a whore and a convicted thief. Ye talked about yer first love being of questionable birth an' character, well, ye don't get much more questionable than that, do ye? Except ye *can*, and after what I were made to do at Newgate, I am." Pip clenched his jaw as the memories threatened to make him retch. "Ye don't get it, do ye? Do I 'ave to spell it out? The guards took bribes t' let men in after dark, men who paid for time with the prisoners. And what they didn't do to us, the guards themselves did, when no one were lookin'. Ye said ye were damaged, but not half so much as me. 'ow can I ever 'ave what I really want with ye, dirty and broken as I am inside?"

Pip clamped his mouth shut then, shocked at what came pouring out of him. He'd hoped all of this was buried and gone, a long time ago, but apparently not.

Ash reached for him, but Pip pulled away farther still, and eventually Ash's hands fell back down to his sides. "Phillip, I will say it as many times as you need to hear it. I know who you are *now*. That's what counts. The rest of it doesn't matter beyond helping me to understand some of the wounds you've suffered. You may have scars, but you aren't tainted by your past, not in my eyes. You are a bright, beautiful, vibrant, *infuriating*, and surprising man. I want whatever I can have of you."

Pip shivered, suddenly aware of the chill in the room now that his earlier temper had fled. And when Ash reached for him this time, Pip didn't pull away. He allowed Ash to guide him back beneath the blankets and didn't resist when Ash curled around him from behind.

"Phillip, you told me you loved me, and I should have said this then, but I was still trying to understand all that you were throwing at me. I'll say it now. I love you. Selfish as I know I'm being, I need you in my life. We can find a solution. If you truly want me as I want you, we can find some way. You only have to tell me what you're willing to accept of what the world we live in will allow. I can't change the world, but you have my word I'll change as much as I can."

Pip closed his eyes and pulled Ash's arms more tightly around his chest. "I do want ye, Ash. I only want to be able to spend as much time with ye as I possibly can. And I promise to try too. I'm just not sure what we can do."

"Perhaps, with a little time, we can figure it out."

They both nodded off then, emotionally and physically drained. They hadn't settled on a solution as to how they would live, but Pip felt as if a huge weight had been lifted from his shoulders now that the truth was out in the open. Ash still wanted him. Ash loved him. Perhaps that would be enough and the rest wouldn't matter so much now Pip had that to hold on to.

Chapter Twenty-Two

THEY WOKE late in the afternoon but neither of them wanted to leave the warmth and comfort of their bed until they absolutely had to. Pip decided they'd talked enough for one day, so despite the fact that they still hadn't decided on a solution, he pounced on Ash as soon as the man was awake and didn't stop their play until they had to dress for dinner.

Carey and Carruthers seemed to sense their mood and did not press them over much at the table. They kept the conversation light, and Pip actually had a fairly pleasant meal. Joining the stuffed shirts at their table was not as painful as he'd always imagined it would be. But after dinner, while Carruthers and Ash took a turn at the billiard table, Mr. Carey pulled Pip aside for a little talk.

"How are you really, Pip?"

"I'm all right, sir."

Carey nodded. "You look better than you have since your return. I will assume that means that this is what you want… to go with this man?"

"It's what I want, but… I'm not sure I know 'ow."

"What do you mean?"

Pip was hesitant at first, knowing how private a man Ash was and wanting to respect that. But at the same time, Mr. Carey was, for all intents and purposes, family. Pip had relied on his advice for years—even if he hadn't always heeded it—and Carey had managed to find a way to be with the man he loved, perhaps not as openly as he would have wished but enough that they both seemed happy. If anyone might be able to help, it would be him.

They took a walk to the library while Ash and Carruthers played, and when Pip was done voicing all his fears, his insecurities, and Ash's, Carey spun on his heel and headed back to the billiard room at a fast clip without so much as a word.

Both Ash and Carruthers looked up in surprise when Carey burst into the room, Pip on his heels. Carey went immediately to the tray and poured himself a whisky before taking the decanter and refilling Ash's glass nearly to the top.

"Right. Drink up," Carey said as he downed what was in his glass and waited for Ash to do the same.

When Ash had finished, Carey said, "The way I see it, the two of you already know what needs to be done, but neither of you is willing to take the chance and blurt it out, so I will. If this is truly what you want, to be together, then you will need to take a new house somewhere, McNalty, someplace a good distance from both Keswick and Penrith, where your neighbors won't know you or Pip."

"It'll 'ave to be a good distance indeed, given Pip's activities over the past few years," Stubbs muttered under his breath from the door.

Pip swung around and scowled at the man as Carey and Carruthers hid their smiles, and Ash looked at all of them in confusion.

Stubbs carried a bottle of port and another bottle of whisky with him to the tray with the decanters and glasses while Carey continued, "As I was saying, find a house. Hire new staff. Interview them yourself so you know their characters and if they can be trusted—we might be able to send out some discreet inquiries ourselves to help. Introduce Pip to everyone in the neighborhood as your personal aid. If you'll forgive me for saying so, Major, your injury will be quite helpful there. Play up your infirmity. It would explain your needing a servant at all hours of the day and night."

Both Pip and Ash began to object at the same time, Ash probably out of pride and Pip wanting to defend his lover's dignity, but Mr. Carey raised an imperious hand cutting them off. "I know you both have enough pride between the two of you for ten men. But I see no other means by which your continued level of intimacy might be explained away." He paused there, holding each of their gazes before continuing. "Pip, as much as you try to deny it, I'm certain you could manage the pretense of being the man's companion or secretary—although you've never been particularly interested in remaining indoors all day—but there would be no reason for you to be in the major's bedchamber at all hours if you weren't his servant. Make your position too low or too high and you put more distance between you. Not only that, but if you're the man's companion, you'd be expected to make calls with him in the neighborhood, creating more opportunities for a slip up." Carey swung to face Ash. "And *you*, Major, if I were in your place, I'd play the bloody invalid to the hilt and damn my pride if it got me what I wanted. It is what you want, is it not?"

"Yes."

"Then what does it matter if your neighbors think you more injured than you actually are? You know the truth of it and so does Pip."

"But who'd ever be daft enough to believe me a gentleman's aid, whatever that is?" Pip blurted out.

Carey swung to face him with that damned eyebrow cocked. "Pip, I will ask you only once more. This is what you want, isn't it?"

"Aye."

"Then it's time for you to stop dithering about and live up to your potential. You know you are fully capable of achieving anything you set your mind to. So set your mind to this, and quit making excuses."

"But… what would I do with meself all day?" Pip asked plaintively, all of his other objections seeming pitiful and unfounded in the face of Carey's obvious confidence in him.

Carey gave him a smirk that clearly said, "Do you really need me to answer that?" And Pip rolled his eyes as Ash coughed uncomfortably into his fist.

"Ye know what I mean," Pip said petulantly.

Carey waved a dismissive hand. "Do as you choose. I would recommend you keep your staff small, Major, as you did in Keswick. I don't know that you'll be as lucky as we are with our Maud and Stubbs here. But hopefully we can find you someone loyal and discreet enough. There will still be plenty of work to be done, and, Pip, you could spend as much time as you wished out of doors. You would both simply establish from the start that you had the right to be above stairs whenever the major might need you. That's all. Not much else would have to change."

Carey made it all sound so easy, but he wouldn't be the one pulling it off. Pip didn't like the labels of servant and master still hanging between him and Ash, but the plan had merit. And if he were honest with himself, Pip didn't truly want to be raised too high in station anyway. He would be much more comfortable as a servant in the house. He'd loathe paying calls.

The group dickered over specifics as they made their way through most of the whisky bottle. But by the end of the night, Pip felt better about the plan. And when they finally went to bed, Ash surprisingly didn't chew Pip's head off for making their private affairs the subject of the evening's discourse.

The following day, Master Carey sent out letters of inquiry, and he and Mr. Carruthers invited Ash and Pip to stay at the farm at least through Christmas, while Ash sent out inquiries of his own after a new house— somewhere a good distance from both Penrith and Keswick, but perhaps not so far that visits couldn't be made back and forth on occasion.

Ash wrote to Mrs. Applethwaite as well, informing her of his plans to stay in Penrith over the holiday and giving her leave to travel if she had family she wished to visit. But he didn't mention any of the rest of their plan in the letter, preferring to wait until he had a new position for her and her husband. Pip felt guilty for putting the woman out of a job. They hadn't exactly been on friendly terms, but she wasn't all bad, and at her and her husband's age, finding further employment might prove difficult for them. Ash assured him, however, that they'd be taken care of. He had an aunt he thought might rub along famously with the woman, and he sent a letter to her along with all the others.

While they waited for responses, Ash thrived in the warmth and comfort of the farm. They spent every night together, and Ash's color came back. Maud's wonderful cooking put a bit more meat on his bones. They ate dinner with the masters each night, which proved a bit uncomfortable for Pip since the masters grilled him on his speech and table manners to prepare him for his new role above stairs. But Pip endured it bravely, knowing that a life with Ash would be worth any hardship.

Part of Pip dearly wished they could just stay at the farm together forever, especially after he got Ash on one of the horses in the stables the first time, but he knew that wasn't possible. A friend staying with the masters for a few weeks or months was one thing, but staying with them for years would definitely draw attention they didn't want.

There were already a few whispers in the village regarding Mr. Carruthers's unmarried state, and even though Mr. Carey avoided the same by playing up the grieving widower that he was, they couldn't afford any more gossip if they wanted to remain where they were. And besides that, Ash was a solitary sort, and Pip couldn't see him wanting so much company for long. The man would want his privacy, his quiet, and his books… and Pip, of course. Pip would be quite happy with that, as long as they were able to come back to the farm from time to time.

Epilogue

December 1826

TWO DAYS before Christmas, all the servants and the children went out to gather evergreen boughs, holly, and hawthorn to decorate the hall. Ash and Pip rode out in a horse and cart to join in the hunt as they rooted about in the small copses between the hills around the farm. And when their baskets were laden with enough greenery to satisfy the children, Ash drove the children back while Pip and Maud and the other servants returned to the house on foot.

The following afternoon, Ash sat warming himself by the fire in the library, reading his letters, while Pip climbed up and down a ladder in the main hall, stringing up the garlands and wreaths the ladies put together the previous night. Pip was humming tunelessly to himself as he worked, happy to the heart of him and not afraid for anyone to know it. He'd spent every night in Ash's bed and every day by his side, and even his lessons with Mr. Carey and renewed lessons with Mr. Pruitt, the children's little mouse of a tutor, couldn't ruin his good humor.

When he was finished in the hall, Pip stepped back to admire his handiwork. The polished wood banister gleamed beneath the red-ribboned garland he'd wrapped around it. Swags of pine boughs were draped above every door and wreaths on every wall. There would be no great ball for the neighborhood. But Pip eagerly anticipated that night just the same. He'd worked hard all day to make sure the decorations were perfect for the feast Maud prepared every year for everyone on the farm.

Christmas Eve was the one night that the servants were invited to dine with the masters. They would all put on their finest and crowd into the dining room. And then after dinner, they would open the doors to the rest of the rooms, and everyone would spill out into the hall and the front parlor and billiard room. Master Carey would play the pianoforte, and they would sing and dance and play games until late into the night. And even if Pip wouldn't be able to dance with Ash, he couldn't wait to share the occasion with him.

While Pip was admiring his work, Ash stepped into the hall and moved to his side. "It looks lovely, Phillip. I can't remember the last time I had a true Christmas at home."

Pip beamed at him, even more pleased that he'd put in the effort. "It'll be the best Christmas yet. I'm sure of it."

Ash smiled at him warmly and Pip's heartbeat quickened as it always did when he looked at the man. Catching a glimpse of the large monstrosity constructed of evergreen, satin ribbons, and paper flowers— the kissing bough—hanging from the ceiling in the center of the room, Pip dragged Ash beneath it and planted a loud wet kiss on his lips. Ash flushed bright red and cast wary eyes about them, making sure they were alone before giving Pip a peck in return and pushing away from him.

"You need to be more careful, Phillip... even here," Ash admonished, but his tone held no real censure.

"I'll be good," Pip replied with a wink.

Footsteps sounded on the stone and Ash put more distance between them as Maud carried a tray with their tea past them and into the library. When she had passed, Ash cleared his throat and said gruffly, "I received a letter from my aunt. She is very interested in meeting Mr. and Mrs. Applethwaite. It will mean a journey back to the cottage soon, but you don't have to come with me if you don't wish. As long as the weather and roads remain clear, I should only be gone a day or two."

"I won't make ye—*you*—travel on your own, Ash. I'll come with you."

"You don't have to, Phillip. I know you were unhappy there."

"I were—*was*—happy sometimes too. I don't have any real love for the place and too many people know me there as I am for us to stay there, but it weren't—*wasn't* all bad."

"If you wish to come, I won't tell you otherwise, but we'll have to be careful with Mrs. Applethwaite. She may not be pleased with what I have to tell her at the start. Although, I truly believe she'll be happier with my aunt than she ever was with me. They are more of a kind, I think."

That night proved to be as grand and merry a time as Pip had hoped, with the goose cooked to perfection and the ale and cider plentiful. Ash kept himself to the outskirts most of the night. But whenever Pip sought him out, he found the man smiling fondly in his direction, seeming happy to simply watch Pip enjoy himself. Pip, Stubbs, and Mr. Carruthers danced with all the girls so that none felt left out, and even the shy tutor, Mr. Pruitt, took a turn or two, though the man flushed scarlet to his hair and tripped over his own feet in his nerves, to the vast amusement of the downstairs maids.

Pip was having a grand time. But when Ash excused himself for the night, Pip was more than happy to follow him.

"Phillip, you don't have to leave. You're obviously enjoying yourself. Stay. I'll be fine," Ash said when he reached the base of the stairs.

Pip moved close to him and whispered, "I'd rather be with you."

Ash met his gaze then, and heat flared in his eyes, mirroring the fire in Pip's. Without further comment, Ash led the way up the stairs and to their bedchamber, where Pip spent the next couple of hours showing him just how pleased he was with the evening and how much he preferred being exactly where he was.

Pip was dropping off to sleep when Ash propped himself on an elbow and said, "I don't have a present for you to open, Phillip, but I do have a bit of news, which I hope will suffice. I've had a letter from the land agent in Kendal. He's found a house for us."

Even though he felt a tiny pang of sadness at leaving the farm, Pip's smile was genuine as he said, "That's wonderful, Ash. When do we leave?"

Ash seemed to ponder the question with an inordinate amount of gravity before he said, "We'll have to see the place before I finalize anything. But, I suppose in a month or two… or three, we could be ready."

"So long?" Pip frowned at him in confusion. The roads were difficult in winter to be sure. But Kendal was not so far that it should take months to move Ash's few belongings there.

Ash smiled at him tenderly and leaned in for a kiss. "I thought, perhaps, you might not mind staying on here for a little, while the worst of the winter passes. Carey and I had a talk, and he intimated that we had not overstayed our welcome as yet, so I thought—"

Pip didn't give Ash the chance to finish his sentence. He threw his arms around Ash's neck and kissed him senseless, whispering breathless thank-yous and I love yous each time they pulled apart to catch their breaths. Pip ended up showing his happiness and gratitude in a number of other ways before they both collapsed into an exhausted and happy slumber.

THEY HADN'T found a new housekeeper yet. They hadn't quite chosen a house. And they both still had wounds that needed healing—oh, and the horse *still* didn't have a name. But the truly important parts were settled. They had each other. They had love. They had time. And they didn't have to face the road ahead alone if they didn't want to, no matter how many twists and turns there might be in it.

ROWAN MCALLISTER is a woman who doesn't so much create as recreate, taking things ignored and overlooked and hopefully making them into something magical and mortal. She believes it's all in how you look at it. In addition to a continuing love affair with words, she creates art out of fabric, metal, wood, stone, and any other interesting scraps of life she can get her hands on. Everything is simply one perspective change and a little bit of effort away from becoming a work of art that is both beautiful and functional. She lives in the woods, on the very edge of suburbia—where civilization drops off and nature takes over—sharing her home with her patient, loving, and grounded husband, her super sweet hairball of cat, and a mythological beast masquerading as a dog. Her chosen family is made up of a madcap collection of people from many different walks of life, all of whom act as her muses in so many ways, and she would be lost without them.

E-mail: rowanmcallister10@gmail.com
Facebook: https://www.facebook.com/rowanmcallister10
Twitter: https://twitter.com/RowanMcallister

Also from Rowan McAllister

http://www.dreamspinnerpress.com

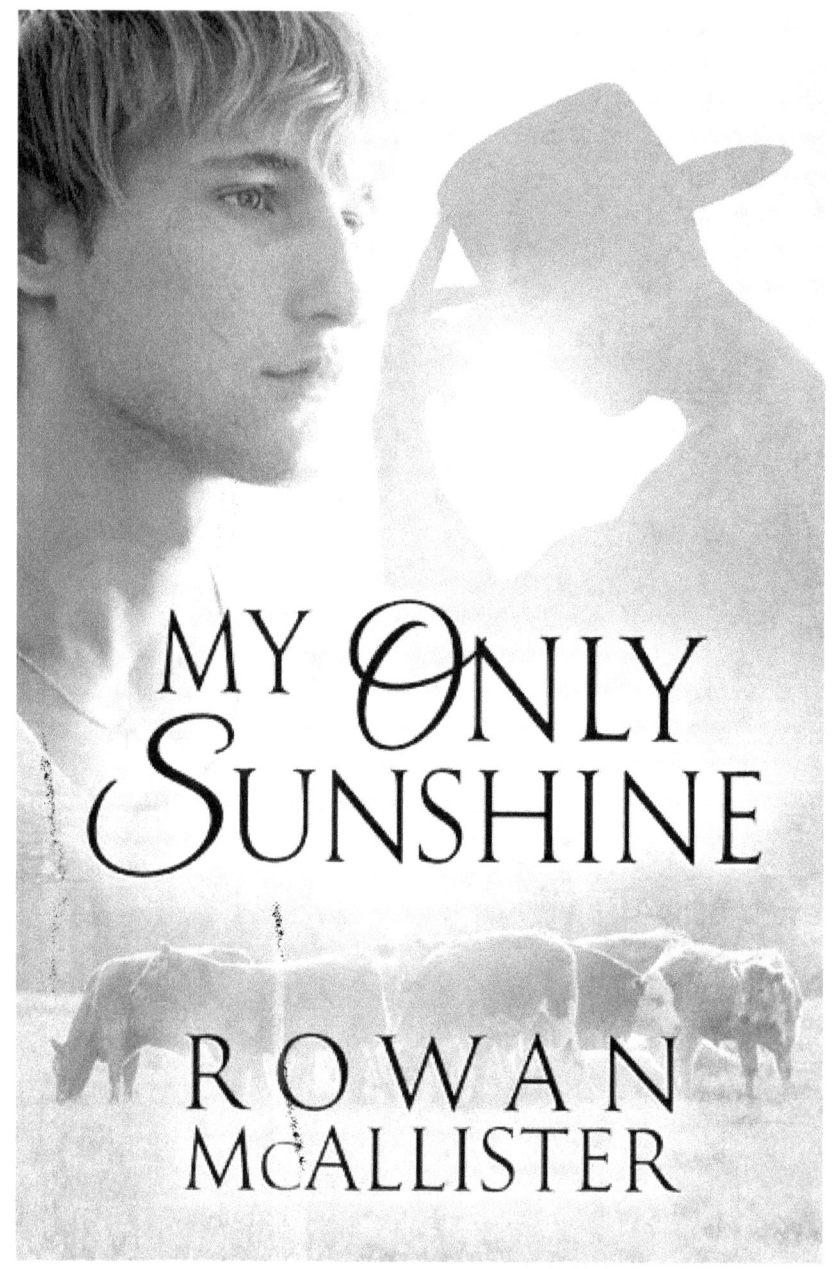

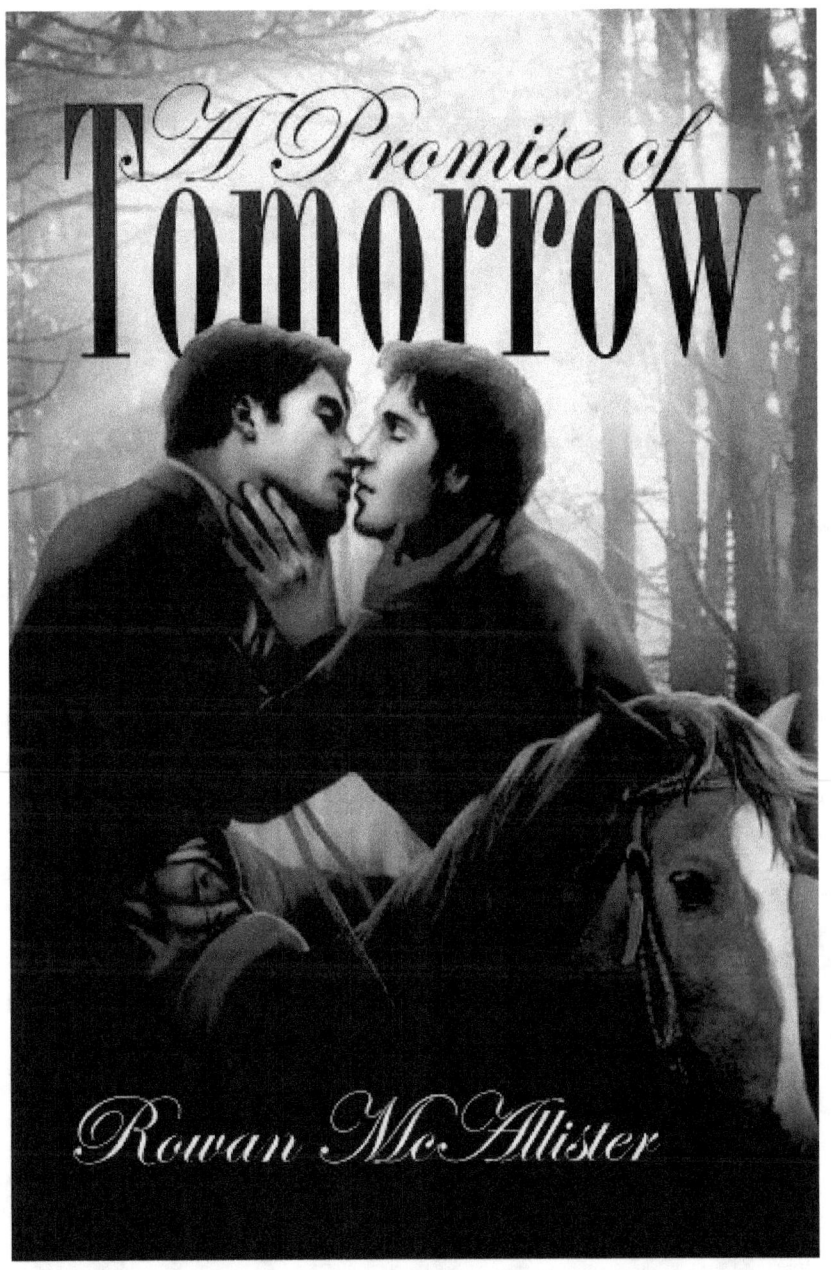

Also from Rowan McAllister

http://www.dreamspinnerpress.com

Feels Like Home

Rowan McAllister

Also from DREAMSPINNER PRESS

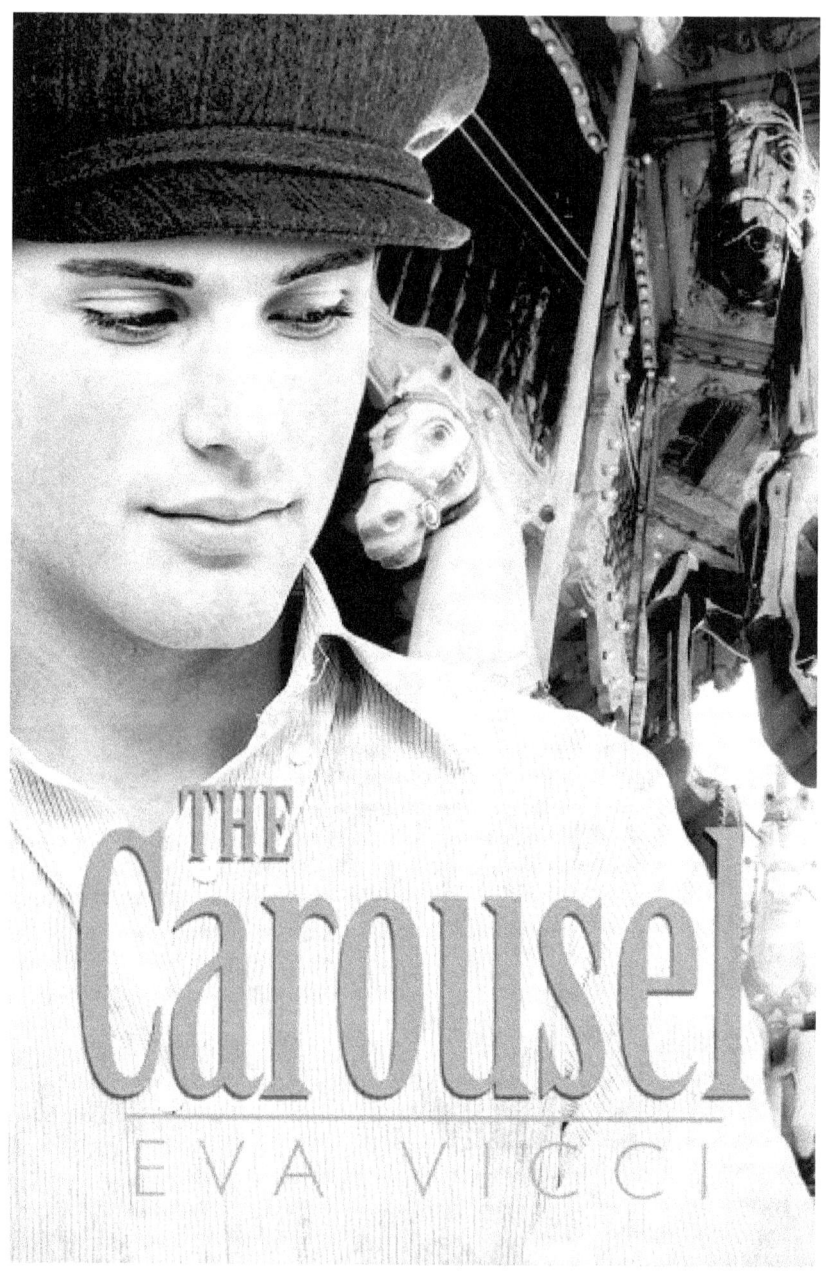

THE Carousel

EVA VICCI

http://www.dreamspinnerpress.com

Also from DREAMSPINNER PRESS

NOBLE'S SAVIOR

Jerry Sacher

http://www.dreamspinnerpress.com